RECON IN FORCE

BOOK SIX OF THE EMPIRE OF BONES SAGA

TERRY MIXON

YOWLING
CAT PRESS

This book was previously published as Reconnaissance in Force.

Published by Yowling Cat Press ®

Digital edition date: 6/21/2023

Print ISBN: 978-1947376625

Large Print ISBN: 978-1947376205

Cover art - image copyrights as follows:

DepositPhotos/innovari (Luca Oleastri)

DepositPhotos/algolonline (C Atkinson)

DepositPhotos/steho (Stefan Holms)

DepositPhotos/Iurii (Юрий Коваленко)

Donna Mixon

Cover design and composition by Donna Mixon

Print edition design and layout by Terry Mixon

Audio edition performed and produced by Veronica Giguere

Reach her at: v@voicesbyveronica.com

ALSO BY TERRY MIXON

You can always find the most up to date listing of Terry's titles on his Amazon Author Page.

Note: the links below (ebook only, obviously) redirect you to my website where you can click a button to go to Amazon. This allows me to participate in Amazon's associates program and earn a little more. Sorry for any inconvenience.

The Last Hunter

The Last Hunter

Bonds of Blood

Alpha Strike

The Enemy Revealed

Command Authority

The Grand Conspiracy

Shield of Humanity

Fog of War

Ships of the Line

Operation Liberty

The Empire of Bones Saga

Empire of Bones

Veil of Shadows

Command Decisions

Ghosts of Empire

Paying the Price

Recon in Force

Box Sets

The Empire of Bones Saga Volume 1

The Empire of Bones Saga Volume 2

The Empire of Bones Saga Volume 3

The Empire of Bones Saga Volume 4

Humanity Unlimited Publisher's Pack 1

Humanity Unlimited Publisher's Pack 2

Want to get updates from Terry about new books and other general nonsense going on in his life? He promises there will be cats. Go to TerryMixon.com/Mailing-List and sign up.

DEDICATION

This book would not be possible without the love and support of my beautiful wife. Donna, I love you more than life itself.

ACKNOWLEDGMENTS

Once again, the people who read my books before you see them have saved me. Thanks to Alan Barnes, Tracy Bodine, Michael Falkner, Michael Goad, Cain Hopwood, Kristopher Neidecker, John Naiser, Bob Noble, Andrew Olivier, Jon Paul Olivier, Bill Smith, Tom Stoecklein, Dale Thompson, and Jason Young for making me look good.

I also want to thank my readers for putting up with me. You guys are great.

1

Admiral Jared Mertz wrapped up his presentation to the senior Fleet officers aboard Orbital One with more than a hint of relief. Everyone had seen the data they'd brought back from Harrison's World about the Rebel Empire, but it was still hard for them to get their minds around. Particularly the scope and danger their enemies represented.

He understood the conceptual challenges they faced. Before the expedition, he'd felt the same way. The Old Empire had died over half a millennium ago. They'd known that all their lives. The New Terran Empire, as Kelsey had come to call them for convenience, was a peaceful civilization. One not ready for a war to the death.

Which was what they found themselves saddled with.

Thankfully, Admiral Yeats wasn't the kind of man to roll over when faced with such an overwhelming threat. He was just the man they needed in Fleet command at a time like this.

The older man rose to his feet. "Thank you, Admiral Mertz."

Yeats looked over the sea of faces as Jared resumed his seat. "This is a lot to have dumped on us with no warning. Even a month is hardly enough time to let it sink in, but we don't have the luxury of sitting on our butts and hoping the Rebel Empire doesn't come calling.

"We could've had the displeasure of an enemy fleet dropping by instead of the forces Admiral Mertz brought home. Make no mistake, those ships are a godsend, but we're still way behind the curve.

"We'll continue receiving repaired ships from Harrison's World, but we need to start building our own. The first of the captured shipyards at Erorsi will be fully operational in thirty days. The other one was badly damaged and will take longer. The ones we're building from scratch will take over a year to become operational.

"The shipyards at Erorsi are small, as well. Each will be able to build two destroyers or light cruisers at a time, or a single heavy cruiser. Nothing larger. The shipyards we're creating here at Avalon will have dozens of slips, each capable of building any size ship we want. Once those are online, we'll start building others throughout the New Terran Empire for redundancy and to increase production.

"As each shipyard comes online, it will begin construction of an initial set of destroyers to make certain all systems are operational and that the personnel are completely up to speed. That first set of ships will take about nine months. I expect the timeframe will be a few months shorter for an experienced construction crew.

"They'll move up to larger hulls once we're confident that everything is progressing well. Expected construction times are as follows: seven months for destroyers, twelve months for light cruisers, sixteen months for heavy cruisers, twenty-two months for battlecruisers, and thirty months for superdreadnoughts and carriers."

He gave them a long, serious look. "That means it will be years before we have anything close to the fleet we want. We'll need to be cautious in how we deploy what we have. Speaking of those ships, Captain Quinn, you're up next."

The slender woman rose to her feet. "We've fully manned the ships Admiral Mertz brought back, but we're running up against some hardware constraints as we work on the rest of the existing Fleet personnel. Boxer Station and the Grant Research Facility have sent all the completed implants they have on hand, but even their reserves are limited. We need to get our own implant manufacturing capability online.

"The factory ships have helped, and we've started refining the requisite materials and building our own implant infrastructure, but that will take at least another month to get fully off the ground just for what we need in Fleet.

"The civilian side will take a year or more to really get rolling here on Avalon. The rest of the Empire will take longer. We're focusing on the critical personnel first.

"We'll have the civilian implant manufacturing capability at Avalon running at full speed inside a year. Updating existing equipment to use them will take longer. Perhaps another year just for the most critical systems.

"I'm estimating that it will take between two and three years before we've incorporated implant usage into every facet of civilian manufacturing and have it all rolled out to the general population. Fleet has priority, of course, so we'll have retrofitted everything in about eighteen months. We've already begun that process."

Yeats nodded. "The basic computer systems on Orbital One have been upgraded to allow us to use implants. We're all no doubt pleased that the administrative tasks go by much more quickly, but the paperwork never seems to end, does it?"

That brought a round of laughter.

Yeats rose to his feet, hands behind his back. "Thank you, Captain."

He focused on the rest of the compartment. "The information that Harrison's World has on the rest of the Rebel Empire is sparse and inconsistent. I'm tempted to believe that some of what they do have is misinformation. In fact, we'll assume it probably is.

"The captured AI didn't have any data on the area outside the sector it controlled. That had to be intentional. Not only does the ruling AI not want its human subjects to know too much, it doesn't want the cybernetic competition knowing it, either. That makes stamping out any rebellions easier, I suppose. Such as what they did at Harrison's World. It doesn't make our jobs any simpler, though."

Jared cleared his throat. "If I may, sir, I think I have a partial solution."

The older man gestured for him to continue. "By all means, Admiral Mertz."

This wasn't going to be an easy sell, but Jared knew the time had come to make his pitch. He sent a command to the screen, and it changed to a picture of their captured Rebel Empire computer specialist.

"Meet Lieutenant Commander Michael Richards, Rebel Empire Fleet. We captured him at Erorsi. It's taken a while, but he's come to the conclusion that we're telling him the truth. That the AIs lied to his people, and that they're slaves. He's ready to help us in every way he can. In particular, he knows the system where they picked up the Marine Raider hardware."

Yeats nodded, but his expression tightened. "Why should we trust him? Forgive me, but the man has to have reservations. If someone switched sides once, they can always change their mind again. How can we possibly trust that he isn't leading us into a trap?"

"Marcus vetted him through his implants," Jared said. "That's where the subject opens up access and allows the AI to verify the truth of his statements. Richards is honestly convinced his people are slaves and is willing to help us."

After a moment, Yeats shook his head. "I need to think about that. I'll want more information on this vetting process, too. If it's as effective as you say, it will be useful with the other prisoners.

"Speaking of Marcus, where are we in building more AIs like him? We could use some help with all this work."

Doctor Leonard rose to his feet. "We've been hard at work reverse engineering the hardware, but progress is slow. Sir Carl tells me that it will take at least a year to design complete plans, and then we'd need to build one as a test. A test, by the way, that will almost certainly fail.

"A realistic timeframe for success might be three to five years. Any serious setbacks—of which there will be a few—will delay the project further. If we could get our hands on the plans somewhere, that would be extremely helpful."

Quinn made a face. "I suspect the odds of that are low. Can't Marcus help?"

The elderly scientist shook his head. "That timeframe already includes as much help as Marcus and Harrison can give. Without them, the time required goes up dramatically and the chances of overall success plummet."

Yeats sighed. "Of course they do. Can you give us an update on the flip-point jammer project?"

"It's not proceeding as well as I had hoped, Admiral," the scientist said. "The people at the Grant Research Facility built the three existing units by hand over a period of years. They didn't anticipate mass production for quite some time.

"While they're working diligently to correct that deficiency, it will be at least six months before we see the first new units roll off the line. It may take longer if they run into problems. Even then, the number of units produced in a month will be low until they get extra production lines working."

Yeats grimaced but nodded. "That isn't unexpected. We'll just have to hope that things stay relatively quiet for a while. Once we can get more of the flip-point jammers, we can start protecting our space from the rebels and even disrupt the sectors we intend to take away from them.

"We have teams going over the maps of the Old Empire you brought back to present various scenarios where we might surgically use flip-point jammers to disrupt the enemy. A number of choke points have suggested themselves."

"There's going to be another supply ship for the AI at Erorsi in about a month," Jared said. "There's also a destroyer due to go report on Harrison's World a month after that. Either one of those situations could blow up in our faces."

One of the officers in the crowd raised his hand. "Are they likely to be suspicious, Admiral? You took out their last supply mission."

Now it was Jared's turn to grimace. That comedy of errors was the late and unlamented Wallace Breckenridge's fault. They'd lost ships and men that hadn't needed to die.

"I think this year is safe," he told the man. "The records

indicate that ships have vanished before. Even warships. That speaks to some other situation that we're unaware of but gives us some breathing room. No doubt, the loss of this second set of ships will cause us more trouble. Our time of being undiscovered is coming to an end."

"Could the alien build flip points into the Rebel Empire?" a woman with captain's tabs asked. "That would allow us to strike anywhere we choose."

Jared shook his head. "Omega says the power requirements are quite steep. He has at least four months of steady charging ahead to recover the energy needed to create even one. I floated the idea of providing him with extra fusion plants and power storage, but the hurdles are too steep. His people designed his hull to stay sealed, so we can't just build a massive exterior station to support him. Everything would need to go inside the station.

"The problem there is that our power generation and storage technology is woefully inferior to his. The word he used to describe our current technology is 'adorable.' We have a team of people working on rectifying that, but it will take time to even understand the principles his people are using."

"We also need to keep in mind that these new flip points are permanent. If we open one into rebel-held space, they can use it to get to us. We should keep that idea in reserve, but I strongly suggest we avoid it until it will have a decisive impact."

"Agreed," Yeats said. "On the plus side, Sir Carl has finalized the design of the FTL coms. We'll begin seeding them throughout the Empire over the next few months and should have reliable, redundant, real-time communication throughout the Empire inside a year.

"Unfortunately, he's discovered that this technology isn't quite as undetectable as he'd originally believed. They do cause a resonance similar to, but far weaker than, a flip point. We will need to be cautious about using them in forward areas. They're a tremendous asset, and we don't want to tip our hand to the enemy.

"That leads me to the next subject. In consultation with our best ops planners, as well as Marcus and Harrison, I've decided that we need to firm up our understanding of the Rebel Empire. We need reliable data.

"The best candidate for that mission is Admiral Mertz, of course. I'm authorizing a reconnaissance in force. He won't be taking *all* the ships he brought back, but we'll send him with enough strength to take care of business if it comes down to it."

Yeats looked around the room. "Fleet has always relied on its commanders to make the hard calls for themselves, and I see no reason to change that. If the Rebel Empire manages to disrupt our new means of communication, we need people willing and able to act decisively. There will be no micromanagement from the rear in Fleet."

That brought a palpable sigh of relief from the crowd.

"We'll send *Invincible* as the flagship on this scouting mission," Yeats continued, "and about half of the ships Admiral Mertz brought back with him. The freshly recommissioned superdreadnought *Gibraltar* will form the core of our new Home Fleet once it arrives.

"And before any of you start casting covetous glances at her, I've decided that I'm moving my flag there as soon as she arrives."

He glared at them for emphasis, earning a rumble of laughter.

"Admiral Mertz, I want you to capture the supply ship intact this time. Preferably the escort, too, but definitely the freighter. Princess Kelsey has been hounding me about needing the supplies it carries. She wants more raiders, as do the emperor and I.

"Then you'll need to scout for the facility that made them. If the information on the freighter matches what Commander Richards told us, I'll revisit my decision about him accompanying you.

"Let me be clear. I not only want you to capture the supplies but to get the technology to make more. The princess's manuals only cover the use of Raider enhancements, not the construction of them. We *need* that knowledge if we're to survive and fight effectively."

Jared nodded. "You can count on me to do my best, Admiral."

"I know I can. We haven't finalized the timeline yet, but expect us to pull the trigger on the reconnaissance in the very near future. As in no more than a week, but probably less than that. We absolutely cannot afford to allow the enemy to know we're here."

The older man smiled. "Also, I've spoken with His Majesty about the current situation on *Persephone*. He said that it is not acceptable to have a civilian in command of a Fleet or Marine Raider vessel."

"Princess Kelsey isn't going to be happy about that, and neither is the computer controlling the ship," Jared said. Unhappy was probably an understatement.

"I know," Yeats said. "So we've decided to commission her as a colonel in the Imperial Marines. She'll find out later today that she's the new commanding officer of the Marine Raiders. If she's going to fight, we might as well get rid of the fiction that she isn't a warrior."

"It's about time, sir. She'll be pleased."

"Major Talbot will be less so, I'm sure," Yeats said with a smile. "I also have something in mind for your carrier and her escorts. It's a bit unusual, but I think it's the best course of action given the circumstances. We really don't have any people trained in fighter operations, so I intend to keep Zia Anderson in command.

"She doesn't have the rank for it, but I'm also placing her in charge of the carrier group. The job belongs to a commodore or admiral, but I'm not quite ready to shift any of the existing flag officers to do that, particularly since they don't have a firm grasp on what being a fighter commander is really about."

Jared felt the corners of his mouth rise. "She's going to feel even more out of her depth. She was only a lieutenant when this all started."

Yeats nodded. "I understand, but we all have to step up. I'm transferring a very experienced executive officer to help her with that. He has a much firmer grasp of running a ship, even with his weakness in fighter operations and unfamiliarity with implants.

"She'll have to bring him up to speed. Once that happens, she'll have someone to share the load. Then we can talk about promoting people. I have some thoughts that I'll share with you about that later."

"Aye, sir."

"Now, we have a lot more ground to cover before we can wrap up," Yeats said briskly. "I've got people waiting outside to brief us on the status of our remedial training on Old Empire technology, the drive to recruit the people we'll need to man all the ships we're planning to build, the greatly expanded ground forces we'll require, our transition to a wartime economy, and more. Get comfortable."

Jared resisted the urge to check the time. This was going to be a really, *really* long day.

* * *

KELSEY BANDAR, heir to the Imperial Throne, banged her head on the table in the Imperial library. She'd gone over everything they still had in electronic form from before the Fall, and there was no reference to the "key" that Emperor Marcus had mentioned his son Lucien having.

It was infuriating. Surely, the words he'd used in his last transmission meant *something*.

She'd spent the last month going through the archives of old equipment. There were plenty of keys of one kind or another but nothing that seemed to have any deeper meaning.

To help sort things out, she'd shanghaied the newly created Doctor Carl Owlet to help. Sir Carl when she was particularly cranky.

He'd examined the data with every tool he'd designed for things like this. Still nothing.

"Excuse me," he said from behind her. "Are you all right?"

She raised her head and sighed. "Yes. I'm just frustrated. I was so *sure* there was something here."

He shrugged. "Apparently not. Is this all the hardware left over from before the Fall?"

"Yes."

"Maybe we need to take a step back and look at the person rather than the gear," he said. "Emperor Lucien arrived as a boy. Perhaps he didn't know what this key was or the person tasked with telling him died in the attack."

She rubbed her face. "His guards shoved him into an escape pod and blasted it free as soon as they got close to Avalon. The rebels still almost killed him anyway.

"He had people with him, but no advisors. He basically arrived with the clothes on his back."

Carl nodded. "Is the escape pod still in existence? Perhaps they hid something inside it. Or even dropped it there during the chaos."

Her head came up. "That's not a bad idea."

"Of course not," he said with a twinkle in his eyes. "I came up with it."

She laughed.

They'd linked the Imperial Library to an Old Empire computer, so searching the records wasn't nearly as difficult as it would've been a year ago.

"Got it," she said as the data came up in her implants. "The escape pod is on permanent loan to the Imperial Air and Space Museum. Let's go give it a look."

Her guards formed up around them as they headed for the parking garage. She hadn't wanted to accept the fact she needed them, but being the heir was part theater. The men and women of the Imperial Guard were the price she paid for being one breath away from the Throne.

Of course, since they'd locked her up a month ago, she'd insisted they get implants and be questioned closely about their loyalty to the Throne and her. That had scared off more than a few applicants.

With reason, it seemed. Ethan had had his fingers deep into their number. Follow-up investigations were still under way.

She knew the men and women assigned to her were loyal. They wouldn't turn on her. They also wouldn't let her wander off unescorted. Dammit.

The trip to the museum entailed her grav limo and two follow cars. Officially. She knew that there were two Fleet fighters circling the area in case she needed heavy backup.

Hopefully, that wasn't going to be a problem here at home, but considering the number of times things had gone badly, she wasn't going to complain.

She checked her internal chronometer. "We don't have a lot of time. I'm supposed to meet Senator Breckenridge for dinner. Probably something political and boring, but the man took a flechette for my father. I owe it to him."

Carl nodded. "That's perfect, actually. Angela and I have a little getaway planned. She rented a cabin up in the woods for some quality time. I'm not supposed to know about it, but she has terrible computer security habits."

Kelsey gave him a stern look. "Just because someone leaves their door cracked open doesn't mean you should walk in and look around."

He made a dismissive noise. "It's as though she left it lying on the counter. She knows I know. I'm not sure what that means, but it's probably important." He sighed. "Relationships are hard."

"Yes, they are. They take work on everyone's part."

Kelsey turned her head and smiled a little. He was right, as far as he knew. His girlfriend, Major Angela Ellis of the Imperial Marines, had arranged with Kelsey to borrow the Imperial Retreat. They'd plotted together to leave enough information lying about to give Carl the wrong impression but not enough to clue him in that they were running a disinformation campaign.

The grav limo landed outside the museum, and her guards formed up around her as they went in. The crowds were just as large as one might expect. Wide-eyed kids and equally interested adults examining the artifacts left over from the Old Empire. There was so much to see. More than she'd anticipated.

It had artifacts from before the Fall and from their slow climb back into space. She imagined it would have a number of new exhibits before long.

She'd come here as a kid herself. The thought darkened her mood. She'd had just as much fun as the people around her at her brother Ethan's side. Now he was dead at her hand. Basically.

He'd tried to kill their father and take the Throne for himself. She'd had no choice. It still hurt. It was like cutting off her own arm. She knew the pain would never fully go away.

A man in a dark suit walked toward her, but the guards stopped him. After a moment, they let him through, though they kept a close eye on him.

He bowed low. "Highness, welcome to the Imperial Air and Space Museum. I'm Director Chandra. How can I be of assistance?"

"Thank you for taking time out of your busy day to meet me,

Director. This is my associate, Doctor Owlet. We need to examine Lucien's escape pod."

He looked a bit confused at that but nodded. "Of course. It's in the main space wing. This way, please."

It only took a few minutes to get there.

The escape pod had no doubt seen better days, but the museum had painstakingly restored it. It sat in a display that looked like a hillside. The hatch was open, and a bold-faced youth stood there looking out. The mannequin was very lifelike, though she knew the boy must've been terrified during the real events.

She started to step over the rope, but the director stopped her.

"I'm sorry, but you can't go inside. It's a delicate relic."

Kelsey smiled at him. "I assure you it's sturdier than it looks, Director. The Old Empire built to last. We believe there might be something inside that the Empire needs."

The poor man looked of two minds, but he nodded. "Please be careful. I cannot overstate how historically important this relic is."

"Sir Carl is our most respected expert in Old Empire technology. I realize this is an unusual situation, but I happen to know we have a number of things we've brought back during the expedition that are in need of a good home."

She could see in his eyes that that made a difference but didn't entirely ease his worry. He let them in, though.

When the guards made to follow her, Kelsey stopped them. "There's not going to be any danger in there. Why don't you focus on the crowd?"

She and Carl stepped past the false Lucien and into the pod. It was a standard Old Empire model that held two dozen people in zero comfort. Much like a marine pinnace, the passengers were strapped to the walls and packed like fish in a tin. There wasn't even a control console.

"Do you suppose the power is still on?" she asked.

"Not a chance," Carl said as he walked deeper into the pod. "The power packs wouldn't have lasted more than a few months."

He set his bag down in front of a large access panel. "The power connections are behind here. I have a small fusion pack in my bag for emergencies."

She knew it wasn't Mjölnir. The high-tech hammer he'd built for her was safely tucked away in her personal armory.

"Exactly what kind of emergencies are you expecting, and why do you need a fusion pack in your bag?"

He grinned at her. "Why do you need the arsenal you carry around? Because it might come in *really* handy in a pinch."

She couldn't argue with that.

It only took him a few moments to open the panel. The power packs were obvious and marked. Their indicators were dark.

Carl pulled out a fusion power pack the size of his fist and started connecting it to the ports. The lights began coming on.

Once she was sure the on-board computer had come online, she linked with it. It wasn't much more than a basic interface, but it had what she was looking for. Records of the descent and landing, both interior and exterior. It also had an encrypted copy of the ship's logs at the time it ejected. Those might be invaluable.

If nothing else, the records were historically priceless. Now the people of the Empire could see for themselves the moment everything changed for Avalon.

The recording started as soon as the escape pod jettisoned. That made sense. Why waste data storage on noncritical periods?

The interior view showed the pod packed with more people than its designers had ever intended. Mostly women and children. Lucien was easy to spot.

Someone—probably a guard—had strapped him in. The boy struggled free of the restraints as the pod raced away from its doomed mother ship, awkwardly helping a woman with a baby into his place.

Kelsey swelled with pride. That was the man he'd become one day shining through.

The external view captured her attention at that point. The pod was moving rapidly, but Kelsey recognized what the mother ship was. A battlecruiser much like *Courageous*. The computer labeled her as *Lancelot*.

Explosions wreathed her as she returned fire at unseen enemies, shielding the escape pods with her own hull and battle screens. Pods continued flooding from her until she exploded without warning.

The pod tumbled badly. A piece of shrapnel from the ship must've struck it. The people inside were thrown around like leaves in a whirlwind. Some died. Kelsey could see that as her heart flew into her throat.

Lucien smashed into the wall and somehow hung onto a harness. The woman inside clutched at him desperately. He looked as though his arm were broken.

The pod straightened moments later and entered the atmosphere at what an observer might charitably call an unsafe speed. The external cameras went offline moments later.

Kelsey imagined anyone on the ground who happened to be looking up saw the pod as a finger of fire racing across the sky.

The pod could still sense the surface, and it braked hard just before impact. That ripped Lucien free from the woman's grip and slammed him into the forward bulkhead.

Once it was safely on the ground, the hatch slid open, and people started trying to get free from their restraints. They had to be afraid death was still coming for them. In their place, Kelsey would've been.

Lucien staggered to his feet and cradled his arm. Yeah, that was an ugly break. In that moment, he looked so much like the mannequin it was spooky. Determination steamed off him. It made her proud.

The woman who'd held him tried to help him out, but he shook his head. Kelsey wished there was sound to hear what he'd said to her.

The boy-emperor leaned against the wall and opened a storage compartment. He dug inside and pulled out a pack. He opened it and partially extracted something, obviously examining it for damage. It was an object she was *very* familiar with. Understanding flooded her.

"Isn't that…" Carl started.

"The Imperial Scepter," Kelsey finished breathlessly. "It must be the key Emperor Marcus was talking about."

2

Captain Zia Anderson was certain the crew thought she was crazy, but she couldn't help herself. Here it was late on third shift and she was wandering the corridors of her new command. Her first command.

The Fleet carrier *Audacious* was both an Old Empire ship—with all the bells and whistles that implied—and a completely new kind of warship for the New Terran Empire. Fighters hadn't made a comeback after the Fall, so none of the so-called wiser heads was really sure how to fit them into their battle plans.

That left it to her to come up with fighter doctrine all on her own. Oh, the Old Empire had a ton of books on the subject, but no living person had ever put them to use. Reading something was not the same as living it.

Ever since Princess Kelsey had promoted her and Admiral Mertz had assigned her to command *Audacious*, she'd been learning and refining what she knew and dragging the crew along with her.

A little more than a month was not enough time to get them even into a modicum of shape in her opinion. The ship's crew was coming along nicely, but the pilots in her squadrons were still learning the basics of their craft. Pun intended.

She was learning along with them, though at a slower pace. She'd never been much of a pilot, but anyone that served on the command crew of a Fleet ship knew enough to take over someone else's station in a pinch. As a tactical officer, she'd sat right next to their pilot—Pasco Ramirez—for years. She could get a ship from point A to B well enough.

That wasn't nearly enough to fly a fighter well, so she'd been spending a lot of time in the simulators. That meant being there when the pilots were mostly asleep. A captain didn't make a big display of her ignorance. She had to seem competent at every aspect of her command.

Now, after drilling for a month, she was about ready to take a real fighter out. It had her both nervous and excited. She'd flown with other pilots before, but only under their watchful eyes. This was her first solo excursion.

Zia walked onto the flight deck and found Commander Annette Vitter waiting for her. Vitter was a comrade from her service on *Athena*, their original ship. She'd been one of their best cutter pilots.

The other woman smiled. "You ready to take her for a spin, Captain?"

The "her" in question was a sleek fighter sitting on the launch rack with the rest of the ready birds. Vitter had had the ready team prep her for flight, but Zia intended to go over every centimeter of the craft before she climbed in.

"You bet," Zia said. "I'll start the preflight."

She couldn't help but look at Vitter's right arm every time she saw the other woman. One day, maybe, she'd be able to forget that the pilot had lost it in a pinnace crash. One that her skill had turned from outright destruction into something barely survivable.

Princess Kelsey had gotten a tourniquet on her quickly enough to save her life, and the doctors on Harrison's World had created this life-like artificial limb that interfaced with the woman's nervous system just as well as the original.

Vitter had been the obvious choice as the lead pilot, and the princess had promoted the woman while she was still in rehab. She'd taken to fighters like a marine to booze and cards, and she was wickedly good.

In addition to her overall command of every fighter on the ship, she personally led Black Jack Squadron. If needed, her second was more than capable of stepping in to take over while the woman guided all of three squadrons in action.

Her title was archaic and hoary with age. It came from the time when the only carriers on Terra were in the wet navy and limited to only atmospheric work. She was the Commander, Air Group, or CAG.

Admiral Yeats had been skeptical of the usefulness of the fighters at first. Then Vitter had led her people on a simulated attack run, swarming Orbital One. Even knowing they were coming hadn't been enough to save the space station. Not then, and not in the follow-up runs he'd ordered.

After that, he'd become a fervent convert, running roughshod over any of his subordinates who weren't as eager to embrace the new technology. He'd taken enough spare fighters recovered from the graveyard to outfit Orbital One, and they were still installing the new flight decks there.

A second carrier would be arriving at Avalon in a few more months, but he wanted to have a ready force to help defend against any threats. Unlike when Admiral Mertz had used his in combat, they were significantly more effective in large numbers.

Zia focused on the preflight. Her implants provided the checklist and could even expand on what she should be seeing, so it didn't take long.

Vitter stood back, watching. She was already dressed in her bulky flight suit. Zia would need to change before they launched.

"I'll go gear up," Zia said once she was satisfied with the external preflight.

"Locker A-1 is reserved for you, ma'am. It'll always have your gear ready to roll."

She smiled a little. "I'm afraid my job is on the command deck, Annette. Sending you people to do what you do best."

"Maybe, but that doesn't mean you don't have a place here. My people respect you."

That meant a lot to Zia. She knew that once they got into the thick of it, all too many of her pilots wouldn't be coming back. It was dangerous work.

"Not any more than I respect them. I'll be right back."

Zia went into the ready room and waved at the on-duty pilots. They were all dressed to launch at a moment's notice but were engaged in everything from sleeping to watching entertainment vids to playing poker.

Those who were awake called out greetings as she made her way to the adjacent compartment with the lockers. She quickly stripped off her uniform and pulled on an under suit. It would keep her alive if all else failed. Princess Kelsey had proven that with the one she wore under her armor at Boxer Station.

Once she had the snug under suit on, she climbed into the bulky flight suit and arrayed her survival gear. The more capable equipment would allow her to survive for up to a day if everything went south. A beacon on her hip would lead CSAR to her or any other pilot who successfully ejected from a crippled fighter.

Not that doing so was standard practice, regardless of what Admiral Mertz had done. The deadly little craft could keep a pilot breathing for a week, just based on the emergency supplies it carried. They'd only bail if it were in danger of exploding.

Her helmet was sleek and aggressive in styling. That fit the mentality of the people attracted to the job. Hotshots, each and every one of them.

They'd decorated her helmet with all three squadron emblems, which filled her with pride. The rear of a pilot's helmet usually only had their own squadron's badge. They had arranged hers in a diamond with *Audacious*'s emblem sitting on top.

She headed back out only to run into a pair of the ready pilots. They checked her gear over matter-of-factly. Part of her felt like objecting, but she knew they'd do the same for one another.

"Thanks, boys," she said once they finished. "Don't break anything while I'm gone."

Their leader grinned. "Who? Us? Have a good flight, Captain."

Vitter was standing next to one of the ready fighters when Zia came out. "Your call sign for this flight is Black Jack One, Captain. I'm Black Jack Six."

Zia nodded. "Got it."

She climbed into her fighter. It only took a moment to bring everything online via her implants, and she got down to the task of checking every system.

Once she was ready, she opened a channel to Vitter. "Black Jack Six, this is Black Jack One. Ready for launch."

"Copy that, Black Jack One. Contact flight operations and launch when ready."

Zia opened a channel to them. "Flight operations, this is Black Jack One requesting a launch window."

"Copy that, Black Jack One," Lieutenant Leo Thomas said. "You are cleared to launch at your discretion."

"Thanks, Control. Black Jack One out."

She sent the command to the magnetic catapult her fighter rested on. It came to life and hurled her down the short tunnel and out of the ship with brutal force, pressing her deeply back into her acceleration couch.

Once clear of the ship, she brought her drive online, and it instantly cut the perceived acceleration down to something bearable.

Moments later, Vitter's fighter appeared off to port. She could see the woman looking at her through her canopy. "Good launch, Black Jack One. Let's put you through your paces. I hope you studied all the maneuvers carefully, because I'm a stickler for detail."

Over the next two hours, Vitter taxed Zia's memory, skills, and endurance. They went through virtually every scenario a fighter pilot needed to perform. Everything except an ejection. That was a bit traumatic for the little craft.

"That's a wrap, Black Jack One," Vitter finally said. "You need to work on a few things, but overall, I'm satisfied with your progress. You're still a greenhorn, but you'll do in a pinch."

Damned with faint praise. Zia smiled. She really was on the low end skill-wise, and she knew it.

"I'll take it, for now, but I'm going to keep practicing."

"Roger that. Contact control and take us in," Vitter said. "You'll only have an hour to get cleaned up and onto that fancy bridge of yours before all the lazybones are up."

Zia called *Audacious*'s flight operations and got them a return vector. They positively dawdled back to the ship. Once they were in the area, Control gave her priority over a passenger cutter inbound for landing.

Unlike most ships, all small ships used the carrier's flight decks rather than isolated docks.

The landing priority apparently didn't sit too well with the cutter pilot. She could hear him arguing with control. He claimed to have a senior officer on board.

Control called Zia. "Black Jack One, this is Control. The inbound cutter is requesting priority in the landing queue. Are you okay with coming around again?"

"Negative, Control. Black Jack flight will land first."

"Copy that, Black Jack One."

The other pilot shut up once he acknowledged Control's instructions, but Zia imagined he was pissed. Too bad.

Zia led the way in and put the fighter neatly down in the designated area. Vitter landed beside her.

The cutter took a spot just up the deck, and the passenger hatch opened as soon as it settled. A large man with wide shoulders and a grim expression exited and headed right for the fighters.

Well, this should be interesting.

She opened her canopy and shut the fighter down before climbing out. The man was waiting impatiently below her. His rank tabs indicated he was a commander.

"What the hell was that? Didn't you hear my pilot say there was a senior officer on board?"

Zia held out a hand, cutting Vitter's hot response off. "I heard you just fine, Commander. This is a carrier. Fighter operations always have priority."

"Helmet off, pilot. When I'm chewing ass, I want to see who I'm talking to."

That really tanned Zia's hide. She had a volatile temper, when she allowed it to rear its ugly head, and this guy was pushing her buttons.

She popped her helmet off and held it in the crook of her arm. She ran a hand through her hair to get it into some semblance of order.

The man glared down at her. "I realize you people think you're all that and a bag of crisps, but the universe doesn't revolve around you. What's your name?"

"Anderson. Call sign Black Jack One."

"Well, Anderson, you'd better be glad I don't have time to deal with you right now. You can be sure that once I've reported to the captain, we'll have another discussion that you won't enjoy nearly as much as this one."

Zia frowned. She hadn't been expecting anyone coming to see her.

"And why would that be, Commander?" she asked.

He smiled a bit smugly. "Because I'm your new executive officer. I don't know how you people have been doing things, but they'll be by the book going forward. Expect my call, Anderson."

He turned on his heel before she could respond and headed for the lift.

Vitter stepped up beside her. "Why didn't you tell him you were the captain, ma'am?"

"Because it'll have a bigger impact if I let him find out the hard way. He wanted to make a point by browbeating me, so now he gets to get the same kind of treatment.

"I'm a bit concerned that I didn't hear about this ahead of time. I knew Commander Leonidas was going to receive his own command, but I thought he had another week."

The other woman smiled knowingly. "The ways of the personnel branch are obscure, ma'am. You know what I think? That if I had orders to a new ship, I'd make sure and at least know what my commanding officer looked like."

"That's because you're a prudent and thoughtful officer. I can see this new guy is going to have a rough time adjusting to how we do business. I should go get cleaned up and get this over with."

Zia called her steward while she stripped her gear off and told him to stall the man. She took a quick shower, dressed in her uniform, and headed back into the ready room.

She stopped in her tracks as soon as she came in. It looked as though every fighter pilot on the ship was there.

Commander Vitter stood in front with a wicked smile on her face. "Captain Zia Anderson, you have met all of the qualifications to be a Fleet fighter pilot. It is my pleasure to welcome you to our ranks, but my sad duty to inform you there is yet one more burden to be borne. Attention on the flight deck!"

Every person in the room stiffened, including Zia. She still wasn't completely used to being a senior officer, and a commander still felt like a superior to the lieutenant inside her.

"The fighter corps has a tradition when welcoming people to its ranks that goes back to before humanity ever left the surface of Terra," Vitter said conversationally. "One that left a mark on all who accepted our deadly burden. Captain Zia Anderson, are you willing to shed blood for your brothers and sisters? To suffer pain for them?"

That was an easy one. "I am."

"Then open your tunic."

That was an odd thing to do, but Zia opened the top of her uniform tunic, exposing her undershirt.

"Once pilots wore wings of metal on their uniforms, not patches sealed into place," the pilot said. "That meant that our wings had bite."

She held up a set of metal wings with two long spikes in the back. Zia suddenly knew what was coming.

"Each and every pilot on this ship has shed their blood with these very wings to join our ranks. Your nanites might heal the wounds quickly, but the pain and symbolism mean a great deal to us."

The woman placed the wings on Zia's upper left chest and used the heel of her fist to pound it into her captain's flesh.

The spike of pain was immediate and intense, but Zia gritted her teeth and made no sound. She kept her expression neutral though her chest was on fire.

Vitter waited a beat and pulled the spikes back out. Another pilot stepped forward with a swab and tugged the under tunic aside long enough to wipe away the blood. He applied two dabs of medical sealer to the aching wounds and stepped back.

"Pilots, I give you our newest sister!" Vitter said.

Everyone shouted raucously and crowded around Zia, pounding her on the back and shaking her hand. It was such a powerful moment that it took everything Zia had not to cry, but she averted that catastrophe. Barely.

Once all the pilots had left, except the ready crew, Vitter shook Zia's hand. "We're glad to have you in our ranks, Captain. We know you'll make us proud."

"That was barbaric but damned powerful."

The other woman laughed. "We're warriors, ma'am. We spill blood for a living. The marines have nothing on us."

Zia couldn't help smiling in return. "Well, I suppose I'd better get upstairs and shed some blood of my own."

She left the flight deck energized. This had been one of those moments that changed people's lives forever, and she'd never forget it. Now she had to go try to inoculate the new guy with the same bug, as difficult as that seemed to imagine at the moment.

* * *

ANNETTE WATCHED her commanding officer walk out with more than a dash of pride. The former tactical officer was shaping up into a fine leader. She still had some growing to do, but that was true for all of them. Particularly herself.

Her assistant squadron commander, Lieutenant Commander Jake Fiennes, stepped up beside her. "She's a good one."

"I was just thinking that. I'm wondering how she'll handle the new guy. They didn't exactly get off on the right foot."

He snorted. "You think? Well, he'll either adjust or get rolled."

She gave him a raised eyebrow. "That isn't the way to think about our new executive officer. I know all fighter pilots are wild cards, but there are limits to the meme. Whatever his personality, we're going to have to work under his orders."

Jake seemed to consider that for a moment and then nodded. "I suppose so. The captain will set the tone, but he's going to do what he does. We have to make sure our boys and girls don't raise too big a stink."

"Good man. How are the deployment plans coming?"

She'd tasked him and the other squadron commanders to devise an attack plan for a fleet action. Fighter deployment was new to all of them, and she wanted to have a number of primary, backup, contingency, and emergency plans worked out and practiced ahead of when they needed them.

The notion that people rose up to meet a crisis was wrong. They defaulted to what they'd trained to do. She didn't want her people to practice until they got it right. She wanted them to be so skilled that they couldn't get it wrong.

"We have a number of basic strategies worked out," he said as they walked into her office. "*Audacious*'s computer had all the plans the previous squadron commanders worked up for various scenarios. We kept that framework in place and broke them down even further so we can practice the basic skills they already had down pat.

"The training we've already gotten will slot into the new plans easily enough. Once we get on station, we can launch training flights to stitch everything together. It'll take years before we're as smooth as they probably were, but we can be effective much sooner than that."

She nodded. "That works. I'll want to see a preliminary training schedule this afternoon. I'll have my comments back to you as soon as I can to refine what you have. After the training run, of course."

"Roger that. If you'll excuse me, I'll go get the squadron ready to launch."

Annette sat behind her desk as soon as he'd left and brought up the Fleet records on Brandon Levy.

Last assigned as the commanding officer on a heavy cruiser. He'd also commanded a destroyer a few years back.

She couldn't access the sensitive parts of his record, but the theme was there for anyone who looked. Levy was a competent officer with solid skills. He'd have a much better grasp of running a ship than Zia Anderson, even though Annette thought the other woman was doing fine.

The new guy would have two strikes against him. First, his attitude. Second, he didn't understand the new technology. Not that the rest of them were as far along as they needed to be, but he'd have more ground to cover. Not just skill-wise, but conceptually. Understanding that something was even possible gave one a leg up.

Or an arm.

She held up her artificial arm. The technological marvel still astounded her. When she'd lost it, she'd known her career was over. She'd become a cripple. Someone to be pitied.

Only that wasn't how things had turned out. The doctors in the command post on Erorsi had the full know-how of the Old Empire at their fingertips. They couldn't build a sophisticated arm like this one with their limited facilities, but they'd laid the groundwork.

The doctors on Harrison's World had built her arm with her piloting in mind. The rehabilitation hadn't been easy, but she came into it determined to regain everything she'd lost.

Months of blood, sweat, and tears had paid off. It was almost as natural as her real arm had been now. She could perform any task she needed to with as much finesse and dexterity as any uninjured person.

Annette knew she'd have to help the new guy if they were to avoid a nasty situation where he didn't grow the way he needed to. The fighter pilots under her command were vulnerable to someone that didn't truly understand their purpose. She'd have to make sure the new guy didn't dismiss them out of hand or file them away as glorified cutter pilots.

Unfortunately, it certainly seemed as though Brandon Levy had already put them in that mental space. Tomorrow, she'd make his acquaintance. She'd be a friendly face and make sure he assimilated. That way she could shape his views before they became a problem.

Well, she could worry about him after the training flight. He wasn't going anywhere. She rose to her feet and headed for the ready room.

3

Kelsey arrived at Senator Breckenridge's home a few minutes early but close enough to be considered punctual. There was an art to arriving to dinner parties that was a bit hard to understand for the uninitiated. It wasn't all about being fashionably late.

Frankly, she'd rather have examined the Imperial Scepter, but with Carl and Angela off on their getaway, it wouldn't have mattered. Only someone with his level of technical expertise could even hope to make head or tail out of something as complex as it probably was.

She'd decided not to tell her father until they had at least a little information. After all, any discovery had already waited half a millennium for them to find. It could hold for a few more days.

The senator's palatial home seemed a little deserted to be hosting a dinner party. She'd expected to find guests already in the landing area and on the balcony overlooking it. The lights were on, and there were uniformed Senatorial Guards, but no guests.

God, she hoped she hadn't misremembered the time. Or the date.

She checked her implants as they landed. No, right on time. Something else was going on.

The Imperial Guard formed a cordon around the air car as she exited. There wasn't any visible tension between them and their senatorial counterparts. They'd no doubt worked together before and coordinated her arrival.

The door to the house opened, and Senator Breckenridge himself came out with a smile on his face. "Welcome to my home, Highness."

She held out her hand. "I was worried I misremembered the date. Where are your other guests?"

"My apologies. I thought you understood it was only the two of us."

Looking back, she didn't think he'd ever said one way or the other. She'd made an assumption. This was a little disconcerting. Not because she worried about being alone with the man. Even discounting her guards, she could handle herself just fine.

"This is all suitably mysterious," she said as she allowed him to escort her inside. "I'm thinking you want to do more than small talk."

He nodded. "We can adjourn to my parlor. There's plenty of room for the guards, though I want to discuss a personal matter that requires some discretion. We can eat beforehand, if you're hungry. That might be best, honestly. You might not be in the mood to dine when we're done."

"That doesn't sound promising. I say we just trot it out and get it over with. If I feel like eating when we're done, we will. If not, I can storm out in a huff with a sandwich."

His parlor was filled with family history, she saw. Old paintings and far too many knick-knacks to count. It seemed like a very comfortable space.

There were two chairs waiting for them near the fireplace. It wasn't cold out, but someone had laid a small fire. A decanter of amber liquid and some glasses sat on a small table between the chairs.

Breckenridge saw her to her seat and poured them both a drink. She sipped hers as he sat. She preferred beer, much to her father's horror, but could recognize the quality of excellent scotch when she tasted it.

"Shall we dance around the meat of the matter for a while, or do you just want to trot it out, Senator?"

He smiled. "I think I like the new you better than the old one. Not that I had any problem with you before, Highness. You've got spine now, though."

Breckenridge sipped his drink. "Though I will admit that doesn't make what I need to say any easier."

She racked her brain but couldn't figure out what had the man all worked up. He'd recovered from his injuries sustained helping rescue the emperor and had firmly advocated for her to become the Imperial Heir, even though she hadn't really cared one way or the other.

"You might as well tell me, Senator. I have no idea what has you in an uproar." She looked over at her guards. "I'd like you to wait outside. Also, please turn off your enhanced hearing."

They weren't happy, but they left as instructed. His guards followed them out and closed the door softly.

Breckenridge set his glass on the table. "I know you've read the report on the rescue mission to save your father, but there were certain details that were left out at my request. I felt that I needed to say them face to face when the time was right. Such as the fact that I provided access to the Imperial escape tunnel."

She frowned. "I looked it over. It was biometrically keyed."

"Indeed it was, but I was the only available person who knew where it was located. I'm sorry to have put this so baldly, but I don't think dancing around it will make any of this easier. I was the empress's paramour."

Kelsey opened her mouth to say something and then closed it again. The news shocked and dumbfounded her, so she was better off saying nothing until she knew what she wanted to say.

After a moment, she started again. "I should be surprised—and I suppose I am—but I already knew my mother had betrayed her vows. I'm disappointed to hear you helped her do it, Senator."

He nodded. "It was a long time ago, but I should've exercised better judgment. I intend to make a similar confession to His Majesty, but I felt I needed to explain myself to you first."

"I don't see the logic in that," she said. "Your apology to him makes a lot more sense than one to me. I'm not affected by—"

Her thoughts screeched to an abrupt halt. If he felt as though his dalliance with her mother was important to Kelsey, that had to mean...

He nodded. "I can see you've figured it out. I didn't even suspect until you came back. The times match up too closely to dismiss. I spoke with Crown Princess Elise, and she had me consult with Doctor Stone. I set up this meeting as soon as I was sure. This is a terrible way to break the news, but I can't think of a better one. Biologically, I'm your father."

* * *

JARED WALKED into his father's quarters without a guard at his heel for the first time. He had no doubt they were deeply unhappy with that, but the emperor had been firm on that point.

Over the last month, he'd seen his father more times than he had since he'd discovered his heritage. It made him uncomfortable at first—even more so than before—but the man had just lost his son. The same son that had betrayed and almost killed him.

Jared supposed that might've played into the Imperial Guard wanting to keep an eye on him. Honestly, he couldn't blame them. The emperor had come very close to dying.

A week ago, the older man had undergone the implant procedure. Doctor Stone said he'd come through perfectly. The Imperial Guard was doing the same, no doubt hoping that helped them keep a better eye on their charge.

Jared found Karl Bandar standing beside the massive carving that Master Vestor of Pentagar had given to the people of the New Terran Empire. The incredibly detailed carving hung on the wall in the emperor's quarters for now. In a few weeks, it would go to the Imperial Gallery so that the people on Avalon could enjoy it as well. Then it would tour the Empire.

The emperor had a magnifier out and was closely examining a particular section. He glanced over as Jared cleared his throat.

"It's simply astounding," the older man said. "I cannot imagine the level of dedication and skill required to carve such detailed work by hand. Have you looked closely at the way he used the wood's grain to his advantage?"

"It is unbelievable," Jared agreed. "And such a large piece. The amount of time it took is staggering."

The emperor put the magnifier down and walked over to Jared. "I've sent him an invitation to come visit. I do hope he accepts. I want to meet the man who can create such beauty."

His father gestured to the same chairs the two of them had used before Jared left on his original mission. "Join me."

Jared sat, more than a little discomfited to have the emperor pouring them drinks. "How are you adapting to the implants?" he asked to cover his own awkwardness.

The emperor handed him one of the glasses and beamed. "They're just as wonderful as you and Kelsey had said. It's only been a week, but I can hardly imagine how I got along without them. Even though I'm not using them anywhere close to their potential, I'm sure. For that, you'll have to find a teenager."

That made Jared laugh. "Too true. Kids always seem to know how to push technology far past where those of us just getting it can imagine. The first class of midshipmen that have had them since their teens are going to be an eye-opening experience, I'm sure."

"More like terrifying, I'd imagine. This technology will change the Empire in ways we can't begin to imagine."

The older man sipped his whiskey. "Jared, I want to thank you for your support during this very difficult time. I understand you never liked Ethan, but what he became wasn't truly him. Not the boy I raised. This has been hard."

Jared nodded. "My support has nothing to do with Ethan, frankly. I care about you and Kelsey."

"Nevertheless, I appreciate what you've done. This has been very difficult for Kelsey. More so than for me, I suspect. She's the one that allowed Ethan to make that one final, fatal mistake. It eats at her, but she won't talk with me about it. I hope she opens up to Talbot or you. That kind of thing can fester."

"She hasn't really talked to me, but I know she's getting counseling. Doctor Stone is also her confidant. She's talking to Talbot, too, I'd imagine. He's not the kind of man that lets someone sit on their butt feeling sorry for themselves without making some noise."

"He's good for her," the emperor said. "I'd never have envisioned that match, but it's a good one. He's smart and determined. I think he'll make an excellent prince consort."

Jared smiled. "Oh, I can't imagine he'll like the sound of that. Just being Sir Russel gives him hives."

"If it's any consolation, he pitched a fit when I told him and demanded the Imperial herald enter his title as Sir Talbot."

That made Jared sputter in the middle of a sip. "I'd say you were yanking my chain, but I know him. Did you do it?"

"Of course I did. The man is an iconoclast. His very personality demanded that I do so. It also suitably distracted him from the fact that I was covertly making him more acceptable to the Senate as the prince consort. Knighthood is not a lofty title, but it technically makes him a member of the Imperial aristocracy. Which brings me to you."

Jared froze, his glass almost to his lips. "Me?"

"Indeed," the emperor said with a slight smile. "I've made a decision you're going to hate as much as Talbot did, but it's for your own good. And the Empire's, too, of course.

"You might never be comfortable with the idea, but you are as much my son as Kelsey is my daughter. Blood never entered into my thinking, so the fact you are biologically mine and she isn't doesn't matter one bit to me. Still, the blood of emperors flows in your veins, and the Empire is in sore need of icons like yourself."

"My heart is filled with dread. Majesty, I am no icon."

The other man's smile widened. "I suppose I did turn this into an emperor/liegeman moment. I hadn't intended this to be an ambush, but I'll just keep rolling.

"Have you considered everything that you did? Imagine, if you will, that someone else had led the mission and done those heroic deeds. Have you read any of the Norse Sagas? Epic is not an understatement for what you've accomplished. As the story gets out, the people of the Empire will see you as a hero, and nothing you can do will change that."

Jared carefully set his glass down. "I can see that, but I'm not sure I like where you're going with this."

"I'm not surprised. You're just as pigheaded as Talbot, in your own quiet way. And as blind. Do you love Elise?"

The question took him by surprise. "Of course I do."

"Do you see yourself marrying her one day? Raising a family?"

"I'd like to think so. Did she have something to do with this?"

Crown Princess Elise Orison of the Kingdom of Pentagar was one of the most politically savvy people Jared knew and wickedly subtle in moving behind the scenes. Much more so than he was.

The emperor made an ambivalent gesture with his hand. "Perhaps, in a roundabout way. If you're asking if we talked about what I'm going to do, the answer is no. Still, she's an incredible manipulator—and I mean that with the deepest of respect—so I suppose it's possible that she helped chart my thinking on the matter.

"She's going to rule her people one day, and even though you're a national hero there, that might make a marriage to you more difficult. Knowing her, she'll run roughshod over anyone who objects, but wouldn't you like to make her life a little easier?"

"Now who's manipulating?" Jared asked. "What exactly do you have in mind? A knighthood like Talbot's? I suppose I can accept that. It's not as though others haven't done so."

The people that had done the most during the mission had all received knighthoods, and he considered the honor well earned. He'd seen his promotion to admiral as a similar reward, but if becoming a knight made Elise's life a little easier, he wouldn't fight very hard.

The emperor nodded. "Always the humble man. It suits you, Jared. No, I have something a tad loftier in mind. I've been doing some research in the library that you brought back. *Courageous* was well stocked with electronic texts, but the list of titles that Coordinator West covertly collected is breathtaking.

"For example, there's a fascinating book on the history of the Imperial line. It contains so much that we never knew. For example, our ancestor Empress Christa the First. She succeeded her father, Emperor Justin, after he died in an unfortunate mountain climbing accident. You really should read all about it. It's fascinating."

Jared felt his eyes narrow at the man's light tone. If the emperor had been one of his subordinates, he'd have told the man to trot the full story out. As it was, he had no choice but to allow him to proceed at his own speed.

The emperor took another sip of his whiskey, slowly and obviously savoring it. "What makes the story relevant is that Emperor Justin was a little free with his affections and also had a son out of wedlock. One that he fully acknowledged.

"Empress Christa and the young man knew each other growing up, and she decided a more formal recognition was called for when she assumed the Throne."

He smiled at Jared. "To bring an already long story to a close, she approached the Senate about creating a new position in the peerage. One I had no idea existed, or I'd have taken this step long ago."

Jared's stomach felt as if he'd fallen off a cliff. "What position?"

"One reserved solely for those of Imperial birth that are not in the line of succession. Tomorrow morning, I'll hold a surprise ceremony officially elevating you to your new position. Well, both of them, actually.

"I'd also decided that some of you needed more recognition than you've already received. Doctor Stone, for example. I'm making her Countess of Hawk's Mount. It's a beautiful rural estate that I'm creating from the Imperial lands on the world you grew up on."

Jared nodded. "I've seen the mountains. I think she'll like that."

"It comes with a large stipend, and I'm going to build the seat of her estate with the Crown Purse. It only seems fair when she so cleverly saved my life.

"I'm also posthumously making Timothy Reese a count. He has no family, so the title won't carry on to his blood, which is so unfortunate, but I have a plan. I'll make Talbot his heir. He needed time to adjust to just being a knight, but I think it's been long enough."

Jared snorted. "I hope you have a five-second delay on any live transmissions. He's going to cuss a blue streak."

The emperor laughed and then inclined his head. "Which brings us to you, Jared. I'm making you Duke of East Bay."

Jared blinked. East Bay was also on his home world of Xander. It was the temperate continent in the southern hemisphere where his mother lived and where Hawk's Mount was.

"I'd imagine Duke Matterson won't be happy about that," was all Jared could think to say.

"Actually, he's thrilled. The population on Xander has grown to the point that he was already in discussions with me about doing exactly this. He'll retain his title, of course, and will assume the duties of Imperial governor there. He'll still be running everything but will help create a staff to rule in your place while you're serving in Fleet."

Jared took a deeper sip of his whiskey and poured himself an unprecedented second drink. A big one.

"I should decline, but I suspect you'll just roll over me if I try."

"That's very perceptive of you. The Empire needs this, and so do you."

Jared sighed. "I could argue the point, but I know when I've lost a fight. Well, I suppose that will make me acceptable to even the fussiest Pentagaran."

"If it doesn't, I'm sure the second appointment will."

Jared frowned. "Wait. I thought that was it. Empress Crista made him a duke."

"Actually, she didn't." Emperor Karl Bandar smiled wolfishly. "She made him a prince of the blood. Welcome to the peerage, Highness."

4

One of the things that Zia liked about *Audacious* was that she was as big as a superdreadnought. She needed to be just to have the space for three squadrons of fighters and a flight deck.

Since her steward had parked the new officer—Commander Brandon Levy—in her day cabin as instructed, that meant she could drop by the flag bridge and see what the hell was really going on.

Her primary office sat directly off the flag bridge, which she also used to control the ship. At some point, she really needed to separate the functions, but she was the commander of both this ship and the carrier group. Combining the functions allowed her to keep an eye on the fighters and the ship simultaneously.

Commander Danny Leonidas was already rising from the command chair as she exited the lift. "Captain, we have an unannounced visitor. He's in your day cabin."

She smiled at him. Admiral Mertz had bumped Danny up from lieutenant, just like her. He'd served on the heavy cruiser *Spear*, but she couldn't hold it against such a dedicated officer. Wallace Breckenridge hadn't tainted everyone.

"I know. Step into my office for a minute, Danny."

"Yes, ma'am."

Once he was inside her spacious office, she gestured toward the more comfortable seats to the left of the desk. "Let's take a load off."

He sat, but his expression turned a bit wary. "This is beginning to sound ominous."

"As if we've never just had a casual chat right here. Though I will admit that I know something you don't. The Admiralty sent me word yesterday that you were getting your own command. I don't even have the orders yet, so I didn't expect your replacement for another week."

Danny leaned back in his chair, his eyes wide. "My own command? I was a junior helm officer just a few months ago. I'm not ready for that."

"I respectfully disagree. Yes, you do need more seasoning, but who among us doesn't. We're all going to miss you, but the light cruiser *Lightning* will be happy to have a man like you in the center seat."

The other officer shook his head as though clearing it. "This is all so unexpected. So, the new guy is my replacement?"

"Supposedly. I haven't seen his orders, either. We crossed paths in the hangar bay, but he didn't know who I was. His reaction to the fighters taking precedence over his cutter concerns me. There was a bit of attempted intimidation, too."

"Boy, did he pick the wrong person to try that on," Danny said with a shake of his head. "And right after boarding. That is not promising."

"Yet I'm going to have to work with him," Zia said grimly. "Maybe I caught him on a bad day. I want to spend a few minutes going over his record together."

Commander Levy's record was a good one, on paper. She knew that didn't always reflect a person's true personality, much less whether he'd be a good fit in an unusual command.

He'd last served as the commanding officer of a heavy cruiser under the overall authority of Captain Alice Quinn. That was to his favor. She knew that Quinn had stood up for Admiral Mertz in front of the court of inquiry following their return. She was an ally.

Perhaps Levy felt that moving from a cruiser command to the

executive officer's slot on a ship like this was a step down. Or perhaps it was her own rapid elevation to command that raised his hackles.

Nothing in his record led her to believe he was generally a problem child, but her instincts told her there was going to be trouble of some kind.

Danny rubbed his chin. "Maybe this was a one-time occurrence. He seems like a great candidate. Better than I'd have been in his place, that's for sure."

Zia smiled. "That's not even close to true. If I'd had a say in this, I'd have kept you right where you are, but I know an independent command is going to do you a universe of good. Fleet knows that, too."

She sighed. "Well, I suppose I'll figure the new guy out in due time. If he makes an ass of himself, I can handle that, too."

He rose to his feet when she did. "Skipper, I want you to know what an honor and pleasure it's been to work with you."

She took the hand he offered and shook it firmly. "Likewise, and I don't think this is the last we'll see of one another. Your cruiser squadron is going to be providing *Audacious* the cover she needs going forward."

Danny nodded. "That makes perfect sense. Shall I go retrieve the new guy?"

"Yes," she said as she headed for her desk. "Keep him in the dark about our earlier encounter. I think this might be a salutary experience for him."

The other officer grinned. "My lips are sealed, ma'am. Be right back."

She brought up Levy's record on her desk comp while she waited. His orders were in the system now, too, so she quickly read them. Fleet had indeed assigned him as her new executive officer.

Zia called her steward. "Jim, it looks like we'll need a going-away party tomorrow. Danny Leonidas is moving on to a command of his own."

The tall man on the screen nodded. "I'm both sorry and excited to hear that, ma'am. Will a lunch timeframe work?"

She nodded. "Yes. Plan on all the senior officers attending."

"The new man will be replacing Commander Leonidas?"

Steward First Class Jim Richmond had one of the best poker faces Zia had ever seen, but there was a flicker of something in his eyes.

"He will. Tell me what you think of the man."

"It's not a good thing to speak ill of senior officers, ma'am. Particularly when they're going to become the new executive officer."

Zia smiled coolly. "You work for me directly, Jim. No need to be nasty, but I really do want to know what your initial take is."

"The man has a temper," the steward admitted. "Apparently, some pilot torqued him off and he's pissed. I didn't ask the particulars, but that seems mighty fast to have an incident. That leads me to believe he's going to stir up trouble this ship might not be the better for. With all due respect, of course."

"That pretty much matches what I've already seen. I wouldn't worry too much. We'll all find a good balance, I'm sure."

"If you say so, ma'am."

The admittance chime to her office hatch sounded. A check of her implants showed Danny and the new guy outside her door.

"I have to go, Jim. Make the party a special one."

He looked mildly affronted. "As if I wouldn't. Ma'am."

She laughed until the man smiled and then cut the connection. Then she put on her captain's face and hit the button to open the hatch.

Danny stepped in first. "Someone to see you, ma'am."

The other officer took two steps forward and came to attention. "Commander Brandon Levy reporting as ordered, ma'am."

Interestingly, his eyes held no recognition. Of course, she'd been wearing a bulky flight suit and helmet, though the latter had come off for a little bit. That wasn't very observant of him.

"Thank you, Commander Leonidas."

Her soon-to-be former executive officer smiled wryly and stepped back out. The hatch slid closed, leaving her with her newest problem child.

Her voice must've triggered something in his memory. She knew the moment that he made the connection because his eyes widened in alarm.

Zia smiled coolly. "It's good to see you again, Commander. We really didn't have much of a chance to chat on the flight deck. I'm looking forward to a nice, long conversation so we can get to know one another.

"I understand you have some concerns about fighter priority, but we should get the formalities out of the way first. I'm Captain Zia Anderson. Welcome aboard the Fleet carrier *Audacious*."

* * *

JARED ALMOST STUMBLED out of the Imperial Palace. He wasn't sure how he'd have gotten home without an official driver.

The man frowned in concern, but Jared waved for him to proceed. He had to pull himself together. "I'm fine. Just some unexpected news. Take me to my apartment."

"Aye, sir," the Fleet rating said.

The man brought the air car out of the palace garage at a sedate pace and headed back toward the city. A second car came in from the left and began shadowing them.

The driver eyed it suspiciously. "We have company, sir. Should I call for backup?"

Based on the events a month ago, it wasn't an unreasonable question. Only this time Jared was sure the men in the other car weren't there to kill him. He had a sinking suspicion he'd just inherited his own detail from the Imperial Guard.

He shook his head. "No. It's fine. I'm not in a position to speak about it, and I'd appreciate your discretion. His Majesty has decided I need a little extra protection for a bit. Nothing to worry about."

The man's eyes narrowed, but he nodded. "As you say, sir. We'll be back at your place shortly."

Twenty minutes later, they pulled into his new neighborhood. Elise had said his old apartment was quaint and a little small for two people.

His new place occupied the top floor of an older building in a stylish neighborhood. One with a pad on the roof where his marine guards could screen visitors.

The door into the building opened as they landed, and Elise Orison stepped out. The driver had obviously signaled ahead. Her guards came out, and their eyes tracked the follow car.

Jared stepped out as soon as his air car settled. "It's okay. They're not a threat." He turned back to the driver. "I'm in for the evening, so head back home."

"Aye, sir," the man said.

Elise stepped up beside him as the car took off and watched the other car come in for a landing. Three people in Imperial whites stepped out: two women and one man.

"Jared?" she asked, her expression tightening. "Why are they here?"

"Let's go in and I'll tell you over a drink. I already had a double, and it wasn't enough."

"You're scaring me."

He slid his arm around her shoulders. "I'm sorry. It's a bit of a shock, but I'm not in trouble. Well, not as you'd define it, anyway."

"You're maddening."

She marched him inside and closed the apartment door in the faces of her guards. They'd be a bit discussing things with their Imperial counterparts anyway.

"Make mine a large glass of red," she said as she sat on the edge of the couch. "The good stuff, mind you. And stop stalling."

"I'm not stalling," he delayed as he poured the drinks. "It's just been a shock."

"Let me see," she said thoughtfully. "What is it that Kelsey says at times like these? Oh yes. Trot it out, mister."

Jared chuckled and handed her a glass of the red she liked. He sat down beside her and sipped his drink. The buzz from his earlier drinking had worn off, unfortunately.

"His Majesty has decided that my promotion is a little light for his taste in rewards, so he plans on having us drop by in the morning for a little ceremony."

Her eyes narrowed and glittered a little dangerously. "Details," she ground out between clenched teeth.

"He decided that a title would be appropriate."

Her face lit up. "That's wonderful news! How can you be so glum? Tell me. Will you have to start styling yourself as Sir Jared? Honestly, with the others that were knighted, I felt a little cheated on your behalf."

"If so, he didn't tell me. That wouldn't surprise me, now that you mention it, though. No, tomorrow morning he's going to bestow a newly created duchy upon me."

She just about spilled her wine as she set it down and pulled him into a tight hug, squealing in his ear. "My God, that's terrific! You'll make a handsome ruler, Your Grace. It's very well deserved."

He tossed his drink back and set the empty glass down beside hers. "I'm afraid that isn't all. After some careful study, he decided there was one more title he wanted me to carry, and it's going to cause me grief. I just know it.

"It turns out there's historical precedent for a special level in the peerage for those of direct Imperial lineage when they aren't in the line of succession. At least those the emperor or empress favored. He's going to make me a prince of the blood."

She did knock her wine over this time when she lunged into his arms, whooping loudly.

Loudly enough to make the guards burst in with their weapons drawn, but that didn't dampen her wild celebration dance in his honor.

He waved them back out and used some tissues to stop the wine from running off the side of the table and staining the carpet. He finished just in time to have her land on him again, pushing him back onto the couch with her body.

Jared tried to speak, but she had different ideas. In moments, he found that he really didn't want to talk about it anyway.

5

Annette walked out of the ready room with her helmet under her arm. "Are we ready?"

Fiennes nodded. "All the birds are prepped, and they're wrapping up the preflights now. I already gave your bird a once over."

She'd still check the most critical systems. Annette trusted Jake with her life, but a warrior didn't delegate the critical tasks to others. She'd flown this morning, so a basic run-through would be good enough.

"Have you passed the flight plan on to everyone?"

"Of course."

"Excellent. Then they'll be completely discombobulated when I do something else."

He shook his head with a smile. "Shouldn't we at least pretend we're following an actual plan in the training?"

"I am following a plan," she said. "I'm teaching them that even when they think they know what's happening, the situation can change for the worse without any notice at all. I'll incorporate what you presented to them, but not in the way they expect things to run."

"You're the boss."

Annette went over her assigned fighter closely. It was uniquely hers, permanently assigned and with her name just under the canopy, along with a jack of spades emblem. She'd gotten used to the specific quirks it had and was very happy with it.

Once she was satisfied the bird was ready, she put her helmet on and strapped herself in. "*Audacious* Flight Control, this is Black Jack Actual. Com Check."

"You're coming in loud and clear, Black Jack Actual," a man's voice answered. "What's on the plate for today?"

"Formation fighting and ugly surprises," she said with a smile.

"Won't you be popular? Orbital One is aware of your sortie, and we'll be watching for those ugly surprises with interest."

"Thanks Control. You'll like it. Trust me. Black Jack Actual out."

She switched to the general squadron frequency. "All Black Jack elements, this is Black Jack Actual. We'll be performing a planetary patrol today. Nothing too complicated, but I want you to pay specific attention to keeping close to your wingman.

"We'll try out several basic formations and maneuvers today. Do not embarrass me. Launch when ready and form up fifty kilometers astern of *Audacious*. Black Jack Actual out."

The Black Jack pilots called in their acknowledgments one by one in numerical order. That was standard so that in the heat of battle they didn't try to talk over one another. They also sent in their acknowledgment via implant, but she liked hearing them. It gave her a better feel for their states of mind.

Flight by flight, they launched. When her turn came up, the launch catapult hurled her down the launch tube and out of the ship. Once the grav drive came online, she nudged her fighter into its assigned position among the swarm that was Black Jack Squadron.

They started off easily enough, cycling through a few changes in formation. They were simple maneuvers but very important. If they didn't shift position in the correct manner, they might risk collision with their teammates.

When she was satisfied they were firmly in the groove, she brought up her simulation override controls. They allowed her to activate certain features in the scanner software on each of the fighters.

She activated the program. Down on Avalon's surface, a strobe lit up, announcing hostile missile launches.

"Vampire, vampire, vampire," she said over the general frequency. "Hostile launches from the planet's surface. First flight, take the missiles out. Second flight, cover them. Third, eliminate the launchers."

With commendable speed, first flight peeled off and dove into Avalon's atmosphere. The fighters took continually shifting positions with each pair watching over their wingmates. They targeted the incoming missiles while Second Flight watched for other fighters.

There weren't any this time. At least, not yet.

Jake led Third Flight down on a strafing run. The area housing the supposed facility was actually a military training range. No one was in danger below, and the ordinance was real today.

She took a place behind Second Flight. If needed, she'd help with what they were doing, but she was controlling what was happening in the exercise today. In a real fight, she'd guide First Flight.

Things went gratifyingly smoothly. First Flight took out the attacking missiles quickly and focused on the follow-up waves as Third Flight dropped down and blew up the target area. The flashes were probably bright enough to be notable in orbit.

While they were still conducting their bombing run, she activated the next segment of the program. Her scanners almost immediately reported fighters launching from the south.

"Second Flight, incoming fighters," she said. "Engage."

"Copy," the lieutenant in command of the group said.

They spiraled out to engage the enemy fighters. These were the ugly surprise. They weren't simulated. They were real.

Scimitar Squadron came racing up to meet them, splitting into elements at the last moment. The fighting—with simulated weapons, of course—quickly turned into a massive snarl, as though a cat had gotten ahold of a humongous pile of yarn.

Their implants made keeping track of all the other fighters possible but *very* difficult. Any particular craft could change course at a moment's notice, turning right in your path.

Like two of the enemy fighters did for her.

"Black Jack Actual engaging," she told her wingman.

She peeled off, brought her antifighter missiles online, and fired. The lead fighter dodged violently, and his electronic countermeasures allowed him to elude her strike, but his wingman was less fortunate. He turned red on her scanners and immediately exited the area.

Her pleasure was short-lived, as two other fighters targeted her.

Annette pushed her fighter into a sharp dive and evaded the incoming strike. Barely. Her wingman had a scary moment when he and one of the enemy fighters almost collided. For real.

"Jesus, Black Jack Seven!" she shouted. "Watch out!"

"Sorry about that," Larry Connors said back. "We jigged the same direction."

She started to answer, but her threat warning lit up again. Annette dodged, but it wasn't good enough. A simulated missile took her out.

And just like that she was dead. Thankfully, not in real life.

A quick consult with her scanner gave her a clear course out of the fight, and she had all the time in the world to observe the battle play out.

Any semblance of order was gone. With everyone fighting for their lives, they'd lost track of the strategic situation. Herself included, she thought wryly. It had turned into a dogfight.

The after-action report was going to be fun. They'd overcommitted, and another ground site was busy shooting down her squadron. Jake did what he could, but they'd already lost. The best he could do was try to extract as many of their people as he could.

Well, they said mistakes were the best teachers. They'd all learn something from today's exercise.

Once the remains of her squadron were clear, she sent the signal to terminate the war game. "All *Audacious* units, this is Black Jack Actual. Exercise terminated. Return to base."

Sorting them all out took longer than she liked, but they eventually headed back for the carrier. She started making notes for the briefing. The fight left her tired but exhilarated. This had been far uglier than she'd planned, but that was fine for now.

Once they finished the briefing, they could get something to eat and get some rest. Then they'd do it all again tomorrow.

* * *

KELSEY WANTED TO SMASH SOMETHING. Or someone. With her physical strength, that wasn't exactly the safest frame of mind to be in.

She shed her guards at the door to the suite she shared with Talbot and headed right for the gym. He wasn't home yet, and that was a very good thing. She didn't want to take her fury out on him.

Since she could literally lift the weight machines, she turned her enhanced musculature off and focused on her regular muscles.

It's okay to be angry.

"I don't want to talk about it," she told the ghostly voice of Ned Quincy. The disembodied copy of the dead Marine Raider lived in her implants, so he of course knew what had happened.

"Screw it," she snarled before he could say anything else. "You're damned right I'm angry. If you want to talk, you can use the projectors. I'm not doing this in my head."

She'd had Carl seed her quarters with holographic projectors, all except the master bedroom and bath. He might live in her head, but she wanted *some* privacy.

The figure of a man in casual clothes appeared sitting on the weight machine beside hers. If she hadn't known he wasn't real, she'd have had no clue he was a projection. The Old Empire had really known how to make good equipment.

Kelsey forced her weights up over her head, craving the burn. "Don't try to calm me down," she told the AI. "I'm not going to be placated."

"The thought never crossed my mind. In fact, you might have better luck on the range."

The mental image of incinerating Nathaniel Breckenridge with a plasma rifle was tempting. Perhaps a little too tempting.

Especially since she had more than a bit of difficulty blaming him for this situation. The evidence that he'd been unaware of their genetic relationship was clear enough. He was too much of a power broker to have avoided using the knowledge a long time ago, even if only with Ethan.

No, she believed the man hadn't known he was her father. That didn't change a damned thing, though. It was a huge stinking mess. As if her life hadn't been complicated enough already.

"I'm better off without a weapon in my hands right now," she grunted. "I'm not sure who I'd shoot first: Breckenridge or my mother."

She let the weights crash back down and slumped forward a little. "Holy hell, what do I do? If I tell my father, he'll make some grand announcement. Shit. Breckenridge might beat him to it."

"While this isn't exactly good news, it isn't terrible either. Honestly, so what if the man sired you? Does that really complicate your life more than being the heir?"

"Probably not," she admitted, "but I'm not ready for some new relationship, especially with the uncle of the idiot that tried to kill us."

"Then don't. It's not like you have to send him Christmas presents or invite him over for dinner. I specifically recall him stressing that. If you don't tell your father, do you really think Breckenridge will leak the news?"

Kelsey sighed. "I have no idea. I suppose you're right, but the bastard slept with my mother. He's probably not the only one, either. I really should query the access list in the secret tunnel."

"That's stupid," the AI said. "One or a hundred, it makes no difference."

"I assure you that a hundred would make quite the difference," she said tartly. "There's a not-so-fine line between harlot and slut. God, I hope it's not a hundred."

She rubbed her face tiredly. "I'll grant you that he readily admitted he made a serious mistake in judgment, but to be fair— which I really don't want to do—he was a young man, and they tend to be easily swayed into mistakes by their hormones. Not that it excuses him, but I'm not sure that many other men in a similar position would have refused.

"My mother was the instigator in this relationship. I'm sure of it. I guess that's who I'm really angry with. She's known all this time that I wasn't Father's, but she still condemned him and dragged us all through the muck when he made a mistake in judgment that he owned up to."

The man nodded. "So, what can you do about that?"

"Not a damned thing, but you can be sure that this is going to result in an epic fight whenever I go to see her. Thankfully, I don't have the time right now, so this is going to simmer for a long, long while. Maybe I can avoid strangling her if I have time to calm down."

Kelsey heard the front door open. Talbot was home. She really wasn't looking forward to telling him about this.

"Time for lights out, Ned," she said as she stood. "I want some privacy."

"Take it easy on him," the man said as he stood and vanished. He'd have other ways of amusing himself that didn't involve using her senses or the equipment in the suite.

She needed to see about getting him loaded into a different system. Carl said he was close. Frankly, it couldn't happen soon enough for her.

Time to get this done.

Kelsey headed for the living room. The door opened just as she reached for it, and she started to say something to Talbot.

Only it wasn't her lover.

"Kelsey! I rushed here as quickly as I could," her mother said as she rushed in. "Are you all right?"

* * *

COMMANDER BRANDON LEVY stared at the woman sitting behind the desk in shock. It was the pilot from the flight deck. The one that had...

He pulled himself together. He'd screwed up. Badly. This wasn't the time to make it worse.

"I'm sorry, Captain. I didn't know that was you."

He knew how idiotic that sounded the moment he said it. Which didn't help one bit.

"Obviously," the young woman said dryly. "We've gotten off on the wrong foot, so I suggest we try again. At ease."

He allowed himself to relax slightly. He'd looked over her record, but clearly not well enough. He should've recognized her on sight.

Only he'd been too angry to try that hard, and that had been a stupid mistake. The kind he wouldn't allow to happen again.

No matter how good her record was, she'd only been the tactical officer on an almost obsolete destroyer. He had a decade of experience on her, but they'd bumped her three grades and put her in command of this tremendous ship.

She considered him a moment then glanced at her comp. "Your record is excellent, Commander. You probably expected the Admiralty was giving you command of one of the new ships. I know this has to be hard, but we have to make the best of it. Are we going to have a problem?"

"No, ma'am."

He wouldn't allow his anger to get the better of him again. She might not have earned this command, but he'd damned well make sure it didn't end badly for the Empire. He might not want to help prop up her inexperience, but he'd do his duty.

"Without judging, this morning's conversation tells me that we need to come to a shared vision on how this ship is run," she said. "This is the first carrier in Fleet since the Fall, and adapting to how she's used is going to be challenging.

"I need you to keep an open mind. If, once you've had time to consider the new situation, you think something needs to change, I'm willing to hear you out."

Her lips thinned. "What I'm not willing to do is accept reflexive judgments on capabilities that you don't fully understand. Yet."

Brandon nodded and even agreed with her to a point. He'd allowed his anger at the situation to color his behavior. That was unprofessional and would not do. He'd listen carefully and keep his emotions under control.

"Yes, ma'am."

She eyed him for a moment before nodding herself. "Very good. Let's address the elephant in the room. Until just a few months ago, I was a lieutenant and a tactical officer. Now I'm in command of this ship. That has to chafe."

He made a mental note to put her in for the Understatement of the Year Award but said nothing.

Once she recognized that he wasn't going to respond, she continued. "As it happens, I know very well that I'm not as experienced as you. I didn't seek out this command, but someone had to do it.

"Princess Kelsey made the decision, in consultation with Admiral Mertz, to promote me and assign me to this command. Something I'm still more than a bit uncomfortable with, but I will carry out my orders."

Admiral Mertz. The thought almost made him snort. Not that he was one of the people in Fleet inclined to hold the man's birth against him. No, he knew Mertz by reputation. He'd more than earned his destroyer command. Honesty compelled Brandon to concede that Mertz should've been a captain years ago.

The man obviously had what it took. He'd read the classified summaries of what had happened on the exploratory mission, and Mertz had more than lived up to anyone's wildest expectations.

Brandon didn't think that entitled Mertz to be an admiral, but he wouldn't have blinked at a promotion to commodore. So one more bump wasn't too much of a stretch. Besides, as he'd heard the story, Princess Kelsey had ambushed him with the promotion. Much like Zia Anderson, he reluctantly admitted.

Logic wasn't going to help him adjust to this situation. Fleet expected its officers to obey their orders, and he would do so. He just didn't have to like it.

"My current executive officer is a good man, though about as inexperienced at his post as I am. He's moving on to command one of the light cruiser escorts for the carrier group. We're having a party for him tomorrow. I think you should be there."

Of course he should be. That was just basic courtesy.

"Yes, ma'am."

"You're not very talkative," she observed. "Well, we'll find our own rhythm as we become accustomed to one another. The part of the job you're going to have to work on revolves around fighter doctrine.

"You're going to have to play catchup on that one, but you're in luck that we're all still getting accustomed to it ourselves. I also see that you don't have implants yet. That's an even steeper learning curve to master, and they will influence every single aspect of your job."

She eyed him. "What do you imagine implants mean for you, Commander Levy?"

"They'll make doing my job easier, ma'am. Allow me to interface more directly with the ship to better manage it."

He had no idea what that actually meant. Even after all the reading he'd done, he still didn't really grasp the full implications of what the new technology could do.

Anderson nodded. "All technically correct, but that sounds rote. Frankly, it can't be any other way. You have no idea the depth and power implants give an officer on this ship. Or honestly even what the ship is capable of. *Audacious*."

"Yes, Captain Anderson," a mellow male voice said from the overhead speakers.

"Attention to orders. Commander Brandon Levy will assume the position of executive officer as of 0800 tomorrow. Note it in the logs."

"Aye, Captain. Welcome aboard, Commander Levy. This unit looks forward to working with you."

He swallowed. He'd never heard of a computer that could sound so autonomous. He wasn't sure if he should answer or not, so he defaulted to the polite thing.

"Thank you, *Audacious*."

"The computer on this ship can run every system in a pinch, except for the weapons," Anderson said conversationally. "Those require a human being by design. He also can't remotely control the fighters, since they're considered weapons. They usually operate too far away anyhow.

"*Audacious* is built on a modified superdreadnought hull and still has two-thirds of her weaponry. The fighters make her far more dangerous than *Invincible*, even without them. The three squadrons we have aboard could take a superdreadnought, though they'd suffer hideous losses. More to the point, they could take every original ship in Fleet present in this system without support from us. But only if they are used wisely."

She considered him for a moment and then stood. "I think a demonstration of both implant and fighter operations are in order. Come with me."

Anderson led him out onto the ridiculously large bridge outside her office. The man he was replacing rose from the wrap-around command console in the center.

"Keep the conn, Danny." Anderson turned to Brandon. "Let's take a seat at the observation consoles, Commander."

He opened his mouth to ask what they were doing when a loud klaxon began screaming and the lighting changed to a reddish hue. The ship had just gone to general quarters.

The bridge crew focused on their consoles as the overhead speakers came to life. "This is a drill. I repeat, this is a drill. Long-range scanners have just detected an incoming Rebel Empire fleet. Come to heading two five zero by one seven five at maximum military power."

It was Captain Anderson's voice. Her lips hadn't moved.

The speed with which the bridge crew performed was amazing. They seemed to be one with their consoles, hardly speaking and only occasionally manipulating the controls.

"The ship is actually still in orbit," Anderson said. "I have the bridge controls in simulation mode. Operations is taking over their regular duties.

"The bridge crew is using their implants to do almost everything. The scanner readings and more are available right in their heads. They should be able to operate without the consoles at all. *Audacious*, cut power to the bridge."

The compartment plunged into darkness, every console going dead all at once. Only the emergency lights remained active. The bridge crew sat back and frowned in concentration. He assumed the ship continued operations without the slightest hitch, which was damned impressive.

"During the battle of Harrison's World, *Courageous* lost power to the bridge, and we would've died without the ship's AI. Marcus is a lot more advanced than our computer. No offense, *Audacious*."

"This unit is incapable of taking offense, Captain."

"Restore power to Commander Levy's console," she said.

Brandon's screen came to life, showing the area of space the carrier supposedly occupied as it sped out of Avalon orbit. The scanners also showed what he assumed was a computer-generated fleet racing toward them. It was almost as massive as the one Admiral Mertz had brought back to Avalon.

Audacious wasn't alone. It looked as though the entire fleet was going out to meet the intruders as a unit. He assumed they were all computer generated.

Over the next hour, he watched as a stupendous battle took place. A preposterous number of missiles raced toward them, and Admiral Mertz's ships returned fire in kind. Then the admiral ordered the fighters in.

The little minnows charged into the enemy formations, almost as fast as missiles themselves. Only they were much harder to kill.

They worked together in ways he couldn't quite grasp but that were obviously practiced. Massive ships perished under their fire, but they took punishing hits in return. It might be hard to swat a swarm of insects, but they died when hit.

When they came streaming back to the carrier to rearm, there were less than half as many as had gone out. That kind of attrition broke units, but these people went about their duty without complaint.

Of course it was all a drill, so they weren't real.

"Is that level of loss normal?" he heard himself ask quietly.

"No. We're making this harder than we think it will be in real combat," she said. "Of course, when the rebels killed *Audacious*, they all died. They went out four times. The last sally only had three fighters."

She turned to face him squarely. "Those people are the ship's real weapons, Commander. In combat, weapons have the right of way, so we always act accordingly. This isn't ego. I didn't tell you to wait for the fighters to land because I wanted to put you in your place. This ship exists as a platform to project their power, and when doing so, they have precedence."

He reluctantly nodded. "I can see I have some work to do before I can understand everything I'm seeing."

"Agreed. Tomorrow morning, I want you to report to Doctor Zoboroski for your implants. You can't do your job without them. It'll be light duty for you tomorrow, but Commander Leonidas can still show you everything you need to know before he leaves for his new command."

Brandon still wasn't convinced she really knew the best way to run this ship, but he was willing to try to open his mind. One way or another, this was going to be a rough transition.

6

Jared had a rough night. Sleep hadn't come easily. He'd lain awake long after Elise was dreaming beside him.

She'd been unreservedly delighted at the news, and not just because it made her life simpler. Regardless of what the emperor said, she'd already flat out told him that she'd marry him if he'd been a normal man on the street because she loved him.

Her fierce determination told him it wasn't posturing either. That made him feel good but did nothing to lessen the nerves he still felt.

He rose quietly and made his way into the bathroom an hour before the alarm would have normally woken him. A long, hot shower at least put him in a comfortable mental space.

Once he was dressed, except for his uniform tunic, he made breakfast. If he timed things well, he'd serve Elise breakfast in bed.

While he started the eggs, he checked his implants for any new messages.

Implant coverage in the capital was spotty, but that would change as more people required it. They'd fully wired his place. Even normal calls went to his implants.

There was a message from Kelsey waiting for him. He checked the time. It had come in right after they'd gone to bed.

Her image appeared in his mind's eye. She looked like she needed sleep more than he did, which was unusual.

"I just saw the message from my father that he wants me at the Imperial Palace in the morning. Do you have any idea what's going on? Also, I need to talk to you as soon as you get up. I have some unsettling news."

He deleted the message and pinged her. If she wasn't ready for a call, her computer would prompt him to leave a message.

An image opened up of her drinking some coffee in her kitchen. She was a little bleary but awake.

"Morning, Jared."

"Morning," he said. "I don't like the idea of unsettling news, though I have some, too. You called, so you get to go first."

She shook her head. "I'm sure mine is more troubling. I had dinner with Senator Breckenridge last night, though I'd hardly call it a meal. More like an ambush.

"He told me that… ahem, he'd been indiscreet with my mother about nine months before I was born. He's my biological sire. Lily confirmed it. Without telling me in advance, which I'm going to have to talk with her about."

He almost dropped the package of bacon he was opening but managed to save the sacred pork. "That's a lot more unsettling than my news, at least to you. I'm not sure what to say, but you knew it had to be someone. At least the man showed some character during the coup."

She nodded, eyeing the stovetop. "That looks good. I'm going to make me some, too."

The way the implant calls worked, it seemed as though she was standing right there, though her kitchen was laid out differently than his. It was as though the two rooms were side by side. It made having a conversation much easier than just voices in one another's heads.

"The news was shocking," she admitted, "but it wasn't the worst part. My mother showed up right after I got home."

Jared, a man who'd faced death in combat without a tremble, blanched. "Jesus."

"Indeed."

"What did you do?"

She laughed without humor. "I resisted the urge to punch her lights out. She is my mother, after all. In fact, I managed to avoid telling her anything and threw her out on her ear, much to her outrage. I was far too angry to have that fight."

"And she let you throw her out? I'm shocked."

"I cheated and had the Imperial Guard handle it. That didn't go over well, as you might imagine. You know how she is."

He smiled a little. "Actually, I don't. She never wanted to see me, and I was happy with that."

Kelsey growled. "See? That's what pisses me off. She's a damned hypocrite. She had the gall to sound all outraged that I wasn't ready to welcome her with open arms. Accused me of holding a grudge over something that happened before I was born."

"Something she conveniently forgot to mention, and that you had to find out the hard way," he agreed.

"Exactly! Anyway, she just wanted to fight after that, so I had the guards eject her from the premises. I did allow myself the pleasure of pushing her out the door and locking it behind her."

He focused on the food for a minute, making sure everything was cooking well. Then he started the coffee.

"You're not going to be able to put her off for long, you know."

Kelsey sighed. "I can try. I needed to tell Talbot first anyway. He deserved to know the truth. Which, I'm still not sure I should tell my father, by the way."

"Why not? He already knows you're not biologically his. I'd imagine he'll have an epic fight with your mother about it, by the way."

"That is his fight," she admitted, "though I deserve to have a piece of her, too. I'm concerned that putting a name to my sperm donor will cause Senator Breckenridge more trouble than he perhaps deserves.

"I've come to the conclusion that his mistake was a long time ago, and that he was young. Christ, look at the things I've done. I'm not in a real position to judge."

She sipped her coffee. "My mother, on the other hand, was a

serial adulterer. Talbot and I flew out to the palace, and I examined the secret exit's computer. I'll bet she didn't know it kept recordings of the comings and goings. Care to guess how many men she smuggled in?"

"I'm told the only way to win this kind of game is not to play."

"Eighteen!" she said, ignoring his response. "And not all of them before my birth! She was cheating on my father right up until they found out about you. Breckenridge was actually one of the shortest affairs in duration.

"One of them lasted two years. He moved out to her new home as the groundskeeper, by the way. I'm not sure precisely which bushes he keeps trimmed, if you know what I mean."

"That was a bit bawdy, even for someone who spent much of their time with marines," he said. "She is your mother. Don't forget mine kept exactly that same kind of secret from me."

Kelsey shook her head energetically. "Oh no, she didn't. I'll lump her with Breckenridge and my father. The excitement of the situation and the person they were dealing with overcame their common sense. That's a far cry from what my mother did. She knowingly cheated on her husband for decades.

"Anyway, I'll deal with her soon enough. What is your unsettling news?"

He started to respond, but the door chimed. "Someone is at the door. Let me call you back."

Jared pulled the last of the breakfast off the heat and headed for the door. He could've checked remotely to see who it was, but the guards wouldn't have disturbed him unless it was important.

Opening the door revealed his own mother. "Jared!" She rushed into his arms. "I got here as quickly as I could."

"Mom, I'm glad to see you," he said, squeezing her tight. "I should've come to visit, but things have been so busy. Come in."

The guards—a mixture of Imperial Marines and Imperial Guards —closed the door behind them. He was going to have to sort out that mess before long, too.

"I just made breakfast."

"Good. I'm starving."

That hadn't been his mother's voice. Elise, her hair tousled from sleep, came out of the bedroom and stopped dead in her tracks. Thankfully, she was dressed, though only in his shirt. It covered everything. Barely.

His mother's face paled a little. "I should have called ahead. Why don't I come back later?"

"It's a little late for any embarrassment," he said with a chuckle. "Besides, today is going to be very, very busy. Mother, this is Elise Orison. Elise, my mother, Patricia Mertz."

Elise smiled as though she hadn't walked almost naked into the room with his mother. "It's a pleasure to meet you, Patricia. You absolutely should stay for breakfast.

"Let me get dressed and we can talk. And, before you start, I don't want any of that 'highness' nonsense from you. I'm Elise." She headed back into their bedroom.

"Let me get us some coffee," he said to his mother. "I have so much to tell you."

"Obviously," his mother said with a twinkle in her eye. "I'd given up hope that you'd ever find someone special with your career looming over you like it does. I hope she's the one."

He smiled. "I think so. I just have to find the right time to ask the question."

"You know I can hear you, right?" Elise asked from the bedroom. "Yes, I'm the one. That's the worst proposal ever, by the way, but I'll take it."

He'd forgotten that she had excellent hearing but smiled anyway. The prospect of marrying her had his heart soaring.

His mother pulled him into a hug. "Oh, my God! I'm overwhelmed! So much has changed."

"You have no idea. Sit down and I'll bring your coffee. I know my message was a bit sparse on detail, but I'm okay. Better than okay, really. So much has changed. Some of which I can't talk about."

She took the mug of coffee from him. "I heard some of it. I always knew you'd succeed at anything you tried, but you've exceeded my wildest expectations."

"I've also exceeded my own worst-case estimates. The situation the Empire finds itself in isn't pretty. I'm not sure if everyone understands that just yet."

"The news services seem to be taking the situation seriously," she said. "I'd only gotten your initial message when the emperor had His Grace virtually shove me onto a fast transport for Avalon. If you sent any other messages, they haven't caught up with me."

"Then you've missed a lot of the story," Elise said as she came out of the bedroom in a sophisticated-looking dress. One suitable for the ceremony later that morning.

Which reminded him that he hadn't gotten around to telling Kelsey what was coming. Well, she'd just have to be surprised along with everyone else.

"I'd planned on asking you to marry me a little more formally," he told her.

She kissed him soundly. "I was almost to the point of proposing to you. You can be frustratingly dense at times. Have you heard how long before you ship out again?"

He nodded. "No more than a week. Possibly sooner than that. Time-sensitive events are in motion."

His mother's face fell. "I'd hoped to have more time with you."

"I'm sorry. I'd like that, too, but if you've heard even the basic story, you know how important this is."

She nodded, her face becoming resolute. "Of course. You know I'm so very proud of you, don't you?"

Jared pulled her into a hug. "I do, and that makes me feel as loved as I could possibly be. You made me the man I am."

He checked his implant chronometer. "I have to finish getting dressed. Elise will make sure you get to the palace, but I have to be there early."

His mother frowned. "But you haven't eaten. Why are you going to the palace?"

Elise smiled, her eyes twinkling. "Oh, just a little get-together." She speared him with a glance. "Eat some breakfast. I have it on good authority that they'll wait for you to start."

His mother looked apprehensive. "I don't know if Jared told you, but I used to work there. After what happened with the emperor, there might be some… hard feelings. Perhaps I should just stay in my hotel."

Elise put her regal face on. "I won't hear of it. Trust me when I say that anyone who is rude to you will have more than enough people leaping to your defense. Any trouble will be very short lived and terribly one sided."

"You can't yell at the emperor."

"I can, actually. Not that I expect him to be anything other than gracious and welcoming."

From his mother's expression, she didn't necessarily share that assessment.

Jared walked into the kitchen and put the food onto plates. "We have enough time to eat, I suppose, but we don't dawdle. We can catch up this afternoon. Let's get some fuel. Today is going to be long and—for me—trying."

7

Zia stepped out of the cutter she and her command crew had taken down to the Imperial Palace. The unexpected trip had thrown off her carefully scripted schedule, but when the emperor summoned his officers, they came and stayed as long as he wanted.

Danny Leonidas and Brandon Levy stepped out behind her, still talking quietly. Annette Vitter and the ship's chief engineer, Tony Hastert, were on their heels. The rest of her officers trailed after them.

The Imperial Guard surrounded the landing pad. They were undoubtedly scanning her and her people for weapons.

A woman in a suit stepped forward. "Captain Anderson, I'm Lisa Devonshire, His Majesty's majordomo. If you and your officers would be so kind as to accompany me, I'll show you to the audience room. Many of your fellows are already waiting."

Zia smiled and nodded. "Thank you."

She ran back over her thoughts as the woman took them inside the tremendous building. It had to be an award for Admiral Mertz. Nothing else made sense. The man certainly deserved them. The promotion he'd gotten didn't even match some of the rewards others had gotten for their parts.

Frankly, she was glad she'd managed to dodge any awkward awards. She enjoyed teasing "Sir Talbot" every chance she got. He was still grumbling about it.

That wasn't to say that she'd gotten away unscathed. The emperor had given a number of people the Imperial Cross: Admiral Mertz, Commodore Graves, Lily Stone, Dennis Baxter, Talbot, Pasco Ramirez, Annette Vitter, Timothy Reese, and herself. It felt like too much in her case, but telling the emperor no wasn't an easy task.

Fleet officers, Imperial nobility, and Imperial Senators filled the Imperial Audience Chamber. She was definitely out of her league in here.

"Zia!"

She turned her head and spotted Charlie Graves and Dennis Baxter heading her way.

Charlie was in command of the battlecruiser *Courageous* now. Her old partner, Pasco Ramirez, was his executive officer. Frankly, she was stunned that he hadn't taken over *Audacious*. He had a lot more experience than she did.

Dennis had been *Athena*'s chief engineer. He was now doing the same thing on *Invincible*.

"Hey, boys," she said. "Any idea what this is about?"

Dennis shook his head. "No, but I haven't seen the admiral. It has to be about him. I think there's going to be a knighting ceremony."

Charlie grinned. "I hope so. I'd love to tease him about it."

She looked around the room. "There are a lot of us here. Not just people from the mission, but senior officers from all across Fleet. Not to mention all the people looking down their noses at us. This feels a little bigger than a knighting."

"What then?" Charlie asked. "Maybe making him a baron or something? That would be wonderful!"

"Zia."

She turned her head and found Crown Princess Elise Orison standing behind her with a vaguely familiar-looking woman at her side.

"Highness."

"This is Patricia Mertz, Jared's mother."

Zia smiled and took the older woman's hands in hers. "It's wonderful to meet you. Allow me to introduce Charlie Graves and Dennis Baxter. We all worked with your son on *Athena*."

"It's such a pleasure to meet all of you," the admiral's mother said. "I've heard so much about you over the years. I feel as though I already know you."

"I have to go meet up with Jared," Princess Elise said. "Would you be so kind as to keep an eye on Patricia?"

"I'd be happy to," she said. "Do you know what's going on? Is it about Jared?"

The other woman nodded. "Yes, but my lips are sealed. You'll like it. I promise." The princess excused herself and hurried out of the room.

Zia focused her attention on Patricia Mertz. "You should be so proud of your son. He saved all of us, and I do mean *all* of us."

Jared's mother smiled. "I couldn't be more proud. This is so overwhelming."

"There are people serving champagne," Charlie said. "Would you like a glass? Everyone?"

At their nods, he hurried away into the crowd.

"There's Princess Kelsey," Dennis said.

Zia turned her head and saw Jared's sister zipping along in the same direction that Princess Elise had gone.

That's when she spotted a looming disaster. The princess's mother was sailing along in her daughter's wake.

"Oh, hell," Jared's mother said.

"Dennis," Zia snapped. "Get people around us right now. If she doesn't see us, there won't be a scene."

"Battle screens up, aye" he said, pulling in people they knew to provide a wall between what would undoubtedly be a matter/antimatter mixture.

"I should leave," Patricia said.

"Bull," Zia said firmly. "You have more of a right to be here than she does. This is Jared's moment. If she starts making a scene, I'll end it."

The older woman looked unconvinced but didn't argue.

The guards at the doorway allowed Princess Kelsey through but stopped her mother. From the sound of it, she was giving them hell, but they held firm. It wasn't as though she were the empress any longer. The divorce had been almost as scandalous as his affair, back in the day. Now, everyone knew the woman was a hypocrite.

Zia kept an eye on where the woman went. This situation still had the potential to go seriously south, so she'd pay more attention to her than the ceremony. Just in case.

* * *

KELSEY MADE her way to her father's dressing room. He was already in the robes of state. The long, flowing purple fabric was stiff and unbearably hot, or so he'd always said.

Half a dozen pages stood ready to assist him, and the Imperial Crown and Scepter sat on cushions close at hand.

She resisted the urge to look at it more closely. This wasn't the time.

"Am I late?" she asked.

"Just in time," he said warmly. "They tell me Jared only just arrived. I expect him momentarily."

"Are you going to tell me what this is about?"

"He didn't tell you? Well, then, who am I to ruin the surprise?"

She planted her fists on her hips. "So that's how this is going to be. Fine, two can play at that game. I know a secret that you desperately need to know. I'll trade."

He laughed. "Always bargaining. I'll pass."

Kelsey sighed. "You really do need to know. Mother showed up at my place this morning. She's here in the palace."

That wiped the humor right off his face. "Grim tidings, indeed. I suppose it was inevitable. I'd been hoping she'd stay away. I really don't want to deal with her."

"Then don't," she said bluntly. "I tossed her out of my place, so she's in a fine humor. There's going to be a fight eventually. A big one. Fair warning, I'm going to cut her off at the knees."

"I may go into seclusion." He rubbed his face. "Well, I don't have time to worry about her now. There are people waiting for me to start. On the plus side, this is going to piss her right off."

"You're not going to tell me, are you?"

He smiled. "And ruin the surprise? Of course not. You and Elise are going to be right there, and you'll know in a very few minutes."

The main door opened to admit Jared, Elise, and the Imperial majordomo.

Her father nodded. "Just in time. Let's go."

He led them to the door in the wall. One of the pages presented the Crown to him. Karl Bandar settled it on his head and took up the Imperial Scepter. In that moment, he became her liege, the Terran Emperor. The transformation still amazed her.

The majordomo waited for his nod and opened the door, walking out first. Kelsey could hear her voice as she announced her father's arrival.

"His Imperial Majesty, Karl the First, Emperor of the Terran Empire. Her Imperial Highness, Princess Kelsey Bandar, Heir to the Imperial Throne. Crown Princess Elise Orison, Heir to the Throne of the Kingdom of Pentagar. Admiral Jared Mertz. All draw close to hear the words of your liege."

They all slowly walked into the audience chamber. There was no rushing when pomp and ceremony were required.

Her father stood before the Imperial Throne. She had a smaller one beside it. It had been her brother's back before things had gone to hell. Jared and Elise stood to one side.

Everyone in the crowd stood at attention, or close to it in the case of the senators and nobles. The only one scowling was her mother. There was a small bubble of space around her. It seemed no one was in the mood to chat. Probably afraid they'd get something on themselves.

Her father gestured for Kelsey to sit. That was not according to protocol, and the majordomo's eyebrows pulled together a tad. It was her version of a fierce scowl.

Kelsey did as he'd indicated and sat. The cushion made the throne a lot more comfortable than it looked. Thank God.

Her father looked out at the crowd. "Over the course of the last few months, most of you have heard many details about the mission into the Old Empire. What you have not heard are the full details that only a few are privy to. Nor have you heard of every event that transpired. Some of them will remain classified for many years to come.

"Many of the people involved have been recognized in one way or another. Some with promotions, others with awards, and a few with grants of knighthood. Those were only the first wave. Others are coming."

He smiled. "In fact, I have a number of knighthoods to bestow upon the unsuspecting tonight. Shall we begin there?"

Kelsey watched as her father called officers and crewmen alike forward. The majordomo read the unclassified parts of their awards and then he used a thin ceremonial blade to tap them on the shoulders in a ceremony older than the Empire itself.

All looked stunned, but none more than Zia Anderson, Kelsey thought. She really hadn't seen this coming. Neither had Charlie Graves, Dennis Baxter, or Pasco Ramirez. They should have. They'd been a big factor in the Empire's successes.

As each person she knew came forward, Kelsey grinned at them, pleased to be part of this moment in their lives.

Once her father finished, he smiled. "And then there are those that did even more. In secret, the Imperial Senate and I have worked to make our pleasure known. Doctor Jerry Leonard. Step forward."

The scientist blinked at them in surprise. Carl Owlet nudged him toward the dais.

"Doctor, you met the challenge of the Old Empire technology head on, marshaling the forces and intellect to turn them into tools we could use to survive. For that, the Empire is in your debt, and we always pay our debts. Kneel."

The scientist actually protested. "Majesty, it was Doctor Cartwright—"

"Hush, Doctor. He's out of the system, but my agents are seeing to his reward today as well. You've earned this."

A low laugh ran through the crowd as her father knighted the befuddled man.

"Rise, Sir Jerry, and accept the accolades of your peers."

The red-faced scientist waved weakly at the clapping crowd in the audience room, much to their amusement.

Her father grabbed the other man's shoulder when he tried to escape back into the sea of people. "Hold up. I'm not done. It is my considered opinion that you've earned far more than a simple knighthood. I am hereby giving you a grant to continue your researches, and forming an institute to assist you in the Herculean tasks ahead of you. I won't be so crass as to mention the amounts, but trust me when I say that you will not want in your work."

The scientist beamed. "Thank you, Majesty! That will open so many doors for us."

"Indeed it will," her father agreed. "So will the Barony of Jackson's Rest that I'm bestowing to you and your heirs. It's on East Bay on the world of Xander, but I'm sure that you'll be far too busy to go visiting it all that often anyway."

"A what?"

It was all Kelsey could do not to whoop out loud. This was perfect.

"Don't worry, Your Excellency. I'm sure Sir Carl will explain it to you in words large enough to make sense."

That did get a laugh from the crowd as Carl came to lead the stupefied man off the dais.

Her father then called Doctor Lily Stone forward and did the same, minus the research facility, but with an upgrade to Countess of Hawk's Mount, also on Xander. She handled it with much more aplomb than Doctor Leonard.

"Your work with Old Empire medical procedures will save innumerable lives, Your Excellency," her father told the Fleet officer. "To facilitate this, I am promoting you to the rank of Commodore and placing you in charge of the medical and research sections of the hospital ship *Caduceus*.

"Captain Justin Guzman will assist you, and Fleet will see that the operations side is filled with the best people. They will support you to the best of their abilities, I'm sure."

Lily bowed. "Thank you, Majesty."

The doctor gave Kelsey a smile before she left the dais.

Kelsey followed her down with her eyes and spotted her mother again. Justine Bandar looked furious. She had no idea over what, but her mother was glaring at Zia, Dennis, and Charlie. Well, good luck with her causing trouble for them.

"Now for an award that it saddens me to give," her father said. "During the mission, one of the major factors for their success were the marines. Until almost the end, they were led by Timothy Reese, who was tragically killed in action. I've already seen that he was promoted to lieutenant colonel and given the Empire's highest award, but that isn't enough.

"He had no living family, but I am raising him to the peerage posthumously. I've selected a very nice area of land for his heir, though. Not coincidentally, also on Xander. I hope you're all seeing a pattern here."

He smiled out at the crowd. "No, this isn't an empty gesture. I believe it's fitting that a marine carry on in his stead, just as someone took command once he was gone."

Kelsey sat up straight, having just enough warning to know what was coming.

"Sir Russel Talbot, step forward in the name of Timothy Reese."

Her fiancé looked stunned, but he didn't argue as he came onto the dais.

That was damned sneaky of her father. Talbot would make a huge fuss over this in his own name, but he'd never utter a peep now. At least not until it was safely done.

"As Lieutenant Colonel Reese is no longer with us," her father said once Talbot stood in front of him, "it falls to you to carry on in his stead in the marine tradition. In the name of the Terran Empire, I grant you the County of Barrett Falls. Not coincidentally, it is adjacent to Countess Stone's holdings."

I'll get you for this, Talbot sent her through their implants.

Don't blame me. This was all his idea. Suck it up, Buttercup.

Once Talbot was safely off the dais, her father turned toward Jared. "And that brings us to the guest of honor. Admiral Jared Mertz was the man who made all these successes possible. He made the right choices. The hard choices. We collectively and individually owe him our lives.

"So, while he'd tell us that his promotion is reward enough, I am forced to disagree. Come forward, Admiral Mertz. Kneel."

Once Jared was on his knees, the emperor took up the ceremonial sword. "A knighting is the least that I can do, so let's get that out of the way." He tapped the blade to Jared's shoulders. "I name you Knight Commander in the Order of Lucien. Rise, Sir Jared."

Jared's face didn't show how uncomfortable he must feel, but Kelsey knew him far too well.

"Now, to the meat of the matter. Your service to the Throne demands a suitable recognition. I'm awarding you the Duchy of East Bay on Xander. Congratulations, Your Grace. As always, you'll be keeping an eye over your most trusted subordinates."

Kelsey saw the woman her mother had been glaring at react, standing there with her mouth open in shock. Zia grabbed the woman into a hug and whooped while Dennis and Charlie grinned.

Who was she? She did look vaguely familiar, but Kelsey couldn't place her. She took an image through her implants and sent a request through the palace system to identify her. The Terran Empire was large, so that might take a while.

"Yet that isn't enough," her father said. "After consulting with the Imperial Senate and verifying that sufficient precedent exists, I am reviving an old tradition. You are my acknowledged son, though you were not born in wedlock, and that has caused you grief. For which I am truly sorry.

"However, it gives me the foundation to make that up to you. Almost a thousand years ago, there was a similar situation, and the Imperial Senate at the time created a level of the peerage to recognize such individuals that the emperor, or in that case, empress, decided were worthy, though they were not in the line of succession. It gives me great pleasure to raise you to prince of the blood. Congratulations, Your Highness."

"No!"

Every head turned at the hot denial from the crowd. It was her mother, of course. Perfect.

Justine Bandar stormed up onto the dais. The guards moved to stop her, but her father halted them.

"I will not stand for this travesty!" her mother snarled. "He is a piece of common trash, and he will not be part of my family."

Karl Bandar smiled coldly. "I'd have preferred not to air our dirty laundry in public, Justine, but I'll not shy away from it. We're divorced. He's not part of your family. He's part of mine."

Kelsey rose to her feet. "And since we're talking about travesties, let's discuss the fact that neither Ethan or I were products of your marriage to my father."

"How dare you? I'm your mother! You will not side with him over me."

"Oh, I assuredly will. I don't know what kind of welcome you expected, but I'm not interested in talking. Guards, see my mother out of the palace."

Her mother looked shocked and tried to shake off the guards' hands, but they efficiently whisked her away.

Kelsey looked out over the crowd. "I'm sorry you had to see that, and even sorrier that I had to be part of it. Father, back to you."

He reached out and pulled her into a hug when she tried to sit back down. "I love you."

Kelsey held him tight. "And I love you."

He held her out at arm's length. "Since you're standing, I have one more thing to do. Kneel."

She gave him an odd look but obeyed.

"My little girl left on this mission as a—forgive me—pampered young woman. The crucible of fire has forged her into a warrior, and it's time I recognized that. I dub thee Knight Commander in the Order of Lucien."

He tapped the ceremonial sword on her shoulders and then pulled her to her feet. "I'm sure that Admiral Yeats was going to tell you himself, but I'll just go ahead and steal his thunder.

"As the only Marine Raider in the Empire, I think we have to recognize that you are only the first. You're in command of the Marine Raider ship *Persephone*, so you need the rank to do so.

Therefore, I'm inducting you into the Imperial Marines with the rank of colonel."

His eyes twinkled. "Perhaps that will keep you from needing to disobey all the military people standing in the way of you doing what you have to do."

Her ears were roaring. No, it was the crowd. The Fleet and Marine personnel were clapping like mad and shouting their approval. She was stunned.

"I'm not a military person," she said. Only her father was close enough to hear her.

"That's no longer true," he said with a smile. "You're a leader. Now you have the tools to make that authority legitimate. Wield it well."

Once the celebratory noisemaking subsided, Elise stepped forward. "If I might co-opt your ceremony, Your Majesty, I also have an announcement."

He inclined his head and stepped back. Kelsey followed suit.

The Pentagaran heir smiled at the people gathered before them. "It is my great pleasure to announce the impending marriage between His Highness, Prince Jared, and myself. May it bind our people even closer together."

That earned another set of lusty shouts from the crowd.

Her father grinned widely. "That is *excellent* news! My most sincere congratulations to you both. Have you selected a date?"

Elise shook her head. "I know that Fleet has imminent plans for him, so I think we should have the ceremony on Pentagar. We'll have to put things together quickly, because I'd like to make sure he's mine before he has to leave."

Jared nodded. "We'll have to get my mother there. She's waited long enough for me to get married. Luckily, we don't need to send very far for her."

Her father blinked. "Patricia is here?" He looked out over the crowd and smiled at the woman Kelsey had noted earlier. "There you are! Come up here and stand with our son."

Kelsey understood now. No need for that identity request she'd sent earlier, and no wonder her mother had been shooting daggers.

She put on her most welcoming smile and held her hand out to Patricia Mertz. "I'm so glad to finally meet you. I'm sure your son will have the grandest wedding you could desire."

"This is all so overwhelming," the woman said softly. "I never told you how sorry I was."

"You don't need to apologize to me," Kelsey said firmly. "We're family."

She pulled the other woman into a hug. Over her shoulder, she saw Talbot grinning at them. That made her smile wickedly, which wiped the smile off his face.

"Count Talbot," she said with her hand extended. "Get up here. Since we're going to be working on a big wedding, we should make it a double."

8

Brandon Levy rode back up to orbit lost in thought. The ceremony had shaken him out of his resentful state of mind. If the emperor thought he needed to knight Zia Anderson, perhaps he had blinders on. Perhaps.

There was a lot to think about.

Not everyone was going directly back to the ship, so the cutter was half empty. As the soon-to-be executive officer, he had a little bubble around him. He was still the new guy.

So he was surprised when a woman moved up and sat beside him. It was the woman who'd been with the captain on the flight deck.

She stuck out her hand. "Commander Levy, I'm Annette Vitter. I'm in charge of all the fighters."

He took her hand and shook it. "I'm sure I made a bad first impression. Can I ask for a redo?"

The corner of her mouth twitched up. "I'm a huge believer in second chances. The two of us are going to be working closely together, so I want to have the best relationship we can possibly have. Might I ask you a personal question?"

He nodded. "I won't say I'll answer it, but sure."

"Is part of your anger with the situation because you don't think the captain is experienced enough?"

"That's damned impertinent to ask," he said after a moment.

She smiled a little. "Impertinence is my middle name. Look, I can't help how you feel, but I wanted you to hear from someone who's served with the captain since before we left on this mission. You'll not find a more dedicated and conscientious officer, or one with a better grasp on what it means to command a carrier.

"Not to turn up my nose at your experience, because it's valid and important, but we've had over a year to get used to working with this equipment and the requisite tactics to use it effectively. The tech is so ubiquitous that you might never know where it is or how it can help you. Case in point." She held up her right hand.

"You've lost me," he said after a moment.

"I was using my arm as an example," Vitter said. "I lost it in a pinnace crash on Erorsi. This is cybernetic."

He blinked in surprise. Her uniform tunic covered her arm, but the hand she was holding up looked completely natural.

"I had no idea. I have to confess that the transfer came so suddenly that I haven't more than glanced at anyone's files. They basically stuffed me into a cutter and sent me over." He gestured at her arm. "May I?"

Vitter held her hand out, palm up. "I was piloting a pinnace full of marines on Erorsi when someone dropped an asteroid on us," she said stoically. "We tried to run for a ridge, but we didn't make it. The blast wave smashed us into the ground."

"And you walked away from that?" He felt her hand gingerly. It felt like flesh and blood.

"More like they carried me out after Princess Kelsey put a tourniquet on me. I'd have died without her quick action. My copilot didn't make it, and neither did some of the marines, in spite of their crash harnesses and armor.

"The folks at Erorsi stabilized me, but it was the doctors on Harrison's World that fitted me with this. It took a while before I could use it well. I thought I'd never fly again. I can only imagine how hard it was for Princess Kelsey to remaster her body after the Pale Ones butchered her."

He'd seen the classified report on what had happened to the heir. That level of modification took his breath away. Just the cranial implants he was supposed to get in the morning scared him a little.

Brandon released her hand. "I can't tell it isn't real. Does it work with your implants?"

"It communicates with them, but it's self-contained and connected directly to my nervous system. It isn't amped up like the princess's artificial muscles, either."

"Does anyone else have anything like this?"

She nodded. "Captain Paul Cooley of *Shadow* lost his legs and suffered a lot of internal injuries. He's still on Harrison's World recovering. I spoke with him a little before they pulled me out of the hospital. He's got a tough road ahead of him."

Brandon had seen that part of the report, too. The Rebel Empire destroyer had savaged the light cruiser. Less than thirty percent of the crew had survived the initial attack, and even more had died when the AI ships had captured the heavy cruiser *Spear*.

Shadow was going to be scrapped. He wondered where the other officer would end up or if he was even capable of serving any longer. Brandon had never heard of anyone with that kind of physical and mental injury making it back onto active duty.

He sighed and decided to answer her overly direct question. "Honestly, I don't know how I feel. I should be supporting the captain to the hilt, but part of me feels like I've been shafted. I have to find a way past that."

Vitter nodded. "She's young. You feel as though they skipped over you. That's perfectly understandable. I'd probably feel the same way.

"What you're not seeing is the experience she has with the new ships and systems. Once you've made the jump, I wouldn't be surprised at all to see you moved to command a ship of your own. Fleet is going to grow like you've never imagined."

Brandon pinched the bridge of his nose. "I hate being so petty. Honestly, I'm sure I'll adjust. I just have to get myself into a new headspace. A little mental distance from the change will make things better."

They had half an hour until they docked, so he might as well make the best of the time. "Tell me about fighter operations. What are your people like?"

She smiled. "They'll give you grey hair, but I couldn't ask for more aggressive, hard-fighting people. They'll make you want to brig them, and then they'll make you proud. Often in the same day."

The two of them settled into a deep discussion of how the small craft worked, and he immediately felt more comfortable. Maybe this wasn't going to be so bad after all.

* * *

ANNETTE WAITED until they exited the cutter to spring her next surprise. She cut Commander Levy off as he was excusing himself.

"Actually, if you have a few minutes, I'd like to give you a tour of the flight deck. It's what this ship is formed around, and you need to know what's down here."

Levy smiled a little. "Now why do I feel as though you sat by me on the cutter just to lure me into this tour?"

"That's not the *only* reason, but it was one. No offense, but your arrival might have cemented certain preconceived notions about fighter pilots. I'd rather have you see us in our element and form a better idea of the kind of people we are."

"Sure."

The landing bay was adjacent to the launch bay so that ships could quickly rearm and get back into the fight, so it was a quick walk to the area where the fighters were arrayed, ready for battle.

"These are Raptors. Mark fives, to be precise. The most advanced fighters the Old Empire had. They're incredibly fast and can be configured for antiship or antifighter roles. That basically means that it carries different missiles to suit the occasion.

"To take out a ship, it needs powerful strikes. It can carry two ship killers, one under each wing. Those can swap out for twelve antifighter missiles on need. They also have high-capacity flechette guns for really close work and taking out missiles fired at them."

He looked at the closest fighter with a quizzical expression. "Wings? Don't grav drives make those obsolete? Not to mention a space fighter doesn't run into air."

"Part is aesthetic design, more is tradition, but in the end, these ships can fight in atmosphere and drives do fail. Do they need wings? Probably not, but they look more ferocious with them."

Levy squatted to look at the missiles. "Only one under the wing, so this must be a ship killer. It's chancy enough getting through with ship-launched missiles. How can these little things hope to compete?"

She smiled. "Because we get in close. The drives on these are short range but very powerful for their size. Think of a sprinter. The charges are shaped to help get through battle screens and armor. One won't kill a ship, but enough stings will take the target down."

"That sounds pretty dangerous for the pilots."

"It is. In an actual combat scenario, we'll lose pilots. A lot more than any of us like. We all know that. That might explain some of the personality types that seem to be attracted to the profession."

He leaned back against the fighter and considered her. "What kind of personality are we talking about?"

"Someone cocky, who pushes the limits. Risk takers and daredevils. And let's not forget the egos. They're the best, they know it, and are always trying to prove it. We're a breed apart.

"I'm not saying that as a way of trying to earn them any slack. Only so that you'll have an idea what you're getting into as the executive officer on a carrier. Especially the first carrier."

"All right. I'll keep that in mind, though I won't promise I'll go any easier on them. At least I've been warned what I'm in for."

She stepped away from the fighters. "Let's go into the ready room. We always have some fighters in a state of readiness. They can launch on a moment's notice and keep an unexpected enemy busy while the rest of us get into flight suits. It's a rotating duty we all pull."

The pilots in the ready room were all awake, though that wasn't a firm requirement, so long as they were suited up. About half of them were playing cards, while the rest were watching a vid.

"Heads up," she called out. "Keep your seats and listen to me. This is Commander Levy. He's our new executive officer."

Their expressions were professionally guarded.

"I've heard a lot of good things about you," Levy said. "I won't pretend to understand what you do yet, but I'm going to learn. That will undoubtedly mean I make mistakes and miss things. When that happens, I'm going to rely on you and your comrades to set me straight."

He smiled a bit wryly. "On the flip side, I'm going to be the guy you get hauled in to see when you get up to any shenanigans, so don't push me too hard. If we can find a balance, we'll get along fine."

She stood back and watched as the new officer mingled with the pilots and started learning who they were. That was promising. Hopefully, he'd figure out the right balance as they went forward.

Once the crap hit the fan, it would be too late.

* * *

JARED SAT DOWN BESIDE TALBOT. The emperor had other things to do and had excused himself. Elise, Kelsey, and his mother were locked into a deep discussion about flowers. He was damned glad he only had to show up and get married. They were giving this more attention than he'd marshalled when they attacked the AI at Harrison's World.

"This is crazy," Talbot said. "I had no idea what I was getting myself in for. Hell, even this morning I thought I had more time to get used to it."

That made Jared smile. "I only knew the hammer was coming down this morning. About the wedding. I had one whole night to think about these titles. Man, they are going to complicate my life."

"Tell me about it," the marine grumbled. "I'm as far away from being a noble as possible. What the devil was he thinking?"

"I'd imagine that a lot of the first nobles were people like us," Jared said philosophically. "The men and women who got things done. The foppish sort only came in later."

Talbot sighed. "Maybe. I still feel maneuvered. The emperor used the LT to make me feel like I had to accept the title."

"It worked, didn't it? Frankly, that was a masterstroke. I'd have bet money you'd have run for the door before they corralled you into this."

The other man laughed softly. "Wouldn't that have caused a scene? Then there's the wedding. Kelsey and I talked around the subject, but she's just like her father. She saw an opportunity and waded in swinging."

Jared looked over at the women. "Is it the wrong decision? If so, now might be the time to say something."

"No, no. Nothing like that. I just envisioned this as something that would happen a little more sedately. A year ago, I couldn't even spell officer. Now I are one."

The last two sentences were said in a stilted voice, and it was a joke Jared had heard before.

"Very funny. You still haven't caught up, though. Once you marry Kelsey, you become the prince consort. Your Highness."

"Shit," Talbot said. "I never even considered that."

Jared laughed. "Did you consider the fact that your bride-to-be is now a colonel in the marines? Major."

"Dammit. This just keeps getting better. Think about who I'll have as a mother-in-law."

"Ouch. Point to you. Your life is going to be filled with plusses and minuses."

They sat in silence for a minute before Talbot spoke again.

"I suppose she's worth it."

Jared laughed again. "Remember she has super hearing."

"She'd have already skewered me if she'd heard me," the marine said with a grin. "Have you considered that we'll be brothers-in-law?"

Jared hadn't thought of that wrinkle, but it was definitely an upside. "I like that. You're a good man to have at my back when trouble comes knocking, and I like to think I have my uses."

"Such as when Justine Bandar comes calling?"

"Let's not get carried away. Bravery only goes so far."

Kelsey came out of the other room and glared at them. "You know I can hear you, right? I'm trying to plan two weddings. With only a few days before we leave, you're a distraction. Out."

Jared wasted no time in pulling Talbot to safety. The Imperial Guards assigned to him formed up around them as he headed for the landing pad. "Let's get out of the building before they find something for us to do."

"An excellent idea," the marine said. "We should make the most of the evening. Where do muckity-mucks go to have a real drink?"

"To the nearest marine bar."

Talbot grinned. "I know just the place. We should celebrate our freedom while we can."

"Speak for yourself, marine. I, for one, welcome our feminine overlords."

9

Zia woke, glad that medical nanites had made hangovers a thing of the past. She showered, dressed, and made it to the bridge right on time. Danny Leonidas smiled at her and rose from the command seat. "I expected you to sleep in, Captain. You were up late."

"You mean that I made the mistake of letting the fighter pilots get me well and truly hammered. Thanks for covering for me."

"It was no problem. I'm going to miss being here."

Zia took her seat and shook her head. "You're going to revel in commanding your own ship. Admit it."

"It's intimidating," he said. "But, yes, I'm really looking forward to it."

"Once Commander Levy has completed the implant procedure, I want you to get him up to speed on basic implant operations and run down everything he needs to know."

Danny nodded. "Aye, ma'am. That's a tall order, but I'll get the process started. I'm sure he'll catch on fast."

She really hoped so. Even more, she wanted Levy to get the chip off his shoulder. She might need his unstinting support very soon now.

Lieutenant Esther Frasier turned toward them. "Excuse me, Captain, but we just received orders addressed to you."

"Send it to my implants."

A small window popped up in her mental view. It was Admiral Yeats. "Captain Anderson, these are preliminary movement orders for *Audacious*. That of course means the rest of Admiral Mertz's fleet, too.

"You'll all head for Erorsi in forty-eight hours. I don't want to chance the freighter arriving before you do. I have no idea what Admiral Mertz's plan of engagement will be, but I'm sure your people will play a big role in it. Be ready to depart on schedule. Good luck."

The message ended, and she shook her head at her soon-to-be former executive officer. "We have preliminary orders. You'll arrive on your new ship just in time to head out with us. We leave in two days."

The other officer winced. "That's not a lot of time to get settled in. As in no time at all."

"Such is the life of an Imperial officer. Get things moving on our end. I don't want any unpleasant surprises."

He nodded. "I'll send out recall orders for everyone that hasn't returned to the ship. We're good on supplies, and I see no reason *Audacious* can't leave on time."

"Pass Levy on to Annette and let her get him up to speed. Time just became too precious for you to focus on your replacement. He'll have to learn as he goes."

"Aye, ma'am. Should we cancel the going-away party?"

Zia shook her head. "No way. We'll make time to send you off in style. Unfortunately, we'll have to stuff you in a cutter and send you on your way as soon as we finish. Get some people to help you pack. I'm going to miss you, Danny."

"I'll miss all of you, too, though I won't be so far away. If you'll excuse me, I need to start moving Heaven and Earth."

Zia spent the next hour going over everything for herself. She knew Danny would handle the details, but the responsibility of being fully ready was hers. She also called for Annette to come to the bridge.

Once she arrived, Zia led her into her office. "Time is short, so I'll get right to the point. We have movement orders. We'll be under way in two days."

The other woman nodded. "Danny told me. We'll be ready."

"What he probably didn't tell you was that he's going to be too damned busy to get Commander Levy up to speed. I'm passing that task on to you. Have Jake get Black Jack Squadron ready. The other two squadron commanders can handle their own birds. Get our exec to where he needs to be."

Annette nodded again. "Will do. He and I spoke on the way up from the ceremony. I think he'll fit in just fine, once he adjusts to the new circumstances."

Zia raised her eyebrow. "That seems awfully optimistic. I'm not sure that he's going to fully accept me as his commanding officer. There's a pretty big gap of experience and, in his shoes, I'd be pissed."

"I told him the same thing. I think he'll manage things, and I'm willing to help push him along. He's representative of the rest of Fleet, you know. All us new kids have a serious leg up on them, and they're going to have to scramble to catch up. Some otherwise fine officers won't make the jump."

Zia grimaced. "We'll just have to win that fight one person at a time. Levy's implant procedure should wrap up shortly. We really need him as a full part of the team. Go do me proud."

The pilot saluted. "Aye, ma'am. One hard-charging executive officer coming up."

* * *

BRANDON SWUNG his legs over the side of the table. The operation had been less overwhelming than he'd expected, considering they were putting things in his head.

The ship's doctor, Commander Zac Zoboroski, checked the readout one last time. "Everything looks good, Commander. Someone will need to show you the ropes, and you're on light duty for the rest of the day. If anything happens that concerns you, come immediately back here and let me have a look."

"Such as what?" he asked. "Frothing at the mouth? My wall screen going on and off by itself?"

The other man smiled. "Nothing like that. Headaches, mostly. Something off with your vision. I don't expect that to happen, but the literature says to watch out for it. Even that only means we need to adjust the settings a little. This is very safe technology. Now that the AIs can't reprogram it, of course."

"How many of these have you seen installed?"

"Hundreds. I was responsible for all the new folks that transferred aboard after *Audacious* arrived in Avalon space. Doctor Stone trained me in it once I had my own set of implants."

Brandon considered the other man. "Do they really make that much of a difference?"

"It's night and day. The things I can do now were unthinkable a year ago, and I'm discovering new possibilities in the library every day.

"None of us is using this new technology at anything like full potential. For that, we'll have to wait for the kids who get implants to grow up. They'll manage things that we'd never imagine because they don't know their fool ideas are impossible."

Brandon shook his head. "It feels like this is impossible, so I suppose that makes sense."

The hatch opened and Annette Vitter walked in. "I see I'm just in time."

"I'll leave you to it, Commander," Zoboroski said as he headed for his office. "Take it easy today."

He stood and was pleased to see he had no dizziness. "What are you just in time for?"

"I'm the lucky soul that gets to show you how to use those new implants of yours. I'll also give you a walking tour of the ship. Commander Leonidas is busier than a one-armed paperhanger. Trust me, I should know."

"I can't believe you're so cavalier about it," he said, stepping up beside her as she walked toward the hatch. "That's got to be a serious mental trauma."

Vitter nodded. "I make light of it because I don't believe in letting something like that dominate my life. I'm damned lucky that they were able to fix me so well.

"The first thing you need to know is that there *is* an instruction manual. I realize as a man that you're genetically disinclined to read the instructions before haring off into unknown territory, but I suggest you give it a look first."

He snorted. "That is so sexist. How did you know I wouldn't flip out about you saying it?"

"I didn't," she said with a twinkle in her eye. "Now I know you have a sense of humor under that dour expression."

"I'm not dour," he said primly. "I'm just a little reserved around people I don't know."

"That's what they all say. Okay, the interface to your implants is surprisingly easy to use. It just takes a little practice. Think of this like a new sense. You can see the corridor, you can hear the people moving down it, and so on. Try to take it all in for a moment."

He instantly saw what she meant. There were little icons scattered along the corridor now, including on and in the people passing by. He focused on Vitter and found several on her person.

"Okay, that's interesting. You have icons on you."

"What about yourself?"

As soon as she said that, he realized that he also had one. It must be his implants. With that frame of reference, he recognized her implants and could separate them from the other gear she had that popped up on his internal radar.

He tried to poke his implants mentally. They responded with something very much like a menu. The first thing on it was labeled orientation. That was useful.

"I found the instructions."

"Excellent," she said as they walked into one of the lifts. "You'll want to spend some time studying it in more detail. Take us to the flight deck."

He reached for the button, but she stopped him. "Tell the controls where to go with your implants."

The next few hours were a real education, and he started to get an idea of exactly how far behind he and all of the other Fleet personnel were. The sheer number of things he could now do with a thought staggered the imagination.

The sheer number of systems on the ship daunted him. Each one allowed the appropriate people to do their jobs in ways that were barely comprehensible. A crew trained and able to do this would have significant advantages in speed and effectiveness.

Vitter left him in his quarters when they were done. He felt guilty about taking her away from her duties when he found out they had orders to leave in less than two days. She shouldn't have wasted time on him. Hell, she shouldn't have had to.

It was obvious that it would take him weeks just to become competent at the basics. Putting him here was a severe disservice to a probably well-oiled crew. Fleet should have left Leonidas in the exec's position.

Well, he didn't have the luxury of telling them that, so he'd better get his ass in gear. If they got into a fight, he had to be ready. If something took out the captain, he had to be able to step into her suddenly larger shoes.

10

K elsey put her hand on Carl's shoulder. "I'm sorry you had to cut your getaway short."

He grinned at her. "Me, too, but we have a rain check from the emperor. Besides, I wouldn't have missed the ceremony for the world. Honestly, Angela got her orders right after we got back into the city, so it wasn't happening anyway. Don't worry about it."

"Where is she going?"

He raised an eyebrow. "You don't know? She's going to your ship, Colonel."

"Ah. Well, I'll be happy to have her."

The Imperial Guards around them seemed faintly scandalized when he picked up the Imperial Scepter from its cushion, she noted.

"We're not going to hurt it," Kelsey assured them. "We just need to perform some tests. You're going to be right there with us. I promise we're not stealing it so we can sell it on the black market."

"How much do you think it's worth?" Carl asked.

"Don't tease them like that," she said repressively. "They leave their senses of humor in their duty lockers."

That got a smile from some of them.

She'd checked with her father about this, of course. She hadn't mentioned the reason she wanted to do it, though. Just in case they were barking up the wrong tree, she wanted to keep that close to her vest for the moment.

Carl's main lab was in the capital at Imperial University, so only a short air car ride from the palace. He'd brought down a surprising amount of technology recovered from the graveyard of dead Fleet ships at Harrison's World, as well as some things from the Grant Research Facility, a very secret weapons research lab that had been the genesis of the rebel forces on Harrison's World.

She hadn't been to his lab since they'd refurbished an entire building for his use. She supposed that the prestige of having a Lucien Prize–winning scientist on their staff, as well as having the Imperial purse foot the bill, made a large facility inevitable.

In this case, Carl's lab wasn't just the outer research area, which was filled with scientists and research students examining various pieces of equipment, but the highly secure inner lab that was his personal domain.

Security here worked like an onion. It took clearance to get past the human guards at the door. Carl had shown them just how easy it was to use social engineering to get into one of their other "secure" labs, so he'd insisted on diligent people manning the entry points.

Once into the outer labs, only those with appropriate clearances could get into any of the more secure rooms. His personal lab had the tightest security of all, only opening to his implants or someone whom he'd approved.

That was a damned short list, considering the importance of the experiments and research in progress there.

He led her and her guards into his private domain. The wide room had a dozen tables piled with partially disassembled gear and almost as many computer terminals. No people, though.

"We'll want to put it under a scanner and see what we can without opening it," he said, heading for a machine with its hood already raised. "I doubt it's booby trapped, but it pays to be cautious."

Carl set the scepter under the scanner head and lowered the hood. A screen behind it came to life, showing them the external surface.

Little points appeared on the image as the scanner determined the composition of the materials.

Kelsey watched it but also used her implants to get a more details. Under the precious metals on the surface, there were additional high-tech materials but nothing that seemed out of place.

The scanner bumped up the power and started looking at the inner makeup of the scepter. She immediately saw advanced electronics very similar to what went into implants.

"I'm not seeing anything that leads me to believe opening it would be dangerous," Carl said. "There is a computerized component, but I'm unsure of what it's for at this point."

He raised the hood and took the scepter over to a worktable. The Imperial Guards hovered a little too close, so he gestured for them to step back. "I'm going to be very careful. Don't worry."

Carl grabbed a headband with a magnifier. "The latches are cleverly hidden. If I didn't know this was meant to come apart, I'd have figured it was a solid unit."

"That makes sense," she said. "You don't want everyone in the Empire seeing that when you use it in ceremonies.

"I wonder if this is the original scepter or one built after the rise of the AIs. If this key was there before the AIs, it might not have anything to do with them." The thin scientist shrugged. "Emperor Marcus seemed to think it was relevant, so it must tie in somehow."

He used a tool under one edge of the handle, and the end of the scepter came off. From there, it was easy to remove the rest of the panels.

The interior of the scepter was made of what certainly looked like a small computer to Kelsey. Her implants detected nothing, not even an operating power supply. After all this time, any power source was likely dead.

Carl plucked the battery out. "I have one that will work here. This is the same model I use in a few other projects."

He retrieved an identical battery from a bin and slipped it into the appropriate socket. The lights on the computer indicated it was booting, but Kelsey still couldn't detect it. It was very stealthy. Her

Raider implants were good enough to sense most equipment at this range.

"I'm not seeing any way to connect with it," she said.

Carl nodded. "That might be intentional. The best way to hide an access point is to make it invisible. You either have to activate it in some way or transmit in the blind. You know, like saying a code phrase and having a secret door open up."

She smiled. "Someone has been watching too many action adventure vids. Can you see any way to trigger the access point?"

"Let me examine the rest of the scepter for a few minutes."

Kelsey stepped back to let him work. She could do other things while she waited for him to wrap up. Like figure out what she was going to do about her mother.

The woman had left a billion messages on her com. The guards had sent her packing twice last night, including once where they'd called the local police to haul her away.

She doubted they'd arrested the ex-empress. That would've taken colossal balls. No, they'd probably taken her back to the precinct and read her the riot act. Not that it would stop her mother for very long.

Not that it needed to. She'd be out of the woman's grasp in two days. Then she'd have weeks or months to come to terms with what she'd learned. Her mother could find her own balance in that time, too.

No, she had to meet this challenge head on.

"I found something," Carl said.

She shook herself out of her funk and walked back over to him. "That was quick."

"That's because it's right in my face. Literally." He lifted the handle a little. "This is a sophisticated scanner. One I'd wager is tuned to scan someone's DNA."

Kelsey snorted. "Then I'm screwed, because it would have to be linked to the Imperial line. My father or Jared are the only possible candidates, or one of the cadet branches of the family. That all assumes that it wasn't set to only recognize Lucien and his father."

"There's only one way to be sure. We need to have one of them give it a try. Perhaps they can add people to the access list. I'm a bit nervous about hacking the computer without trying other options first. If it's *really* secure, it might wipe itself if someone unauthorized attempts to get in by force."

She nodded. "Get together with Jared and see what you can find. Since I'm not actually required for this, I should probably deal with my mother."

He shook his head. "I don't envy you that task. Her behavior at the ceremony last night was all the morning news could talk about. I'll grab some portable gear and head up to *Invincible*. Good luck."

"You have no idea. I'm considering wearing my powered armor. Just to be safe. Send the details to my implants once you figure something out."

"Will do."

Kelsey collected her guards and headed back out to the air car. Finding her mother wouldn't be hard. All she had to do was listen to any of the ranting messages to get the address where she was staying.

* * *

ZIA THOUGHT THAT COMMANDER—SOON to be captain—Leonidas's going away party was a smashing success. Jim Richmond had outdone himself. The food was light yet very scrumptious. Probably fattening, but medical nanites could help with that. Thank God for technology.

Danny Leonidas looked at turns sad and happy. That pretty much defined how they all felt. Except for the new guy. Brandon Levy looked depressed.

Zia wasn't sure about what. With him being so new, it could be just about anything. She hoped he'd settle down once he was actually working his new position.

Annette Vitter slid over beside her. "He's really not that bad once you get past his dour and occasionally officious exterior. I mean seriously, he's a lot less abrasive than Commodore Meyer was when the admiral had to deal with him."

That was certainly true. Then-Commander Sean Meyer had had trouble walking with that stick up his butt. He'd been arrogant and closed-minded on the best of days.

The events of Harrison's World had proven that even the most obnoxious person had a good side, and she had to admit that Meyer was more than dedicated to his job. Even if he was snootier than the local nobles.

"Here I am being as closed minded as I accused him of being," Zia said sourly. "Being in command has a lot of challenges. Like giving him the benefit of the doubt until he gives me reason not to."

Annette turned so that her back was to Levy, who was chatting with Tony Hastert. The swarthy chief engineer seemed to be telling one of the tall tales he was known for. He seemed to think that a story worth telling was worth embellishing.

She had to admit he had a real talent for it. He could spin out the story of *Spear*'s destruction into an epic tale of tragedy and loss, which of course it was.

"I wouldn't let it get to you," Annette said. "He has got a chip on his shoulder, but he's starting to understand why things are the way they are. Once he's up to speed with the new technology, he'll find himself in command of one of the salvaged ships."

"Sure, after we spend all the time training him," Zia said grumpily.

Annette laughed. "All it takes is one look at the manpower requirements going forward even five years and that becomes inevitable. We're going to be hideously short of experienced command personnel."

That was even truer than Annette knew. Zia had been there for the full-day briefing with Admiral Mertz. The scope of the new Fleet was vast.

They'd already broken ground on a new academy but were aggressively recruiting new people to stick into makeshift classes all over the planet. The current crop of junior officers was going to be learning on the job in positions they'd never have dreamed of getting for years.

The situation with the senior officers was even worse. Fleet had never been huge to begin with, so it taxed the current manpower levels just to crew all the ships they'd brought back. A number of older vessels were in parking orbits, bereft of everything but a caretaker crew. They'd probably be decommissioned in the near future.

That wouldn't even begin to be enough. Recall orders would go out to former Fleet personnel and those who'd retired. That would help, but it wouldn't fill the gap. It was going to be challenging.

Well, that was a problem for another day.

Zia picked up a fork and rang it against the glass of champagne in her hand. "Your attention, everyone. As much as we're all enjoying this, Danny needs to get his butt onto the cutter for his new command. Danny, we're going to miss you."

She raised her glass. "I give you Captain Daniel Leonidas, commanding officer of the Imperial Fleet light cruiser *Lightning*."

Everyone raised their glasses and shouted their congratulations.

Danny smiled and saluted them with his glass. "I'm sorry to leave you all, but I know the ship is in good hands. I won't be too far away, either. To the Empire! May she never falter!"

Zia smiled and repeated the toast. He was going to be a great captain. Now she had to get Brandon Levy into similar shape.

"It is also my duty to welcome our newest companion. As of this moment, Commander Brandon Levy is officially *Audacious*'s executive officer. Welcome aboard."

The clapping was much less boisterous, but that didn't seem to bother Levy. He smiled and nodded to all of them. "I'm sure this is as sudden for you as it was for me, but I'll do everything I can to get up to speed quickly. I look forward to working with all of you."

Zia clapped but decided to reserve judgment on that. Annette was good at reading people, but only time would tell. They were going back into harm's way, and there was no room for petty jealousy.

"Danny, if you'll say your goodbyes, I'll walk you down to the bay," she said. "I think Annette has arranged a little escort to see you safely to your new command."

11

J ared examined the Imperial Scepter closely. It was just as impressive as he'd expected, plated in precious metals and glittering with cut gems.

"What do you need me to do?" he asked Carl.

"The handle has a sophisticated scanner that I think is keyed by DNA. Nothing happens when I pick it up, but I'm hoping you get a different result."

"With my luck, it'll be an electrical shock."

The young scientist laughed. "No chance of that, Admiral. It's safe."

Jared grasped the scepter by its handle and lifted it. The thing had more heft than he'd expected. It would make a decent club.

"I'm not feeling anything," he said after a moment. "What am I missing?"

"See if you can connect with it. You might not sense anything to ping, but try anyway."

Jared didn't feel as though the scepter was available, but he tried to insert his implants into it anyway. After a few tries, he sensed something. It felt as though the device were looking back at him. He received a connection request through his implants and accepted it.

Identify yourself, a computer voice whispered into his mind.

I am Jared Mertz, Fleet admiral and prince of the blood. He'd added that last since it seemed appropriate.

The key recognizes your bloodline, Highness.

That seemed a little underwhelming. *Am I authorized to use you?*

This unit will work for anyone of the blood that possesses it.

"It says I'm authorized, but I have no idea what it does," he told Carl. "What do you want me to do?"

"See if it will describe what it does. What kind of key is it?"

Tell me what you do, he instructed the device.

This unit is the key. It unlocks the repository.

This wasn't the smartest computer he'd ever interacted with. *What repository?*

The Imperial Vault.

"It says it opens the Imperial Vault," he told Carl. He connected with the ship's computer and ran a search.

The original Imperial Palace on Terra had had a massive vault with many, many treasures from all across the Empire.

Do you mean the treasure room under the Imperial Palace?

Yes.

Do you have any other data that I can access?

This unit has no further information to share, Prince Jared Mertz.

Can I instruct you to allow contact from another computer?

Yes.

Open a connection.

He felt the connection appear in his implants. "Marcus, please connect with this computer and see what information you can get from it."

"Right away," the AI said. "Connection established. It's remarkably restricted. It literally only knows what it just told you."

He scowled. "Then why have a sophisticated computer?"

"It seems the processing power must be in the function it performs," Carl said. "If I wanted a lock that no one else could pick, this might just be the way. Whatever it does will mesh with the computer in the vault in some manner.

"Without the key, the vault won't open. Since it's restricted to

Imperial blood, no one can steal it. Well, not anyone that isn't related to the Imperial line."

Jared shook his head. "That seems silly. What if the emperor died without an heir? How would they open the vault?"

"Brute force and ignorance," Carl said matter-of-factly.

"You've spent too much time with Angela. I'm fairly sure that won't work out well for the burglars."

He set the scepter back on the padded rest. "I'm not sure what would be so important to Marcus or Lucien once the AIs kicked them off Terra."

"Perhaps Emperor Marcus put something into the vault that's critical to stopping the AIs once and for all."

"It would've been nice if he'd left a note about that." Jared sighed. "He may have hoped to turn things around. At this point, we'll probably never know. Visiting Terra is somewhat low on our list of priorities."

"Admiral, I have found a segregated piece of memory inside the scepter," Marcus said. "It's locked and I cannot access it."

Computer, what is in the segregated memory?

This unit is aware of no segregated memory.

"Interesting. It doesn't know about it. Is it part of the computer?"

Carl frowned. "Hang on. I can see it through Marcus. It's located in an area that is read-only for most computers. There's no reason for something so basic to be protected so well."

"Can you unlock it?"

The scientist shook his head. "No, but you might be able to. Just like you don't need to sense the computer to link with it, you might not need to directly access it."

"You know that doesn't make sense, right?"

"Think of it like a blind connection. The computer can't sense the memory, but if you tell it to access the sectors I give you, it might be able to do so. A function it doesn't even know it has. One that only someone actually able to use the scepter could even fathom, but most would never think to look for. Marcus is a lot more observant than the average computer."

"Thank you," the AI said.

Carl gave Jared a series of numbers, and he instructed the computer to read the area. An image immediately appeared in his head. It was Emperor Marcus. He appeared very much as he had in the transmission Kelsey had found on Pentagar, but he was now seated behind a desk.

"Son, I'm sorry that I can't be there for you. I can only pray that you've managed to escape the notice of the rebels and have arrived at Avalon safely. If not, I suppose you won't be seeing this.

"Maybe when you're older, you'll understand why I couldn't take you with me. It's not because I didn't want to but because I couldn't bear the thought of you dying with me. Which, I have to assume, is the most likely end."

The man sighed tiredly. "We're about to pull out of Terra. We can't hold the system. Based on their tactics, the rebels will destroy everything in space and use EMP blasts from orbit to kill most of the technological base. The death toll is going to be hideous.

"We've pulled as many people as possible onto the ships with us, but the rebels will keep pursuing us. We'll try to give the civilian ships as much lead as we can before Fleet turns and fights, but freighters and personnel transports can't match a battlecruiser's acceleration."

Marcus leaned forward intently. "Once they pacify a system, they don't leave a lot of force there. They start infecting the population through their implants and move on. That's why they can keep using so many of the ships they've captured.

"I'm hoping that once they've moved past Terra, you can strike back for me. I never spoke with you about the AIs, but they have a weakness. One specific unit in a system called Twilight River controls them. If you can co-opt it, you can end the rebellion and reverse the infection in everyone."

Jared smiled sadly. The man had no idea that the rebels would find Lucien and pursue him right to Avalon's atmosphere. They'd destroyed every Fleet vessel, and it had taken longer than Lucien had lived to regain the lost technology.

The boy emperor hadn't had the benefit of medical nanites. They didn't implant the devices until someone was in their late teens because they could interfere with the early development of a growing body. The Empire had relied on their advanced medical care to correct any issues before then. He'd only had a normal human lifespan.

"The scepter will get you into the vault once you slip back into the Terra system. They might flatten the palace, but you know the other ways in. Don't do anything to alert them to your presence.

"Inside the vault, you'll see an amazing number of things. Treasures sent to the emperors from all across the Empire since the very beginning. You'll need to move to the rear of the vault and look for a plain wooden crate on the floor. It's not big, but be careful with it. The contents are irreplaceable."

An image of a small crate appeared in the corner of Jared's vision. He'd recognize it if he ever saw it.

"That crate contains the only override for the AI that exists. Or, perhaps I should say, that still exists. There was one on the station at Twilight River, but I'm sure the AI saw to its destruction at once.

"One of the scientists was visiting the nearby Fleet base to consult with a colleague and broke every security rule to give her a peek. They managed to escape with it when the AI infiltrated the Fleet base."

Emperor Marcus rubbed his face. "I understand that leaving it in the vault probably seems stupid, considering that we know the AIs will overrun the system, but I can't take the chance that they destroy the ship carrying it.

"It may be possible for me to send some Raiders to recover it if we're more successful than I imagine. They'd have to break in, but that isn't impossible if I give them the plans. Which, by the way, are appended to this message."

He smiled wryly. "I know this is a terrible final message for a father to leave his son, but all our hopes ride with you. I love you, boy. Always remember that. When you have a family of your own, you'll understand. Godspeed."

The message ended, and a file uploaded to Jared's implants. It had a very detailed map of the Imperial Palace on Terra, exquisite specifications on the vault itself, and a listing of the contents. The sheer number of priceless historical artifacts in that massive chamber stunned him.

After a moment, he set that aside and looked at the plans. He didn't know that much about breaking and entering, but this wouldn't be easy, even with inside information.

He had no idea what the situation was really like on Terra. Olivia West said that the AI had given up on subduing the population and bombed it back into the Stone Age. The Imperial Palace might not even exist anymore. Yet he now knew they had no choice but to make the journey.

If there was any chance at all they could turn this around, it would require the override. Otherwise, every AI in the Old Empire would keep fighting. Hell, there was no guarantee that they could even get to the Twilight River research station. The AI probably had a massive fleet there to defend itself.

"That was useful," he told Carl and Marcus once he'd digested everything. "Here's what I got." He sent them the message and the plans to the vault.

"Too bad there weren't plans for the override itself," Carl complained. "Then we could build our own."

"Probably not," Marcus said. "Much like the key, it's probably all tied up in the specific computer programming and custom hardware. We'll need the actual override to plug into the master AI. What I wish the emperor had mentioned was who was behind the attack in the first place."

"I'm pretty sure that whoever they were, they lost control," Jared said. "Otherwise, the AIs wouldn't still be running everything."

"We'll need to brief the emperor. When the time comes for our trip to Terra, we'll have to appropriate the key. For right now, that's a low priority. We have to capture the freighter and make sure the escort, if any, doesn't make it home."

He smiled at Carl. "This time we're ready. All we have to do is get into place and wait for them to obligingly come calling."

* * *

ANNETTE TOOK Levy down to the launch bay and into the ready room. "Now that you have implants, I think you need to see how they can affect things like flying a ship. It also gives me an opportunity to show off the fighters for you."

"That doesn't sound like light duty," he said with a smile. "I think the doctor is going to be annoyed with me."

"I'll take it easy," she assured him. "I only make people throw up when they're feeling good."

"Thanks. Seriously, isn't the acceleration going to be a problem?"

She shook her head. "I had them relocate a training fighter to the landing bay. We'll go out nice and easy."

"Training fighter?"

"It's easier to show you after we get you suited up."

Jake Fiennes was waiting to get Levy into flight gear, so she let them go while she mentally reviewed her planned excursion. There'd be no in-atmosphere flight or hard acceleration. It was basically a joyride. One that would allow the newly implanted officer to interface with the small craft and get a feel for what that meant.

Fifteen minutes later, Jake brought Levy back out. She nodded approvingly. "You look ready. Okay, let me give you the safety spiel first. If for any reason we have to eject, you need to keep your hands in your lap and sit up straight. The grav drives in the seats are not light duty by any stretch of the imagination, so we'll try to avoid that.

"Second, while on the fighter, I am in command. If I give an order, it is for the safety of the vehicle, and you need to obey without argument. Clear?"

He nodded. "Perfectly. I won't be a problem."

"We can cover the rest while I'm doing the final preflight. Come on."

She led him back to the landing bay. The training fighter was very similar to the regular version except that it had an extended body and a second cockpit in front of the normal one. That allowed a trainer to observe everything a new pilot did while not seeming like they were hovering.

"This is the trainer," she said. "You'll be in the front, so it'll feel like you're alone. That's by design. I'll be communicating with you the entire time."

Annette gave the bird a good preflight and showed Levy how to enter the cockpit. Once he was seated, she made sure he was firmly strapped in.

"Before you put your helmet on, there are a few other things," she said. "The fighter has a lot of emergency supplies onboard, so unless the fighter is in danger of exploding—which is exceedingly unlikely—we'll be fine in the event of trouble. We're not even going that far away from *Audacious*.

"Also, your controls are locked out unless and until I activate them. In the also unlikely event that I'm somehow disabled, the controls will activate for you. The fighter keeps good track of our health. You've piloted a cutter before, so I know you can get back to the ship if you have to."

He nodded. "Got it."

"Strap your helmet on and connect it to the life support system. In the event that the cabin loses pressure, you're still going to be fine. I'll settle in back and take us out. Once we're clear of traffic, we'll get started with your familiarization."

Annette got herself situated and linked with the fighter's on board computer. The cameras in the front cockpit allowed her to see Levy. She'd make sure he could see her when they got out.

The fighter didn't have standard controls like a cutter or pinnace. Pilots controlled these high-tech marvels directly through their implants.

That scared a lot of new pilots. What if something went wrong?

In fact, this way was a lot safer for the pilots. All the fighter's systems were in range of the implants, even without the amplifying effects of their helmets. Each system had multiple control interfaces in case of damage. The only way to lose contact with a system was the destruction of the system in question.

On a cutter, an unlucky bit of damage could take out a control run and leave systems offline. Even with multiple dedicated runs, those craft were more vulnerable than the Raptors.

The other weak link in the control chain was the pilot's implants.

Since they were in their heads, the loss of their implants wasn't that much of a concern. They wouldn't be caring if they were dead or unconscious.

The lack of a control panel also meant that the pilot wasn't tempted to use the less efficient manual controls. The implants were so much more versatile.

With the fighter amplifying their implant range, a pilot could directly control someone else's fighter if the on-board computer detected they were disabled and the rescuer had the appropriate authorization.

The command pilots—those with the highest level of training and authority—had override codes. They could literally take over another fighter from close by, even if the pilot wasn't disabled.

She smiled. That usually unnerved the hell out of the new guys. It was also useful in simulating systems failures.

None of this was important for the moment, though. Commander Levy probably didn't have what it took to be a fighter pilot. This was just an orientation run.

Annette cleared her departure with Control and lifted them off the deck. A light touch on the grav drives sent them coasting out of the bay at a leisurely few hundred meters a second. With the drives online from the start, there was no feeling of acceleration.

She opened an audio link to the other cockpit. "Okay, we're clear of the ship. If you open your implants up, you'll detect an access point for the fighter. As I said, I've locked out your controls, so you're not going to do anything if you stretch your wings. You'll be able to use its scanners to see what's going on around us."

His eyes widened. "Holy cow. I can see every status on the fighter without searching around for it, and the view is unreal. It feels like seeing, but it's not really visual. More like a 3-D tactical display."

"That's a good analogy. You can see me if you try. We could communicate solely by implant, but that makes a lot of people uncomfortable."

He nodded. "I see you now. How do you keep everything straight without displays to monitor?"

"I treat the fighter like my body. It takes a while to get used to it, but it's incredibly natural. You can also tell it to create virtual displays through your implants. That's usually how most people learn to fly, so it's comfortable.

"In this case, I want you to do this the hard way. Look at our course. See how we're coming up on some geosynchronous satellites? I want you to turn us a few degrees to either side of our present course. I've released the flight controls to you, though I have override authority."

The course change was more abrupt than he'd intended, she was sure. That was a natural mistake for a first-timer. They didn't realize how sensitive the controls were.

"Sorry," he said. "I overcorrected."

"You didn't know what to expect. I'm going to throw a waypoint onto the scanner readings. Change course for that and increase our speed by ten percent. We're positively dawdling."

Over the next hour, she gradually added systems to his control until he had a very good idea of the complexity of what it meant to pilot a fighter. He handled them better than she'd expected. Maybe he had what it took after all. That was something to explore at greater length later.

"Okay, I think you have the basic idea," she finally said. "Now it's time to give you a demonstration of what it means to be in the advanced course."

Annette brought up a dogfight simulation. Empty space suddenly became a 3-D nightmare of ships going every direction at maximum speed, all while shooting at one another.

"Holy shit!" he blurted, trying to dodge the fighter around an oncoming enemy. Proximity alarms blared as he almost collided with their fictional wingman.

That's when someone dropped in behind them and fired missiles. The end was quick.

"Oops," she said. "You're dead. Don't feel bad. I got blown up just about that fast the first time, too. Being a fighter pilot is dangerous business."

He stared at her out of the mental screen. "How the hell do you keep all of that straight? With all the other fighters, I couldn't even tell which ones were on my side, much less where any of them were going."

"Training and practice. We have to keep all of the variables in our heads. I ran an ambush yesterday where most of my squadron died, including me. We train hard so that doesn't happen when things get real, but up close and personal, a lot of us will die anyway. That's what we do."

He frowned hard. "I said I knew what you meant about being a fighter pilot, but it turns out I had no idea. I'm going to have a lot of work ahead of me to understand not only what it means to be a fighter pilot but to command them from the deck of a carrier.

"On the plus side, I think I have a good idea of how implants work on a small ship like this. The capabilities are a lot more intuitive than I expected. I'm sure this is only the start of my education, but I get it. Hopefully, I'll pick up the critical things more quickly. Thank you."

"My pleasure. Now, since we're done, I'll let you find *Audacious* and take us home. Try not to get us killed on the way," she added with a smirk.

12

Kelsey stood outside her mother's hotel room and dithered. She had a lot of nerve coming here after what had happened at the ceremony. Kelsey was going to catch hell, even though she was the wronged party here. Her mother would never admit fault. That simply wasn't how she worked.

Well, time to start the fireworks.

She turned to her guard commander. "There's going to be yelling. Things will get broken. I'm a Marine Raider. She's not going to hurt me. Under no circumstances are you to come inside that apartment unless I signal for you to do so or you see blood seeping out from under the door. Is that understood?"

The man looked deeply unhappy, but he nodded. "Yes, Highness."

Kelsey pressed the buzzer on the door and waited. Moments later, her mother yanked the door open and glared at her. "Finally. Get in here and leave these people outside. The time for childish behavior is over."

"I couldn't agree more."

Kelsey stepped inside and closed the door behind her. "I can't imagine how you expected this to go, but I'm not the little girl you abandoned all those years ago."

"Don't be ridiculous," her mother said. "I didn't abandon you. You came to visit as often as you liked. I blame your father for turning you against me."

"Then you'd be wrong." Kelsey put her hands on her hips and stood there, not wilting under her mother's glare. "I know what you've done. What's worse, I know who you did it with. There's no unseeing something like that."

Her mother shook her head. "I have no idea what you're talking about. All I did was come back to make sure you were okay. A daughter needs her mother after a trauma like you went through."

Justine Bandar had no conception of what Kelsey had been through. They'd decided that the public didn't need to know the gory details of her implants or how she'd gotten them.

"You cheated on my father. How could you?"

Justine Bandar threw up her hands and started pacing. "How can you ask me that after he cheated with the help? Worse, how could you stand by that bastard in the first place?"

"Call Jared Mertz a bastard at your peril," Kelsey said in a low, dangerous voice. "I like him far better than I like you at this particular moment, and I don't see that changing.

"As for Father, he admitted what he'd done and paid the full price for it. You're still busy denying everything and hoping no one realizes the true extent of your betrayal. The fact that you'd had no idea he'd slept with Jared's mother while you were sleeping around doesn't exactly help your position, either."

Her mother started to say something, but Kelsey held up her hand. "I'm not finished. I've seen the train used for escaping the palace. Nathaniel Breckenridge showed it to the people that rescued me from Ethan.

"Maybe you never realized it, but it records every trip. I've seen exactly how many people you've slipped into your rooms over the years, and how long your infidelity went on. Do *not* try to pull the wool over my eyes. I know who you are now."

Her mother dropped into a comfortable-looking chair with an audible huff. "That changes nothing between us. I'm your mother, even if Karl isn't your father. It doesn't mean I don't love you."

Kelsey shook her head. "Maybe not, but it severely limits my sympathy for you when you go after my brother."

Justine Bandar's eyes hardened. "He is not your brother. Jared Mertz killed your brother. He's a monster."

Kelsey shook her head slowly. "You really should watch the news more often. I killed Ethan."

Her mother waved her hand as though she were dispersing smoke. "So those idiots on the news said. I don't believe it. You're not capable of something so terrible. Your father convinced you to take the heat off his precious by-blow. You don't need to lie to me."

"You have no idea what I'm capable of," Kelsey said coolly. "Ethan was mad at the end, paranoid and dangerous. I gave the order that let Ethan run to his death."

Her mother blinked. "What?"

"The flip point he ran through went to an area of space filled with deadly radiation. I kept my mouth shut and let him go."

To her credit, her mother looked horrified. "Why would you do that?"

"Because he was going to start a civil war that would kill more people than either of us can comfortably count. I loved him, but it was him or the Empire. I'll live with the consequences of my decision for the rest of my life, but I wouldn't change it."

"Ethan was your brother."

"Ethan was a mad dog that had to be put down," Kelsey said regretfully. "I don't know when he became a paranoid monster, but you don't leave unexploded ordinance lying around where anyone can set it off. He was the heir, and the Empire wouldn't have survived him ascending to the Throne."

Her mother's frown intensified. "Did you kill him so you could take his place?"

That actually made Kelsey laugh bitterly. "Hell, no. I'm still so disgusted with things that I'd have happily renounced my claim and become a commoner. I have important work to do that doesn't involve egomaniacal senators or other nobles. Political backbiting is one thing I could cheerfully live without."

"Why not just capture him?" Her mother finally sounded somewhat normal, just a woman hurting for the loss of her son.

"He was too far away and had a destroyer with him. If I'd warned him, he might have been able to escape. I'll admit that was a low-order probability, but he'd just poisoned Father and blamed me, so I wasn't feeling very forgiving.

"Which brings us back to you. I counted eighteen different lovers over a period of decades. That's a little more serious than an ill-considered fling. Yes, it's between you and Father, but it hurts me, too.

"If you want to continue having a relationship with me that doesn't involve shouting and recriminations, I'd lose the chip on your shoulder.

"Jared and I have been to hell and back, and we've worked out our differences. He's my brother in every way that matters. I can't stop you from being a bitch to Father or me, but if you go after Jared Mertz, I will make you deeply regret that mistake. Am I clear?"

Her mother said nothing for a long moment, examining Kelsey's face closely. When she did speak, it was much more calmly. "You've grown harder. You were always so soft when you were younger."

"Hard times either toughen you up or they kill you. The past is gone, Mother, and so is the little girl you could manipulate. If you want to continue having a relationship with me, you're going to have to accept that. Grow. Up."

Justine Bandar nodded slowly. "I can see we have many things to discuss."

Kelsey turned toward the door. "It will have to wait. I'm shipping out in a day and a half and have far too much work to do before we leave. I'll give you a chance when I get back. It might be several weeks or several months. You'll just have to be patient. I'm far too angry to be reasonable, and so are you. We'll talk then."

She more than half expected her mother to try to stop her, but the other woman let her leave without a word. The guards surrounded her, and they headed back to her air car. She only relaxed when she was on the way home.

Her mother probably thought she'd find a way to talk with her tomorrow, but Kelsey would be back on *Persephone* by then. She had a meeting with Carl Owlet, and then they'd be leaving for Pentagar. Maybe by the time they captured the freighter, she'd feel a little calmer. Probably not, but one could hope.

Kelsey's implants announced a message from Jared. She listened with interest as he explained what they'd discovered about the Imperial Scepter. Even though it wasn't useful right now, it gave them a long-term goal that might bring the AIs down.

If they could subvert the prime AI, it could order its subordinates to surrender. Considering how badly the Old Empire had lost a straight-up fight, they'd need to be sneaky in fighting this war. A full-on confrontation would be fatal.

She'd tell her father what they'd found and let him incorporate the details into his planning. Once they'd dealt with the freighter, they could map a more considered path forward.

Frankly, she had to admit she badly wanted to see the birthplace of mankind. Even in the condition it was in now. Her mind was already working the angles, and that beat the heck out of being pissed at her mother.

* * *

JUSTINE BANDAR CONSIDERED the door that Kelsey had just closed with barely contained fury. How dare her daughter treat her this way?

The urge to shriek and smash furnishings was strong, but it wouldn't serve her purposes now. If her little girl thought she could put her mother at arm's length for months, she was sorely mistaken. A plan was already taking form in her mind.

She smiled, looked up a number, and activated her room's com. She spoke in her most sultry voice. "Jackson? Justine Bandar. Are you free for lunch? Oh, and perhaps the afternoon? I have a favor to ask, and I'm willing to do anything to get it. Anything at all."

* * *

BRANDON MADE a point of visiting with each of the department heads that evening. He'd read their status reports for the last month, but he wanted to hear them tell him what was important to them. Some things didn't make it into reports, and he didn't want them to have any unpleasant surprises on this mission.

The rush wasn't anyone's fault, but that didn't stop him from resenting it. The stakes were so high. Failure might mean the death or enslavement of everyone he knew. No pressure.

The most interesting conversation was with Lieutenant Commander Elizabeth Givens, the ship's tactical officer. Since Captain Anderson had made such a big deal about how the fighters were their weapons, he hadn't expected *Audacious* to be so well armed.

It might not pack the punch of an Old Empire superdreadnought, but it could take a couple of battlecruisers for a hard ride if the need arose. The missiles were a lot more capable than he was used to, and beams and battle screens were wholly new to his experience.

Tactical doctrine called for the carrier to have a protective group of battlecruisers, cruisers—both heavy and light—and a screen of destroyers. In the Old Empire, they'd have more than they did now, but that would change as they acquired more ships.

Everything Captain Anderson had told him about controlling the ship was true. He could—and had—accessed the scanners from his bed. With his overrides, he could have taken the ship to battle stations and done just about anything that normally required being at a console on the bridge.

Watching the crew work with the ship's computer was a humbling experience. He had a lot of learning to do just to understand what he didn't know.

That didn't mean that he had nothing to offer this ship, however. He took guilty satisfaction in making a list of things he could tweak to improve the way the crew worked together. Neither Anderson or her former exec had had the experience to see how sloppy some things were.

These were modifications that didn't have a thing to do with implants, just interdepartmental functions. If either of the other officers had served as an executive officer, they'd have had a better grasp of what needed doing.

His experience still counted for something.

He spent a good part of the night at his desk working up a grueling training regimen for himself. He had a number of Fleet primers on how the implants influenced tactical and strategic operations. He also knew the basic functions—and the advanced ones —that he'd need to learn just to catch up with his peers.

Then there were the esoteric theoretical possibilities. He had a nephew that was a wizard with technology. He'd sent him an unclassified note asking what kinds of things he'd imagined were possible. The boy had been voraciously reading up on the civilian implant data and had immediately sent him back a long, rambling letter with tasks ranging from the mundane to the mythical.

The next wave of Fleet trainees would upend everything people like him imagined possible. Better yet, the first wave of people with implants—like Zia Anderson—would be in exactly the same boat.

He shouldn't feel satisfied about that, but he did. Small and petty was fine, in private and limited in scope so that he didn't let it bleed into his working relationship with the others. As it had already done.

About an hour and a half before he was due on the bridge, he gave up the pretense of trying to sleep and headed to the gym. To his surprise, he found Annette Vitter there lifting weights.

"Morning," he said as he started stretching.

"Morning," she agreed. "Are you feeling overwhelmed yet?"

He snorted. "You know I am. This is an impossible task, but I'll get it done. The only question is how long that takes and how many mistakes I make along the way."

She set her bar on the stand above her head and sat up. "No matter how badly you screw up, you'll never reach the epic heights that Wallace Breckenridge managed on the same mission we're trying to do over."

Brandon stopped a second snort. Barely. "I could hardly do worse. That man screwed up by the numbers. At least this time we have a lot more ships, and we're on the same footing technologically."

"Don't be so sure," she warned him, wiping her face with a hand towel. "Those people have been using implants their entire lives. Even our most experienced people still default to doing things manually. We don't know all the tricks."

"I was thinking about that earlier. We need to get a bunch of kids implanted and put them in simulators. They'll adjust to the new capabilities far more quickly than we can, and they'll come up with things we never thought of."

The fighter pilot cocked her head. "You mean like full-up ship simulators? I hadn't ever considered that. I was only thinking about general tech."

He nodded. "If we set up classes of kids, taught them the basics of ship operation, and let them play ship simulators in combat, they'd take to it fast. Make it a competitive game and they'd swarm to it.

"We have all the manuals of what tactics the Old Empire used, but we're still short on knowing how they did a lot of things so naturally. The kids could teach academy cadets, who'd pick up a lot of what they were hearing."

Vitter nodded slowly. "That's a pretty good idea. I'd write that up and send it to Fleet headquarters before we ship out. It might make a big difference."

"I probably will," he said as he stretched his calves. "Do we have any idea what role we're going to play in the ambush?"

"Yup. We're the backstop. We'll be positioned in the system on the other side of Erorsi in hiding. Once the freighter and any escorts go by, we'll cover the exit. If someone gets away, we'll make sure they don't get any messages back to the Rebel Empire."

"That seems a safe bet with this ship's capabilities, not even considering the fighters."

"Admiral Mertz isn't the type to take chances if he doesn't have to. It's like Talbot always says: If you aren't cheating, you aren't trying."

He laughed. "That sounds like a marine. Did you know him all that well before this mess?"

They fell into talking as he started working out. Maybe integrating wasn't going to be as difficult as he'd feared.

13

Jared examined the layout of the task force via his implants. Everyone was in place at the Nova flip point. They'd make the jump into the hellish system and almost immediately to Pentagar.

If Ethan Bandar or Wallace Breckenridge had only known how close safety was, things might have turned out a lot differently.

"Take us through, Marcus," he ordered. "Send a greeting to Omega and then take us to Pentagar. We don't have a lot of time to chat."

"Aye, sir," the AI said. "The task force will flip in thirty seconds."

His mental countdown went smoothly, and they made gut-wrenching transition from Avalon to Nova. In just an instant of time, they travelled hundreds of light-years through the gravitational anomalies they called flip points.

The fact that this one was artificially created didn't seem to change how it worked. It hadn't changed in the months since the alien had used its station orbiting the black hole at the center of what had once been its people's solar system to bridge the distance between not only it and Avalon, but also to Pentagar.

In practical terms, that meant that a fast ship could get from

Avalon orbit to Pentagar orbit in a matter of hours. Once they had more freighters rigged up to stand the incredibly deadly environment around the black hole, trade would no doubt keep a stream of traffic making the journey.

"Omega sends his greetings and wishes us the best of luck with the ambush," Marcus said. "I estimate five minutes until everyone is in place for the next flip."

They could've done it faster, but there was no need to rush. Better to arrive in good order.

"Have we got any idea what's on the other end of the rest of the flip points in this system?" Jared asked. "Other than Harrison's World, of course."

Omega had given them a map of the flip points it could detect using its linkage to the black hole. No one had really been able to explain exactly how that worked, though Omega had tried. The science was incomprehensible. Much like the fact the alien station had once created portals into other realities. Science fiction made real.

Just like the transport rings he'd gifted Carl Owlet. The smaller pair made for a useful science experiment, but the openings were maybe a quarter of a meter. The two larger pairs were useful for people and cargo. Both had the range to take someone to the other side of the planet or even a ship in orbit.

Admiral Yeats wanted his own transport rings to make getting people and equipment to Orbital One easier. That was one of the projects Carl's team was working on. They just needed to understand them first. That would take a while, even with Omega's guidance.

Marcus's answer pulled him out of his micro-reverie. "One of the flip points leads to Harrison's World, of course. Admiral Yeats sent scouts through the other two. Those systems appear to have never been occupied by anyone.

"There are normal flip points exiting from there, but the admiral decided that they didn't need to be examined at this time. Omega's map does show some of the potential of that new branch, however.

"One thing the map does not explore is the potential for other destinations through the weak flip points. Doctor Leonard still believes that fine-tuning the flip drive's output might generate a different outcome. Thus far, though, he hasn't tested his hypothesis."

"That would certainly change things if he's right," Jared said. "It's not applicable to us at this moment, though. Are we ready?"

"All ships ready to flip, Admiral. Commencing in thirty seconds."

Less than a minute later, they were in Pentagaran space. A number of Old Empire ships that they'd gifted to the Pentagarans were on guard duty at the new flip point. Jared thought that was a prudent precaution.

"Incoming signal, Admiral," one of his staff members said, turning in her seat. "Admiral Sanders."

Walter Sanders had been a Pentagaran commodore when Jared and Kelsey had first arrived, but after the attempted coup, Elise's father had speedily promoted him and put him in command of the Pentagaran Navy.

"Put him on," Jared said.

The main screen switched from a strategic map of the Pentagar system to a view of a bridge identical to the one Jared was on. The older man in the center seat grinned like a boy. "It's good to see you again so soon, Lord Admiral Mertz."

"I thought we were on a first-name basis, Walter."

"Well, I thought after your recent social promotion that a little formality couldn't hurt. After all, you're now engaged to the heir to the Pentagaran Crown! Perhaps I should call you Highness."

Jared grimaced. "I'd rather you didn't. I'm already tired of the bowing and scraping when I leave the ship. Seriously, how do you people manage?"

"We somehow get by. Fine, I'll call you Jared. In private. At least until you become the prince consort. Then we'll have to fight about it some more.

"Meanwhile, I'd like to thank you for this fine new ship. Her name is *Resolute*, and she's a superdreadnought just like *Invincible*. I'm in love, by the way."

Jared smiled. "They make nice flagships, don't they? You're very welcome. It's the least we could do after you helped us so much."

"I seem to recall the help being a bit tilted toward you helping us.

In any case, you're going to want to head to Pentagar, so I'll accompany you. We need to sit down and plan the ambush in more detail. We have forces in place at Erorsi, so there's no danger the Rebel Empire will sneak in like they did last time."

That, too, had been Wallace Breckenridge's fault. The man had had an absolute talent for doing the wrong thing. If he'd just followed the plans Jared and Sanders had worked out, they'd have caught that first freighter with its pants down.

"Maybe so," Jared said, "but I'm not going to feel comfortable until we have everything securely locked down. Right now, the flip-point jammers can keep us safe, but we could really use some Marine Raiders. With the supplies from that freighter, we'll be able to keep Kelsey out of the fighting."

The other man smiled. "Good luck with that. She seems like the lead-by-example kind of woman, heir or not. I'll have to congratulate her on her promotion as well."

"Well, we'd at least have Talbot and the rest to help defend her," Jared sighed. "Actually, I'm going to send Elise over to one of your ships to get to Pentagar. We're all heading for the Erorsi flip point."

Sanders nodded sharply. "Of course. You're in command of the operation, and I'll feel better when we're ready, too. I'm not sure Princess Elise will feel the same way. She has a wedding to plan, and you're one of the mandatory attendees."

"I suspect more goes into organizing and executing a state wedding than we've put into the ambush."

"I'm not sure Her Highness will appreciate the comparison of her upcoming nuptials to an ambush," Sanders said dryly. "Yet your point about the planning is well taken. I'm sure many details will take time to work out and get into place. With such an important event, no one will want to see any aspect left to chance.

"I'll hop in a cutter and make my way over. We can review the plan and current positioning of the assets over dinner."

"That sounds excellent," Jared said. "I haven't chosen a steward yet, but my new rank allows for one. For the moment, we'll just need to make sure we don't starve ourselves."

"It's a good thing you have a lot of space on that ship," the other man said with a gleam in his eye. "One steward might do for an admiral, but the prince consort of Pentagar will have a few more servants to keep around. We monarchists just love to have hangers-on."

Jared sighed helplessly. "I'll never understand that. They'd better not try to help me get dressed, or I'll space someone. I'll see you in about half an hour. And Walter, it's good to see you again. It isn't very often we get a chance to correct a serious blunder. Let's make everyone proud."

The older man's smile widened. "Then we're in complete accord. I'll see you shortly, Jared."

* * *

KELSEY WALKED into the briefing room on board *Persephone* with a purposeful stride. The men seated at the table rose as she stepped to the head of the table.

She smiled. "Gentlemen, as you've probably already guessed, I'm Kelsey Bandar. For simplicity, let's set aside any excess formality. We're all here to carry out a very difficult mission, and I don't want anything to trip us up. Are we good with that?"

The men glanced at one another and nodded.

A group that looked less like military personnel was hard to imagine. None of the men wore uniforms of any kind. In fact, most had never served in any branch of the Imperial service. Their elite status came from the other side of the sheets, so to speak.

The fourteen men around her specialized in recovering spacecraft that someone had either stolen or that had failed to maintain their payments. Recovery agents were what they called themselves. The next best thing to pirates, but staying on the legal side of things. Mostly.

Talbot's original plan for capturing the freighter was predicated on boarding with marines and shooting everything in sight. While she'd become a big fan of that kind of thing, they absolutely had to capture the freighter—and its cargo—intact.

That included the computer and crew. Lieutenant Commander

Michael Richards, the Rebel Fleet officer they'd captured, thought he knew where they'd picked up the cargo of Raider implants and gear, but it would be best to have independent confirmation.

It would be even better to have people that had been inside the facility, and she intended to get those people, no matter what it took. With that in mind, she'd already decided to speak with her father about including Richards on the mission, even though Admiral Yeats disapproved Jared's request.

They still had time to make that happen, so she'd get her hands on the freighter first. The follow-up mission would flow from what they learned.

"Before we get started," she continued as she sat, "I'd appreciate it if you'd introduce yourselves and tell me a little about what you do."

Everyone resumed their seats. A taller man with brown hair going grey at the temples spoke up. "I'll take the lead on that, then. My name is Cain Hopwood, and I'm the lead partner of Recovery Incorporated. Been getting ships back from folks that shouldn't have them for twenty-five years. Most of these fine folk have been with me since I started.

"And I'm not sure a listing of skills would be much help. We're jacks-of-all-trades sorts. You kind of have to be. You might find yourself needing to do all sorts of things on a recovery operation. Just assume we can all handle any aspect of hijacking this ship you can think of, and plenty you can't."

She smiled. "I like the sound of that. The wrinkle that concerns me most is that this ship will have implant-capable equipment. You've all received corresponding implants, but you've never had to anticipate the kind of security obstacles they might entail."

An equally tall man, this one pale of skin with dirty blond hair, shook his head. "Jason Young. That probably won't be much of an obstacle. The crew will feel all safe and secure. The first hint of trouble they'll have will be someone stunning them. Great things, those stunners. Beats the heck out of darts."

A tall, balding man shook his head. "Best not to get too cocky. What if someone wipes the computer or sets off a self-destruct charge? Oh, I'm Alan Barnes. I usually pilot the skiff."

"That's the kind of thing we absolutely have to prevent," Kelsey said. "Mainly to keep from dying, but also to be sure the Empire keeps breathing."

A tall, bookish-looking man with brown hair smiled. "Bob Noble. I usually secure the target's computers. I've been working with Sir Carl, and we've modified some of our standard tools to do the same kind of thing on the new technology.

"That might not be good enough for a military system, but it should be fine on a civilian freighter. Once we're in, they won't be able to wipe the computers."

"I can say the same about the engineering spaces," an average-sized man with a receding hairline said. "If I can get to the engine room, I can lock them out of propulsion. Michael Falkner here."

A redheaded man spoke up from the other side of the table. "Dale Thompson. I'll take the lead in searching for and locking out any demolition charges."

"Very good," she said.

A tall, white-haired man half raised his hand. "I guess I'm next. Bill Smith. I'm an intrusion specialist. If anyone locks themselves into the bridge or other space, I'll blow the hatch and get us in."

An older, slightly balding man cleared his throat. "I'm Jon Paul Olivier and the young man beside me is my son, Andrew. We're takedown specialists."

She smiled at the two men. "What does that mean?"

The father smiled. "We sneak even better than the rest. Have you ever seen a vid where someone gets whisked away right out from under the noses of his friends? That's what we do."

Hopwood nodded. "And let me introduce the rest of my team. Raise your hands when I say your name. Tracy Bodine, Michael Goad, Kristopher Neidecker, John Naiser, and Tom Stoecklein."

"Well, I'm sure you're all good at what you do," Kelsey said. "You have a stellar reputation for success. Rather than me telling you what the plan is, why don't you tell me the best way to make this work?"

Hopwood nodded. "The challenge here is that the freighter might have an escort. That makes sneaking up on it very hard to do without the warship spotting us. That would probably be fatal.

"We're lucky that your ship has very stealthy pinnaces. If the warship isn't on a heightened state of alert, we should be able to lie in wait for the freighter and slowly match course and speed. Space is big. If they don't see us, we'll be able to attach to their hull. If they *do* see us, we'll have blown everything and need to run like hell."

"Let's assume we manage to succeed, because failure drops the ball into Admiral Mertz's lap. Once we attach, what next?"

The man grinned. "We bypass an airlock and let ourselves in. The men split up and head for the critical areas of the ship: the bridge, engineering, and the computer room. Once we're in position, we seize control of everything. The details vary, and sometimes the execution is tricky, but if we get onboard that ship, we'll get things locked down very quickly."

She nodded. "We'll have a team of Marines in the pinnace to back us up with armor and heavy weapons, if needed. They'll make sure everything stays friendly once we gain control.

"The optimal solution leaves any possible escort in the dark about the change in management. Taking it out is Admiral Mertz's job. Once we signal him that we're in control, he'll kick off stage two of the ambush. He'll use his ships to separate us from the warship and then defend us from any attempts to shoot us."

"How likely is that?" Thompson asked.

"The last time, the destroyer abandoned the freighter. It didn't seem at all concerned about us capturing it. My guess is that this will play out similarly.

"We'll be over in the Erorsi system in a few hours. Once we're in position, we'll use a freighter and destroyer of our own to do test runs until we have everything working perfectly. Or the bad guys show up and we run out of time."

She brought up the deck plans for the kind of freighter they'd likely encounter. "While we wait, let's go over the plans and start making some broad decisions."

14

Zia studied the layout of the system just beyond Erorsi. A white dwarf burned hotly in the center of the system, orbited by uninhabitable rocks and debris. The system was empty of Rebel Empire vessels, which was exactly what she'd expected to find.

That didn't keep her from taking every precaution. She left two probes in the flip point to Erorsi to take back word if they found anything. She also had several probes watching the other flip point in the system with passive scanners from a distance. When the freighter arrived, they'd relay a tight beam back to *Audacious*.

Since the carrier and her escorts were the plug that would keep any Rebel Empire ships from escaping Admiral Mertz's ambush, she had to make sure they didn't see her. The single asteroid belt would be more than enough to conceal her ships from any scans that came their way.

The carrier, two battlecruisers, four cruisers, six light cruisers, and a dozen destroyers floated in a loose array, powered down to standby and moving with the slow orbit of the belt. She had fighters out to keep an eye peeled for significant debris, but that wasn't likely to be a problem. Unlike what the vids usually said, objects in an asteroid belt were extremely rare and far apart.

Her carrier group was overkill for a destroyer, or even several cruisers, but she didn't mind having more than enough force at hand to convince an enemy to surrender.

"How long until we expect the freighter?" Commander Levy asked.

She looked over at where he stood beside her console. "The time interval is variable. The likeliest timeframe won't be for another few weeks, but they've come early before. Or they might not come until three or four months from now. We might as well settle in."

He grimaced. "I hate the waiting, but more practice time is useful."

"How are you adjusting to your implants?"

Levy shrugged. "They aren't that hard to master, with someone to show me what I need to do. It's thinking ahead about how to best utilize them that's hard. I can't seem to break the habit of doing things by hand."

She nodded. "That comes with practice. We're so used to doing things one way that we default to that first. That's why we keep practicing until it becomes second nature. When the fecal matter hits the rotating oscillator, we'll do what we've wired into our reflexes.

"On another note, I've looked over the changes you made to the interdepartmental workflow. I have to confess that was never my strong suit. The interaction seems to be a lot smoother now. Well done."

He smiled a little. "That comes with time and practice, just like everything else. I've been studying the Old Empire map of systems beyond this one. Based on what Commander Richards said, there isn't a lot of habitation out this way. Not anymore."

Zia knew that hadn't been true five hundred years ago. At the height of the Old Empire, almost every system had some kind of population. After the rebellion, the remains of humanity had been concentrated into relatively few systems so the AIs could keep an eye on them.

Commander Michael Richards, the AI specialist they'd snagged on the disastrous mission to capture the last freighter, had some familiarity with this sector of space. Even so, they couldn't completely trust what he said. The AIs kept their slaves in the dark about a lot of things. It was far better to assume the worst and be pleasantly surprised when things worked out as expected.

That happened rarely enough at the best of times.

"Right. The nearest known inhabited system is three flips toward the Imperial core. We can't count on all the other places being empty, though. Just because the AI tells them nothing is there doesn't make it true. Remember the hidden ships at Harrison's World."

Unknown to the inhabitants there, the AIs had placed a facility inside the atmosphere of a gas giant with four computer-controlled battlecruisers in standby mode. Any system could be seeded like that. Even this one.

Which was one of the reasons she'd sent probes all over it as soon as they'd arrived. Since it had never had a real population, she considered the odds of hidden ships low, but in a space battle, the worst surprises weren't what you didn't see. They were what you saw that turned out to be wrong. Lord knows Admiral Mertz had used that fact against any number of opponents while she'd served under him.

She liked to think she'd learned a few things from the experience.

"Status change," one of the sensor techs said almost two hours later. "The stealthed probes at the other flip point report activity. Two ships have transitioned into the system."

"They're early," Levy said, seemingly a little surprised. "Really early."

"Good thing we're already here waiting for them. Another win for the admiral's cautious streak. Do we have a reading on what kind of ships they are?"

"Yes, ma'am," the tech said. "A freighter and a destroyer. Just like last time."

"What's their ETA to the Erorsi flip point?"

"Eight hours at their current speed."

"Excellent. Send one of the probes through to Erorsi with the news. The more time that Admiral Mertz has to get into position and hide his ships the better. We'll shoot the second one through just before they could possibly detect it flipping."

She used her implants to go over the scanner readings from the spy probes. The resolution was crappy, but without going active, they'd need to rely on the emissions from the ships themselves. The destroyer seemed like a Zombie class, just like before.

The little destroyers had been ubiquitous in the Old Empire. They were very utilitarian and filled a number of roles with ease.

The freighter was larger than the last one, and the power output was a tad higher, but that was fine. With a missed shipment, they'd probably brought enough to make up for the loss.

"Remind me why we're not using those fancy FTL coms that Sir Carl developed," Levy said.

"Because it's possible they'd detect the signal. It does generate a small but noticeable gravitic signature. They might not be able to tap into it like Omega did, but we don't want to take any chance of tipping them off that we're here.

"There's also the fact that Sir Carl is still putting them together. We thought we'd have longer to get ready."

He nodded. "I really hope we don't need it this time."

"Thankfully, we only have a destroyer and freighter to worry about."

She settled back into her chair. In half a day, this would be over. One way or the other. She hoped they captured the freighter intact. That was just the kind of break they needed to have a fighting chance.

* * *

JARED HAD to admit he was surprised by how early the freighter was, but the records they'd recovered from Erorsi had a few occurrences this early in the year. He was damned lucky he'd been conservative.

Though, to be fair, even if his forces had missed the arrival completely, the Pentagaran forces were well situated to take care of the two ships.

With Zia's early warning, it was no problem at all to get the various ships in the Erorsi system into hiding. *Invincible* was in Erorsi orbit, taking the place of the destroyed orbital.

With the two shipyards there, that made three objects with fusion plants for the approaching destroyer to detect. Since that was what it expected to see, he'd made sure they could mimic the old orbital's output as closely as possible.

It only took a moment to access the strategic map of the Erorsi system. Some of the ships were out of place but racing to get in position before the freighter and its escort arrived. There was plenty of time, so long as the warship didn't outpace its slower companion, and that seemed unlikely.

Persephone was just about in position. The Marine Raider ship was almost undetectable when either moving slowly or stopped. She would sit behind the flip point.

The plan was to launch both of the Marine Raider pinnaces ahead of the expected arrival and get them inbound. That would reduce the required acceleration to match courses. It also meant they were vulnerable to being spotted or possibly failing to catch up if the target ships took a different course in.

He'd worked extensively with Marcus in playtesting the attack runs. They had a very high chance of being on the proper course and almost a two-thirds chance of escaping detection.

Those were odds he could live with. The chancy part came when the boarding parties seized the freighter. That's when everything could go to hell.

"If the ships bump their speed ten percent, how long until they transit, Marcus?"

"A little more than five hours, Admiral."

He nodded. All their assets into place in less than three. That worked.

Now it became a waiting game. One with a chance to increase their overall odds of success dramatically in the war against the Rebel Empire. Unlike the last time, they had the edge in firepower now. If needed, they could saturate the destroyer's defenses and obliterate it without risking any marines.

* * *

Kelsey didn't wait for *Persephone* to get into position before she launched the stealthed pinnaces. She, of course, went with them.

Major Angela Ellis—her former bodyguard and new executive officer—would rather have had her stay on the ship, but that reduced the chances of quietly capturing the freighter by almost twenty percent. Too great a risk to take.

Of course, Angela had sicced a new minder on her. Lieutenant Regina Paulson wasn't as physically imposing as Kelsey's tall friend, but she was a tough and determined marine. Kelsey was sure the dark-headed woman had secret orders to keep her as safe as anyone could in a firefight.

The princess was in her Raider armor and outfitted for war. Not that she expected to need most of her weapons on this mission, but she'd been caught short far too many times to skimp when she had the chance to prepare in advance of the trouble.

Half of the recovery team was on this pinnace, along with three dozen marines in unpowered armor. The other pinnace had the other half of the recovery team and another set of marines. If only one pinnace managed to rendezvous with the freighter, they could still carry out the mission.

Kelsey sat at the pinnace commander's station on the marine deck. It gave her a wide console to oversee a map of the system. Even though she was completely comfortable using her implants, there was something about seeing the data laid out like this that made it feel more natural. She doubted that would ever change.

This feels like old times, Ned Quincy said.

"You can use your outside voice," she said aloud. "Everyone, Ned Quincy is an AI that is going to appear beside me. Don't be alarmed."

The marines already knew Ned, but she hadn't had any reason to tell the recovery team. She probably should keep his existence secret, but she'd grown tired of talking to him in her head.

His image appeared beside her, made to look solid by the emitters she'd installed. He waved at the goggle-eyed recovery agents. "Afternoon. The princess should also mention that I'm classified. Keep this under your collective hats."

They nodded and kept watching the projection curiously. Lieutenant Paulson wandered over from the rest of the marines.

Ned turned to face them both. "This isn't the first time I've done something like this. Sneaking up on other ships is a stock in trade for the Raiders. The destroyer complicates matters, but if they aren't looking too closely, they'll miss us. Even at point-blank range."

"Any last-minute advice?" Kelsey asked.

"Commit. Once you're in, push through hard and fast. The worst-case scenario is getting onto the freighter and having word get out while you're still capturing it. Make sure you don't give anyone time to yell, either in person or over the com."

Kelsey nodded. "Good advice. We'll be in position by the time the destroyer and freighter flip into the system. It's all a matter of waiting for them to catch up with us. Piece of cake."

Her gut put the lie to her casual words, though. Being able to make more Raiders was riding on this mission. If anything went wrong, they might not be able to recreate what was done to her, and they desperately needed more people with her capabilities.

She took a deep breath and let it out slowly. This wasn't her first rodeo. She'd make it happen, even with the inevitable surprises along the way.

15

Brandon was sitting at one of the spare consoles on the flag bridge practicing with his implants when he spotted an unusual reading from the freighter. At first he thought it was the relatively unfocused nature of the passive scanners themselves, but the more he refined the data, the more certain he became that there was actually something different about the ship.

"Captain, I may have something," he said.

She turned in her seat and gave him her full attention. "What is it?"

"I've been using the passive scanner data to practice using my implants, and I think there's something different about the freighter. Not as in just different data based on the class, either. Something that shouldn't be there."

As the ships had come closer, they'd been able to narrow down the classes until the probability was over ninety percent. That was just about a certainty, considering the limited number of possibilities. He had a very good idea of what the readings from the freighter should look like, but there was something off.

"How so?" she asked.

"We're almost certain it's a Yeager class freighter, but I think I'm seeing more than one fusion plant. There's the ghost of a second one in the data."

Anderson's eyes unfocused for a moment and then she frowned. "I think you're right. It's shielded, I think. Not as well as it could be, but easy enough to miss if you're not looking closely. Good catch."

She tapped her console. "Most freighters only have a single fusion plant. This must be some kind of custom job. I wonder what they need the extra power for."

"Could it be a weapon?"

As a former tactical officer, he knew she had to be thinking along those lines, but it was his place to ask the question.

"I suppose so, but I'm not seeing the reason. They have a destroyer right next to them. Against the ships the Pale Ones used, it's more than capable of handling the job. Even if they wanted to give it some punch, they'd go with missiles. Beams are too short ranged to give an otherwise unarmed ship."

"Maybe they gave it battle screens."

"That might make more sense, but again, why? It's a freighter. The cost and space required for the second fusion plant would eat into cargo capacity and make it a lot less profitable."

One of the women monitoring the consoles around them stiffened and turned in her seat. "The destroyer just went to active scans."

"Are we in danger of detection?" Anderson asked.

"No, ma'am. We're too far away for a normal return from our hulls, and with the fusion plants at standby, they won't be able to detect the reduced power output. The drones we have shadowing them came from *Persephone*. They're heavily stealthed, and I don't think they'll see them either."

"Then what are they doing?"

Brandon tapped into the appropriate scanner feeds and examined the raw data. "It looks like the scans are stronger in front of the ship. I think they might be giving the flip point to Erorsi a closer look. We don't have anything there to detect, so we should be safe."

The captain frowned. "It must be worried about an ambush of some kind. That might make sense with the loss of the last freighter and escort. Their suspicion is going to make the princess's job harder, though."

He shook his head. "Do we have any idea why the Rebel Empire is so cavalier about losing ships? They run the Empire. If someone was taking out my destroyers, I'd be worried."

"Commander Richards didn't know. He wasn't on the command track, so they restricted the information he had on certain things."

The destroyer seemed satisfied after about fifteen minutes of scanning and went back to passive.

They watched it get closer to the flip point over the next few hours. The last thirty minutes were the hardest. Brandon knew the captain probably wanted to get their fusion plants back to full capacity, but they couldn't afford to jump the gun. They'd wait until the ships were gone before they even started the process.

"Status change," the ship's computer said. "Passive scanners are picking up other vessels in the system."

The captain sat bolt upright. "What? Where? How many and what kinds?"

"Numerous vessels have transited the other flip point into this system. With this unit's probes shadowing the original vessels, the passive scanners did not detect them until they engaged their drives at full power. This unit is detecting twenty-six ships accelerating at military speeds."

Brandon accessed the feed through his implants. There wasn't much data at all for him to examine.

"We need to launch other probes to intercept the new forces," he said. "The destroyer was looking for anyone at the Erorsi flip point that could detect this task force."

Anderson nodded. "That has to be it. Why? This has never happened on previous supply runs."

"Then it isn't a supply mission," he said grimly. "It's an ambush. One we can't warn the admiral about."

She shook her head. "Worse, we can't stop the princess from boarding the freighter. With that extra fusion plant, it must be some kind of Q-ship. It looks like a cargo hauler, but they've converted it into a warship. She's going to sneak on board looking for supplies and probably find an armed military crew."

* * *

KELSEY WATCHED the freighter and its escort flip into the system through the passive scanners with satisfaction. The game was on.

Once the two ships had begun accelerating into the system, she was able to get a better idea of their course and speed. It wasn't as firmly nailed down as an active scanner reading would get, but close enough.

She opened a general frequency. "Okay, people, we're on. They're actively scanning the area around the flip point. That'll probably die down as they become more comfortable with their surroundings.

"They're on a course for Erorsi that pretty well matches our estimates. If everything goes according to plan, we'll board in about an hour. An attack that far out from any planet will be so unexpected that we should be able to seize the freighter without too much trouble. Then we'll signal Admiral Mertz, and he'll ambush the destroyer."

One of the recovery agents, Andrew Olivier, spoke up. "What if the destroyer isn't happy with our signals once the fighting starts? We can't trot out the original crew. They'll tip our hands. We can't make them suspicious."

"I've thought of that," she said. "The ambush will kick off with one of our destroyers shooting at the freighter and almost missing. The debris from the missile explosion will miss us, but we'll pretend it knocked out our drives and communications. There will be enough uncertainty that our people should be able to separate the two ships. Then the ruse won't matter."

They spent the next half hour going over the details. Once they'd made a few last-minute tweaks, they settled into their restraints. Now was the critical moment. The approach and boarding could go wrong in so many ways.

They'd approach with the freighter between them and the destroyer, maximizing their chances of going undetected. Once close to the hull, the two pinnaces would split up and attach at predetermined locations.

Time crawled as the freighter grew large in the passive scanners. No one on board seemed to notice them, but her heart was racing. It didn't slow until the pinnaces split up and attached to the hull.

The most dangerous part of the operation was over. They'd snuck up on the target. Now all they had to do was get on board and incapacitate the crew.

Kelsey unstrapped and lowered the ramp. The radios they were now using were low powered, but she didn't even want to chance that. She used hand signals to get everyone moving in the manner she wanted.

The recovery team took the lead to the targeted airlock. It was one used for emergency ingress. They used a very similar procedure to what the marines had done when they'd attacked Boxer Station. They cut the metal around the controls and bypassed the sensor wires.

She made a mental note to have that particular security flaw corrected on *Persephone*. If someone snuck onto *her* ship, she wanted to know about it.

The hatch opened soundlessly into the vacuum. It was a standard emergency airlock, so there was room for half a dozen suited people. Two of the recovery agents and three marines joined her inside.

The recovery agents did some more work on the interior controls before they cycled the airlock again. Probably making sure the inner door didn't signal the bridge.

Maybe she should have them do a security review on *Persephone* to identify weaknesses she hadn't considered.

The airlock opened off a corridor. It was empty. She attached a remote to the bulkhead and kept everyone together as the rest of the team came inside.

Once the rest of them joined her, she consulted her implant map for the ship class. Her subgroup was responsible for securing the bridge and computer center. There were some crew quarters on the way that they'd bypass and deal with after they made sure no call for help would be forthcoming.

They ran into a problem almost immediately. The corridor dead-ended without the lift she'd expected.

Why close off the corridor like this? There wasn't any cargo area in this part of the ship. This made no sense.

Well, they didn't have time to figure it out. She backtracked and found a set of stairs that took them up three levels. The bridge and computer center were on the same deck, adjacent to one another.

That's where they ran into their first crewman.

The woman came out of a compartment almost as soon as Kelsey entered the corridor. She was dressed in a dark coverall with a tool belt strapped around her waist. Best guess was that she was in maintenance.

Kelsey had been ready for this and had her stunner out. The pale blue beam took the woman in the chest while she was still gaping. She collapsed at once, making a little noise.

"Lisa?" a voice called out from inside the compartment. "You okay?"

A glance inside showed a man in a similar coverall working on an air handler. He had no more warning than his friend did before Kelsey stunned him.

The marines hauled the woman into the compartment and tied them up.

"This is a stroke of luck," Hopwood said. "We can use these coveralls to get our people closer to the bridge without raising suspicions. These two don't have implants, so I won't need to use the jammers Sir Carl worked up on them."

"Jammers?"

He nodded. "To keep prisoners quiet. Think of it as a little helmet with a chinstrap. Once we have them tied up, that would keep officers from screaming for help electronically."

"That's a good idea," she admitted. "Too bad we don't have something that works over a larger area. Preferably without silencing us."

The man grinned. "I think he's working on something like that."

"Won't the crew recognize strangers?" she asked. "They won't have a lot of people to remember. We don't look like these two."

"We only need a moment's confusion. If you see someone in the kind of clothes you expect, acting as if they have every right to be there, you wonder if you somehow missed a new guy. That's human nature.

"Andrew and I will lead the team forward and hit the bridge first. On a freighter like this, we'll probably only have a couple of folks to contend with. Those stunners make for much faster work and are a lot less chancy than shock weapons. Alan will come with us to take over running the helm.

"The other team will hit the computer center. Your people will be right behind us in case there's trouble. Once we've secured the bridge, we can lock out the com systems. That'll keep anyone from screaming for help right away. The team hitting engineering will make sure the drives stay the way they are. With those two areas secure, you and your marines can hunt down the remaining crew."

She nodded. "Excellent. The other team should be close to engineering, so let's be about this."

They stripped the two prisoners out of their coveralls. The woman's would be tight on one of the men, but it only had to stand up to a momentary glance.

The recovery agents checked the corridor and sauntered toward the bridge. She kept the marines far enough behind them so that anyone they encountered wouldn't see them. The other agents brought up the rear. They'd hit the computer center at the same time as the bridge team went in.

Hopwood stopped by the bridge hatch and hefted his stunner. Once Andrew was ready, Hopwood triggered the door mechanism and went in. The low hum of the stunners sounded. The rest of his bridge team went in after him.

Then shouts of dismay and gunfire erupted.

She came in fast with her stunner up, searching for targets. Of which there were far too many for her taste.

The bridge wasn't the small affair the plans had led them to expect. It was as big as the one on *Persephone* and had almost a dozen men and women at the control stations. Not just regular crewmen, either. Most of them were in Rebel Fleet uniforms and were armed.

"Civilians down," she shouted over her com as she shot the closest armed woman. She dropped, but flechettes started ricocheting off Kelsey's armor even as the marines poured into the room behind her.

Kelsey shot the man at what would be the com console next. He'd turned back to his controls, and she didn't want a cry for help to get out.

The fighting was brief but intense. When the enemy was down, she checked her people. A few of the marines had minor wounds, but Hopwood was crouched over Alan Barnes. The man had taken a flechette to the chest and was in a bad way.

"Medic!" she shouted.

One of the marines crouched down beside the wounded man and ripped open his medical pack. It looked bad, but they had a chance to save him.

A loud alarm began hooting over the overhead speakers. She walked around the bridge and made sure everyone was out. Then she started examining the consoles.

"This is overkill for a freighter, and they certainly don't need armed Fleet officers. Something is very wrong."

16

Zia watched the fleet approaching the Erorsi flip point with frustration. There had been no way to send a warning drone without someone detecting it. The gap between the lead destroyer and the fleet was too small. She really wished they'd had the time for Carl to finish deploying the ship-to-ship FTL coms.

"Once that fleet flips to Erorsi, I want us moving as soon as possible," she said. "We have to follow them through and hold the flip point. How long to get the fusion plants back up to normal output?"

One of her staff checked something on her console. "Twenty minutes, ma'am."

"Tell Tony to try for fifteen. I have no idea what kind of situation is going to develop at Erorsi, but we have to count on some of those ships heading back into our system before we get to the flip point.

"If not, we'll probably pop over there to find a battle already in progress. Have we nailed down what the fleet consists of?"

Commander Levy nodded. "I make out two dozen destroyers. The remaining eight seem to be a mixture of light and heavy cruisers. *Invincible* can probably handle all of them, though it would hurt."

Zia shook her head. "No, those ships can scatter. No one in their right mind goes head to head with something our size if they can help it. If any of them get away, we might not be able to catch them all without a huge mess."

She grimaced. "Besides, we don't know their plan. Is this something to deal with the rogue AI, or is it an all-out attack on Pentagar? The ships in Pentagaran space are up to the task of defending themselves, but it only takes one ship to devastate a planet."

The time until the enemy task force reached the Erorsi flip point counted down with syrupy slowness. If they left any ships on this side, that would severely limit the amount of support Zia could give Admiral Mertz.

She cursed when the enemy ships flipped. Two icons tagged as destroyers remained on station in the flip point. The enemy commander was covering her backside.

"Dammit," Zia muttered. "Why the hell did we get a competent bad guy?"

"Because idiots make you sloppy," Levy said. "Then you get your clock cleaned when the good ones show up."

Well, they weren't going anywhere at speed now. They'd have to sneak up on the ships as best they could.

"The most important thing is to prevent them from getting a warning back to the Rebel Empire," Zia said. "I want a net of ships between them and the other flip point. If they shoot off any drones, I want them swamped."

He nodded. "We can move ships into position while we have an ambush team creep as close as possible. We won't be able to stop them from seeing us, but we can stop them from warning anyone at home."

"I suppose that's the best we can hope for, but it's going to delay our arrival at Erorsi. Admiral Mertz will be on his own. If we're going to do this, let's do it right. I want enough force to be sure that anyone that comes running back from Erorsi can't overwhelm us with drones. We'll plug this system."

"Aye, ma'am."

Getting all the ships back up to full combat power took a little over twenty minutes. She'd be having a long discussion with certain captains about that.

If the enemy fleet came rushing back into this system, she didn't have enough ships to be certain of stopping them all. That meant she needed to plug the other flip point. To be sure nothing got past the blockade, she split her escort and assigned a battlecruiser, two heavy cruisers, four light cruisers, and six destroyers to the task. They should be able to stop anything that got past her.

The aces up her sleeve were her three squadrons of fighters. Gnats carrying sledgehammers, Annette had once called them. Added into her force mix, she could kill most of the ships she'd seen earlier if she had to.

With her reserve blocking the only other exit to the system, she could hunt them all down. Ugly and messy, but doable.

Right now, she needed to get the destroyers into position to block their enemy counterparts in case the initial strike failed. They were harder to detect at slow speed than her heavier units. The plan was for them to get as close as possible before the primary attack took place.

Once the blockading force was far enough out and ready to shoot down the inevitable drones, she ordered her main task force into motion. The destroyers led the way while the heavier ships cut in to interpose themselves along the most direct route of retreat for the enemy.

Admiral Mertz was the inspiration for the attack method. He'd once used a single fighter to ambush an AI destroyer. He'd rammed it, but Zia knew she could do better. Rather, she knew that Annette could do better.

* * *

ANNETTE TOOK her fighter out to join the combat space patrol. Once she was flying along beside them, she brought her low-powered com online. They could do all the interfighter communicating they wanted until they got close to the destroyers watching the flip point.

Dozens of fighters were already on a ballistic course toward the Erorsi flip point. They'd coast into range and launch antiship missiles as they soared past. If they didn't kill both destroyers, they'd certainly cripple them. Hopefully before they took any shots in return.

After all, a fair fight indicated lack of planning on her part.

For once, she had a stroke of good luck. The enemy rear guard must've been certain they were alone. They only used their active scanners every once in a while, so the fighters made it very close. When the risk of detection became too high, she ordered her people to launch.

The first inkling the enemy had that they weren't alone was a swarm of missiles blossoming to life in their faces. The small grav drives spiked to life at ridiculously short range, hurling their explosive passengers into the stationary destroyers.

One of the enemy ships exploded outright in a bright flash as its fusion plants failed, creating a momentary sun right next to its companion.

The other destroyer was luckier. It survived the explosion and the missiles blasting into its hull. It was no doubt wrecked but still functional enough to launch a pair of drones toward the distant flip point and to vanish. It had flipped to Erorsi.

Annette cursed under her breath. Bad luck had ruined the surprise. The fight around Erorsi was going to be ugly.

"Back to *Audacious*," she ordered, bringing her fighter to full power and swinging around. "Rearm and get ready for immediate launch. We're going to war, boys and girls."

* * *

JARED WAITED IMPATIENTLY AS the freighter and its escort slowly flew more deeply into their trap. His view from Erorsi orbit was time delayed, but the other ships were far enough past his net that they wouldn't be able to escape.

The destroyer captain had already communicated with them, never guessing that Marcus was mimicking the now-dead computer they'd been dealing with. With the full transcripts of every interaction it had ever had with the Rebel Empire, it was child's play to construct a convincing message.

In fifteen minutes or so, his trap would close, and one of his hidden destroyers would carefully fire missiles at the two ships. One would be aimed at the freighter. It had to be convincing but still cause as little damage as possible. He wanted his people alive and that ship intact.

Other ships would then open fire on the destroyer, forcing it to separate from the freighter. He'd prefer to take it alive, so he was hoping the show of force he'd planned would intimidate them into surrendering. He wasn't holding out much hope, though. These people were damned bloody minded.

"Status change," Marcus said. "The probes monitoring the enemy flip point have detected a number of ships transiting. There are too many to be Captain Anderson's carrier group."

Jared realized almost at once what it had to be. The Rebel Empire had sent an ambushing force of its own. He didn't have time to ponder the reason for that. He had to deal with the situation as he found it.

"What kind of numbers are we talking about?" he asked. "What course are they taking?"

"Thirty ships moving slowly enough to avoid detection from Erorsi. It looks as though a third of them are heading toward us. The remainder are angling for the Pentagaran flip point."

"Can you assign classes to the ships?"

"Tentatively," the AI said. "Most are destroyers, but eight are likely cruisers of some kind. Two cruisers and eight destroyers are following slowly behind the freighter and its escort. Six cruisers and fourteen destroyers are angling for the Pentagaran flip point.

"I'm concerned about Princess Kelsey and her forces. If we delay much longer, our hidden ships will be out of position to support them."

"There's nothing we can do about that now," Jared said. "We have to let the new ships get further into the system so we can bottle them up. If we attack now, they'll run back through the flip point. Zia doesn't have enough ships to be sure of stopping all the runners."

He considered the layout of the forces he had on station. If they allowed the first destroyer and the freighter to proceed past the ambush, they wouldn't be able to intervene if the warship figured out something was happening on the freighter.

The two ships would enter *Invincible*'s range in roughly three hours.

That allowed the force headed toward Pentagar to get almost to the flip point, even if he attacked early. If he waited for the right time in Erorsi space, the other ships would have transitioned to Pentagar.

Well, at least the Pentagarans had a sizable fleet of their own and kept a very diligent watch, even over the secured flip point to Erorsi. They could handle the attack.

"Are any of our ships in position to fire a probe through to Pentagar without detection?" he asked.

"Possibly," Marcus said. "One of our colliers is stationed in that direction. If we signal it now via tight beam, it could possibly get a probe to the flip point before the attackers arrive. Unfortunately, there is a significant chance the enemy will detect the probe. That might endanger the collier."

Jared brought up that ship's location and considered the distances involved. A second option presented itself.

"If the collier bolts for the flip point as soon as it receives our message, she might beat the missiles they fire at her. It'll tip our hand, but their ships will be committed by then. It doesn't matter what they think."

The AI seemed to consider that. "Our fleet will not be in an optimal position to engage the enemy at that time. They will be able to elude us. Except, perhaps, the closest destroyer."

"Send the collier."

"Aye, sir. Orders transmitted."

Jared felt a little hollow. This entire mission had gone sideways, and no matter how this played out, people were going to die.

He hoped one of them wasn't Kelsey. He had no way to warn her that she was in significant danger or to tell her what the new plan was. He had to count on her to understand what the aborted ambush meant and to act accordingly.

"Status change," Marcus said. "A new ship has arrived at the hostile flip point. It's transmitting a signal. Passive scanners indicate it has battle damage."

"Go active," Jared snapped. "Spring the ambush."

17

Kelsey hit the com to the other team. With the alarm ringing, the crew knew something was wrong.

"Report."

"We're fighting for engineering," Lieutenant Paulson said. "There are a lot more people down here than we expected, including armed Rebel Empire Fleet officers.

"The layout is radically different, too. Someone spotted us and sounded the alarm. We have the control consoles, but we're trying to nail down the Rebel Fleet personnel before they can shut off the drives manually."

Not optimal, but better than some possible outcomes.

"We have the bridge and presumably the computer center. They aren't getting a warning out. Stop them as fast as you can."

"The marines are pushing hard. We'll get it done, but people are going to die, ours and theirs."

Kelsey grimaced. "It can't be helped. Do the best you can. Something is very wrong with this ship, and we need someone to tell us what it is. The bridge crew will be out for hours."

"Roger that. I'll call you back when we're secure down here."

Kelsey pointed at the bridge hatch. "Watch for crew trying to retake the bridge. Send out teams of marines to locate and incapacitate the remaining crew. I want this ship under our complete control as soon as possible."

She turned to Hopwood. "Is the computer center under our control?"

He nodded, rising from where the medic was still working on Alan Barnes. "I just got the word. They had a few people inside, but we stopped them from purging the system."

Finally, some good news.

She nodded toward Barnes. "How is he?"

"It's not good, but the medic thinks he can stabilize him. The ambush should kick off soon. We'll transport him back to one of the pinnaces in an emergency bubble. He and any other wounded can get care more quickly that way."

Kelsey shook her head. "We're going compartment by compartment, so we'll find the medical center soon. They'll have what we need. If we can take the medical staff without stunning them, we'll get them to work on all the injured, theirs and ours.

"Before we do that, we need to figure out what the hell is going on with this ship. The layout is off, and there are a lot more people than we expected. Rebel Fleet shouldn't be manning a civilian freighter. This makes no sense at all."

Hopwood stepped over to a console. "They were still running the ship, so this isn't locked. They never expected anyone to just pop in unannounced like we did. Let's see what I can find."

He worked his way through the console's screens. He must've been studying hard to know what he'd need to do.

"Weird," he muttered. "The engineering controls show two fusion plants. That's definitely nonstandard. It had to eat into their cargo space."

Kelsey looked over his shoulder. "Is that what was blocking the corridor we tried to take?"

The man checked a few other screens. "I don't think so. The second fusion plant is forward of engineering, but not that far. Let me toggle through some more panels."

She watched him going from screen to screen and stopped him when he found one she wasn't familiar with. "Hold up. What's this?"

"I'm not sure," he said. "It's almost like a weapon control system, but not like any I'm familiar with."

Kelsey used her implants to interface with the console. Since they hadn't locked it, she had no problems accessing it. Another potential security issue on *Persephone* to talk over with the recovery specialists.

It *was* a weapon. There were munitions, but they weren't missiles. It was something she'd never seen before.

A check of the targeting system gave her more insight. The range was less than twenty thousand kilometers. Very, *very* short range in space. The weapon also required orienting the ship to fire, because it had control over the attitude thrusters.

"This looks like an orbital bombardment weapon," she said at last. "It fires solid slugs at high velocity, but the targeting is only for short range. Like from orbit to a planetary surface."

She stared at Hopwood. "This isn't a supply run. It's an ambush. They want to take out the computer on Erorsi before it knew there was a problem."

He scratched his chin. "If that's the case, then the destroyer is going to be on higher alert than we'd expected. It might not shoot us when the admiral springs the ambush, but we might not get away clean either."

"The destroyer also might not be alone. A single destroyer couldn't take all the ships that the Erorsi computer could field before we smashed it. If I were them, I'd send more ships to back it up.

"They also have to secure this system against an attack from Pentagar. Probably by sending a force large enough to take them out as quickly as possible. It's what I would do."

The man stared at her. "What do we do now?"

She shrugged. "We follow the plan. If Jared springs the ambush, we separate the freighter. If he doesn't, then we know there are other ships in play and he's improvising. We'll have to do the same.

"Once we have the freighter locked down, I want the holds examined. They might not have any Raider implant supplies. If so, that's a very bad break. If there are some, I'll want as much as possible shifted to the pinnaces. We might have to bail, and I don't want to leave any of it behind if I have a choice in the matter."

He nodded. "I'll see if I can find a cargo manifest. It might tell us what we need to know without a thorough search. There's no reason they'd fake it. It isn't as though the computer here sent a customs party to inspect them."

"Actually, that isn't a given. We don't know if it sent Pale Ones to check the supplies. I find it hard to believe the paranoid device would let Rebel Fleet humans onto its stations. Let me know what you find as soon as you find it."

She stared pensively at the main screen. They'd know in just a few minutes if Jared was going to attack. If he didn't, she needed a new plan. Time to come up with it.

* * *

BRANDON CURSED as the destroyer escaped. "We need to get after it. The ambush is blown."

"Flank speed to the flip point," Anderson said. "Get to operations, Mister Levy. You'll fight the ship while I focus on fleet and fighter operations."

"Aye, ma'am."

He raced for the lift and impatiently waited for it to get him to the operations center. On *Audacious*, it was where a normal superdreadnought's main bridge was. He had to admit it was significantly larger than what he was used to.

A full crew had already transferred control of the ship from the main bridge. He understood the need to segregate operations, but he still thought they were going around their elbows to scratch their butts.

The flag bridge should be reserved for this all the time, and the operations center should be where the ship was controlled. Of course, that meant that a carrier needed a flag officer rather than a captain in command of everything, but that was a fight for another day.

"Status," he said as he took the center seat.

The helm officer partially turned in her chair to face him. "We're on course for the Erorsi flip point. We'll arrive just in time to recover our fighters and make the flip. Call it fifteen minutes."

"The cruisers and destroyers will precede us," the tactical officer said. "The captain ordered them to follow the destroyer as closely as possible and take it out."

He wasn't sure that would help very much. The cat was out of the bag.

"Has one of the destroyers launched a probe through the flip point?" he asked.

"Negative. They're flipping. They'll signal back via probe."

"I want to see the layout in the other system as soon as we get the data."

"Aye, sir."

Brandon checked the ship's systems. Everything was in the green and all hands were at battle stations. The fighters were queued up and ready to launch as soon as they emerged.

The basic plan for the fighters was to launch them a squadron at a time. It would take about a minute to get the next fighter on the launch rail once the previous one was gone. So, a total of two minutes to get everyone out. Three minutes when all three squadrons were aboard.

Missiles were armed and ready. The beam weapons were in defensive mode, ready to cut down any missiles fired at the carrier. They'd be at their most vulnerable when they flipped. If the other ships didn't take out the crippled destroyer, it might shoot them up. If it could.

"They don't know what kind of force is after them," he said after a moment. "They saw the fighters and the lead destroyers. The rest were off his scanners. He might think it's a grand idea to wait for his pursuers to come through and shoot the hell out of them if they can. I know we're going through after the rest, but I want us ready for any unlikely surprises."

He watched the two lead destroyers make the flip. The rest of the ships were still more than ten minutes out.

Three minutes passed before a probe came through and a data

update came back. They'd found exactly what he'd worried about. The destroyer had been waiting for them.

Luckily, the commanders of the two destroyers had been ready for something like that. They'd taken some hits, but they'd eliminated the other ship. Too late to stop the bastard from sending a warning, Brandon was sure. The enemy force had split with almost two-thirds of their number on the way to Pentagar.

When *Audacious* finally flipped, they arrived to find the system in turmoil. It looked as though the ambush on Pentagar was off. That group had turned and was on its way toward the carrier and her escorts. The ships headed for Erorsi were still on course, though.

"Signal from the flag bridge," the tactical officer said. "Cry 'Havoc!' and let slip the dogs of war."

Bright sparks of light lit up the tactical plot as the fighters launched.

"Shakespeare," he murmured approvingly. "Vitter will appreciate the comparison. Raise battle screens, but make sure the launch and landing approaches are kept clear," he said. The screens were not conducive to launching small craft in their most protective mode. "Go to active scans. I want to know everything we can about the incoming ships."

"Aye, sir," the tactical officer said. "I see six light cruisers and fourteen destroyers coming our way. They're almost in extreme missile range."

He smiled coldly. They'd turned around before the carrier had come through. They probably expected a pair of destroyers. Then that jumped to four destroyers and two light cruisers. They'd still outnumbered the Imperial ships three to one, so they were coming in hot to deal with the problem.

Then *Audacious* had flipped. If the enemy didn't use fighters, they might be surprised at how much combat strength a carrier could put on the board.

The fight was going to be hard but winnable. They'd take some hits, but that was the price they paid. Even if someone broke through, they'd never get back home. The ships Captain Anderson had left behind would make sure that no one escaped.

Captain Anderson had sent out fleet instructions to the escorts, who were forming up around the big ship. The two destroyers had minor damage. The ship that had tried to jump them was an expanding cloud of debris and escape pods.

"Enemy ships launching missiles," the tactical officer said.

Brandon checked the flight time versus the fighter's launch sequence. The final squadron would clear the bays in time for him to raise the battle screens completely. Barely.

"Once the last of the fighters is clear, full power to the battle screens and fire back. Use your best judgment on targeting."

The fight was on.

18

K elsey dragged the man from the freighter's command chair and sat down. With the marines guarding her back, she could focus on the situation around them. Data was finally coming in. A fleet of Rebel Empire ships had come into the system, and a battle at the flip point was getting under way.

Part of the force was headed toward Erorsi. The freighter and its escort had come deeper into the system than they'd planned, so the ships they'd had ready to pounce on the destroyer were further away and at a disadvantageous angle.

"Incoming signal," Hopwood said from the helm console. "It's the Rebel Empire destroyer. Orders to come about and make tracks toward the outer system."

"Do it," she said. "The longer we can keep them in the dark about our identity, the better chance we have."

The new course took them even farther away from the ships they had lying in wait. If only she had a way to deal with the destroyer herself. It didn't even know she was flying along at point-blank range, but she didn't have any ship-to-ship weapons.

But she wasn't unarmed.

Kelsey brought up the targeting system for the bombardment

weapon. Its range was ridiculously short for this kind of thing, but it had the power to take out a warship if they got close enough. Currently, the freighter was too far away to make it work.

"Cain, edge us closer to the destroyer a bit at a time. Be casual."

"I have no idea what a casually drifting freighter looks like, but here goes."

He altered their course just a fraction, and the range between the two ships began shrinking. At this rate, it would take a few minutes.

With some time to spare, she tapped into the ship's interior monitors. The battle was still raging in engineering, but it looked as though Paulson was pushing the defenders ever farther away from the critical equipment.

Elsewhere, a few crewmen were putting up a struggle, but most of them weren't armed. It shouldn't be more than a few minutes before the last of them was down.

One thing she saw that looked promising was the cargo bays. They weren't completely empty. Perhaps they hadn't failed. There might be *some* Raider implants in there.

Her stomach jittered a little as the freighter crept closer to the escort. They were just crossing into extreme range. She'd get one shot at this.

That was when one of the escape pods jettisoned.

"Dammit!" she shouted. "I locked those down!"

A signal pinged them from the destroyer, but she ignored it, focusing on the targeting software. Kelsey took over the helm remotely and brought the nose of the freighter onto target. The moment it came to bear, she fired.

The results were spectacular, to say the least. The kinetic weapon was much, much faster than a missile. There was no dodging it. The oversized flechette quite literally blew through the destroyer, entering amidships and coming out aft in engineering.

While the other ship didn't blow up, the damage was extreme. His drives cut off, and he tumbled, out of control.

Kelsey cut their drives back and changed course. The weapon had no provision for automatic reloading. If the other ship got its act together, he'd fire missiles at her. To call her antimissile defenses pathetic was an understatement.

One of its fusion plants was spiking, which was very, very bad, but the Rebel Empire destroyer still managed to fire a single missile before it blew up. The damned thing raced toward Kelsey and the freighter.

She fired everything she had at it, which perhaps annoyed it enough to miss them. That was the only thing she could think of at this ridiculously short range. It had almost scarred the freighter's paint, but it *had* missed.

"Colonel, we've secured engineering," Lieutenant Paulson said over the com. "My people are making another pass to look for hidden hostiles."

"Be sure to check the escape pods," she said. "One ejected at what I would delicately call a critical moment. We're safe for the time being, but we have enemy ships in route to our position. Probably no more than an hour out."

"Copy that. Paulson out."

Invincible was under power from Erorsi orbit. Maybe she would gather more of the bad guys' attention. To make things harder for the Rebel Empire fleet, she boosted the freighter to maximum speed and made sure the course took them away from the ambushing ships.

They might not have clearly seen what had caused the freighter's escort to explode, but they had to be suspicious. Particularly when she failed to follow their inevitable orders to head their way.

The freighter had a lot more drive power than she'd expected. They'd probably intended for it to get away from Erorsi as fast as possible once they'd sprung their surprise.

She was so focused on the strategic situation that she jumped when someone whooped over the com.

"Who is that?" she said sharply. "Report!"

"Sorry, Colonel. It's Corporal Galloway. I'm down in one of the holds looking at a crate full of what certainly looks like Marine Raider pharmacology units."

"Which hold? I'll be right there."

Kelsey headed for the hatch as the man gave her a hold number. "Mister Hopwood, you have the conn."

"Yes, ma'am."

If there really were Raider implant supplies on this ship, she might be able to get some of them out to the pinnaces. They could drop away and go stealth. They might go unnoticed.

She sprinted toward the lift. Time was not on their side, but this was worth the risk.

* * *

THE DECK CREW had rearmed Annette's fighter by the time *Audacious* flipped, so she was ready when her time came to blast out of her launch tube.

"All *Audacious* squadrons, this is Black Jack Actual," she said over her com. "Focus on the lead ships. Cover your wingmates on their runs. Black Jack will take lead. When we pull out to rearm, make your runs in sequence."

The goal was to have fighters coming in waves. One wave should be attacking, another should be covering them, and the third should be rearming. Somehow, she didn't think this was going to be that easy.

Part of her was relieved that no fighters came screaming out of the enemy formation. That would've complicated an already dangerous situation. The rest of her was disappointed not to test her mettle in a real dogfight.

She sent a final targeting set to her people and pushed her fighter up to maximum acceleration. The six light cruisers were their targets. They posed the greatest threat to the carrier and her escorts. Not that fourteen destroyers would be a walk in the park, mind you, but they'd be very hesitant to engage without their big brothers.

Annette focused on her designated target while keeping an eye on the overall tactical situation. The big ship probably wasn't going to waste missiles on fighters. His antimissile flechettes were going to be the big threat, and his beam weapons.

That was another reason to take out the cruisers. The destroyers didn't have beams. They'd be limited in their response.

She noted how their battle screens were layered and picked a weak point where two overlapped. When her targeting scanners had locked on, she fired both her missiles and pulled away.

The cruiser fired a burst of antimissile flechettes, both at the missiles and her fighter. It had a dozen other fighters to deal with, too, since she'd split her squadron of twenty-four to attack only two light cruisers.

Her fighters proved a lot more maneuverable than the shooters expected, but that didn't mean the good guys escaped unharmed. That only happened in the vids. Two of her fighters exploded, and one veered out of control before the pilot ejected. Once the battle was over, they'd send search and rescue after him.

The ship killers they'd fired exploded all over the targets. They'd launched in waves so that the screens had time to fail. The leading missiles ruptured the battle screens where they overlapped, creating fissures that the rest exploited.

In the end, their fire was overkill. Both cruisers died in flame, gutted by the fiery swords that disemboweled them.

Space was full of chaotic violence as she pulled her squadron back toward *Audacious* to rearm. They'd learn from that mistake fast. This was going to be ugly.

* * *

JARED GRINNED when he saw Kelsey punch the destroyer's lights out. He had no idea what she'd done, but the results were gratifying. The destroyer exploded and left her ship running for empty space.

"Go to active scanners."

"Aye, sir," Marcus said. "It'll take a few minutes to get a return from the inbound force."

"Go with worst case. Two heavy cruisers and eight destroyers. Have the ambush force that was originally supposed to cover the freighter try to protect her."

He checked the tactical plot. At full speed, it would take the enemy almost an hour to get into missile range of *Invincible*, if the enemy were obliging enough to keep coming in their direction. They'd be able to fire on his ambushing force in half that time.

The Rebel Empire forces outnumbered Jared's ambushers about three to one. *Invincible* had more firepower than all of the enemy ships combined, but it wouldn't be able to bring them to battle if they ran.

Of course, in this situation, that might not be the worst outcome. They could hunt down the stragglers. Probably.

If any of them headed out into deep space, that might make them hard to find. He could take steps to make that outcome unlikely.

"Marcus, have our ambushers launch probes to shadow the attacking force. I want enough coverage to be sure each ship has no less than three probes that are out of weapons range and hopefully undetected."

"Aye, sir."

He could see the battle forming up at the hostile flip point, but only through the gravitic scanners. It would take a while longer to see the specifics of what was happening out there. Probably long after the fight was over.

"The collier has made the flip to Pentagar," Marcus said. "Perhaps once we have more force in the system, that will convince the enemy to surrender."

"I hope so, but I wouldn't hold my hypothetical breath if I were you. A single destroyer wasn't dissuaded when we chased it down with a battlecruiser, and the sight of a superdreadnought coming their way isn't deterring these boys.

"I'm also afraid that trying to intimidate them over the com would backfire. They don't respond well to us. That programming in their officers' implants makes them go all violent. That might be counterproductive."

"I submit that that might work in our favor," the AI said. "If they are driven to attack, then we can be certain that no stragglers become lost in the system.

"By now, they are aware of the battle taking place at the flip point they came through. I have no doubt it will be resolved in our favor, though probably at heavy cost. They will not try to fight their way back through."

Jared shared the AI's opinion about the likely cost of the battle but wasn't sure he followed the rest of his logic.

"Are you saying they'll go suicidal? I'm not sure this is that simple."

"Perhaps suicidal is the wrong word, Admiral. I think they will try to take us out, but I have no absolute proof that is true. What I am relatively confident of is the fact that they will likely not try to escape."

He considered what Marcus was saying and shrugged. "There's only one way to find out. Record an outgoing message."

Jared faced the main screen resolutely. "This is Admiral Jared Mertz. We have you outgunned and in a poor tactical position. My superdreadnought has more than enough firepower to take out your entire force. I call on you to spare your crews and surrender."

19

Zia watched the brawl just inside missile range with a mixture of awe and dread. The fighters had obliterated all six light cruisers, but they'd taken heavy losses. Five pilots had ejected from crippled fighters and thirteen others were gone, their pilots almost certainly dead.

Annette was rearming now and would rejoin the fight in a minute. Unless Zia ended it first.

Her tactical officer turned toward her. "We're inside the designated firing range."

"Fire," Zia said coldly.

Audacious and her escorts billowed missiles toward the light war craft. The carrier had fewer missiles than a superdreadnought but far more than even a heavy cruiser could boast. In a standup duel, the destroyers would lose.

The enemy returned fire, streaming almost as many missiles back toward her. That's when they found out another ugly truth.

Fighters could shoot down missiles with their flechettes. Almost half of their salvo never made it past the swarm of little ships around the destroyers.

With their attention split between the fighters and the incoming missiles, their defenses were far weaker than they'd probably expected.

Explosions lit up the space around them. When the scanner readings cleared, they'd blown up or disabled all but six destroyers. This fight was almost over.

"Incoming signal from the hostile ships," the com officer said. "They're surrendering."

"Pull the fighters back," she ordered. "Cease fire, but maintain targeting locks."

The fighters disentangled themselves from the remaining enemy ships. Some headed back to *Audacious* for rearming, but the rest kept the surviving destroyers under their guns.

"They've dropped their battle screens," the tactical officer said. "I still have the officer on the com."

"Put them on the screen," Zia said.

A smoke-filled bridge appeared on the main screen. The woman in the command chair had a long gash down her cheek and had a number of black smudges on her face. She looked furious. In her place, Zia couldn't blame her.

"I am Commander Veronica Giguere, commanding officer of the Imperial Fleet destroyer *R-7322*. We surrender. I don't know what the hell you bastards are playing at, but we surrender."

Zia nodded. This had to be hard for the woman. She knew it would be if the situation were reversed. Now she just needed to handle this without triggering the buried programming in the woman's corrupted implant code. She wanted live prisoners, not a ravening fight to the death.

"We accept your surrender, Commander. You've done the smart thing, even if it doesn't feel that way right now.

"Keep your screens down and idle your fusion plants. No targeting scanners, either. No destruction of your systems or booby-traps. My prize crews will meet any resistance with lethal force, and that won't change your situation one bit.

"You made the right call. Now don't screw it up. Gather all your crew in the mess areas. No weapons. Not even a folding knife. We'll process you all as quickly as we can and get you safely removed to our ships."

The other woman shook her head slowly. "This is treason. You'll hang for this."

Zia smiled a little wryly. "Don't think you know everything that's going on in the Empire, Commander. Let's just say that not all our leadership has been read in on every operation. Unfortunately, you stumbled into something you aren't cleared for."

An outright lie, but one that would hopefully keep her thinking Zia and her people were part of the Rebel Empire fleet.

"I have no idea what the hell you're talking about," Commander Giguere assured her. "We will follow your instructions, but rest assured there *will* be hell to pay over this. I don't care what faction you represent, the Lords will quash you like a bug. *R-7322* out."

The screen cleared, reverting to a view of space.

Zia opened a channel to operations. Brandon Levy appeared.

"Yes, Captain?"

"The enemy in our area has surrendered. I want you to organize prize crews to take control of the ships. All the prisoners come to *Audacious*, and you'll keep enough people over there to move the ships if we need to.

"I've instructed them not to destroy systems or set booby-traps, but we can't assume that's the case. At the very least, I expect they'll purge the computer systems. I would. You'll have to be thorough, but don't give them any reason to suspect who we are. Keep conversations down to instructions, don't give names of ships, and stomp on any resistance."

He nodded. "I'll get right on it, ma'am. What about the rest of the system? Are the other ships still actively hostile?"

"It looks that way. We'll find out soon enough. If Admiral Mertz can't handle the rest of the hostiles, we'll come in and help."

"I get it now," he said softly. "I understand why this ship revolves around the fighters. They really turned this fight around."

She just wished it hadn't cost so many of them their lives. "You had no way of knowing. Now you do. Welcome to the club. CSAR will recover the pilots who ejected, and then we'll have to help them put themselves back together again. Losing friends is never easy."

* * *

KELSEY ARRIVED in the cargo bay and took stock of what it held. There were a number of cargo containers. Her implants could read the manifests easily enough. If they were accurate, this hold held enough Raider implants to upgrade about a thousand people.

More than they had with them, but far less than she'd hoped to get.

The rest of the crates held sundry other high-tech replacement gear. Mostly things they already had in large measure.

Being the untrusting sort, she opened a few crates to verify their contents. The ones labeled communications gear were a surprise. They contained all the parts to construct an AI.

That made sense. They'd obviously intended to obliterate the computer and put a real AI in command.

The find put her in a quandary. They had enough space in the pinnaces to take the Raider implants or the AI. Not both.

"Dammit," she said under her breath. "Get the crates labeled as communications gear onto the pinnaces."

The corporal frowned. "I don't understand. Aren't we here for the Raider gear?"

"Yes, but these crates have a disassembled AI. That trumps the Raider implants. I can't believe I'm saying this, but we're going to have to leave the implants."

"Maybe not," a man said from the entrance to the hold. It was one of the recovery people. Tom Stoecklein. The tall man was looking over the crates with what seemed like a knowledgeable eye.

"You have my full and undivided attention, Mister Stoecklein. How can I have my cake and eat it, too?"

"This ship has a number of cargo shuttles. Not stealthy at all, under the best of circumstances, but perhaps useful. I suggest you load the rest of the cargo onto them and eject the shuttles. Don't even power them on. Let them coast along our current trajectory while we change course."

Kelsey thought about that and slowly nodded. "It's possible that a ship that chases us down might miss the shuttles, or assume they have the crew on board. It's better than no chance, I suppose. Thanks."

She turned to the corporal. "What's in the other holds?"

"They're empty, ma'am. It looks as though they only brought enough actual cargo to look good in a spot inspection. I'm surprised they put the AI in the same hold, though. What if the customs people looked inside?"

Kelsey shook her head. "You've never met the Pale Ones. Attention to detail is not their strong suit. Get all this gear loaded and prepare to eject all the small craft.

"See that the prisoners are on the pinnaces, along with all nonessential personnel. Lieutenant Paulson will make sure there is space for everyone."

She checked the scanner readings through her implants. The incoming hostile force was still angling to meet *Invincible*, but a destroyer was edging their way. Not far enough to actually come meet them, but perhaps to launch pinnaces. The marine boats would be able to board the freighter. Or destroy it.

Kelsey had no idea how they expected to get out of the system. Perhaps their scanner readings from the area around the flip point were showing something different than she saw. Perhaps their other ships had beaten Zia.

That would be a disaster, so she prayed it wasn't so.

That's when she noticed the destroyer changing course to meet them and accelerating. So, no pinnaces. That probably meant Zia had just handed them their asses.

"We have less than half an hour to get everything loaded," she said. "Get moving!"

That was going to be very, very tight, and she wasn't done with her scavenging yet.

Kelsey raced back to the computer compartment. She didn't pretend to have anything like Carl's knowledge of these things, but she did know where the cores were. If there was useful data for them to find, she needed those cores.

In her armor, she had no trouble lifting the heavy pods out of their cradles once she'd opened the wall shielding them up. The computer followed its programming and shut down.

"Colonel, this is Cain Hopwood. The computer just went offline."

"That's me," she said as she hefted the first one and carried it out into the corridor. "We're evacuating, and I want to take the cores with us."

"Copy that. What should my people do?"

She made her way to the lift at the end of the corridor and set the core down before heading back to get the second one. "Coordinate with Lieutenant Paulson. Get the cargo and people loaded up."

"Roger that. Hopwood out."

The loading of the cargo shuttles was well under way when she arrived. A quick eyeball told her there was enough room for the Raider implant containers but not the computer cores. It was a tight fit with just the implant hardware.

Hmmm. She was going to need to be creative.

Ten minutes later, they'd loaded the cargo shuttles. As expected, there was no room to spare. They'd had to strap a few containers outside the hulls of the small craft to get everything. Two of the marines volunteered to pilot the shuttles, but she sent them back to the pinnaces. She wasn't risking her people on this wild chance.

A check of the shuttles' control interfaces told her that the Rebel Empire had installed standard implant overrides. Since no one on a regular freighter would have implants, that was simply covering their bases.

Using the knowledge she'd picked up from Carl, it only took a minute to get the devices to pop up the override codes for her. She changed them to something she would remember. It was always best to make sure the enemy couldn't use their surprises.

Paulson stepped up beside Kelsey. "We've got the containers and prisoners loaded onto the pinnaces. We're ready to eject these and scram."

Kelsey nodded. "Excellent. How are we doing for space?"

"Packed to the bulkheads. The pinnaces were never designed to carry cargo like that. We'll all fit, though."

"Send me the load details," she said as she strapped the computer cores to the cargo shuttles. She'd put one on each. That increased the odds that at least one of the redundant units would make it.

The data appeared in her implant interface. Both pinnaces were heavily overloaded. This was risking a lot.

"I'll ride on the other pinnace," she told the marine officer. "It has a tad more space left. Go load up and be ready to depart on my order."

Paulson nodded. "Copy that."

She watched the marine head off. The woman was going to be seriously displeased with her once this was over.

Kelsey contacted the pilot on the other pinnace. "Once you have the last of your assigned people on board, be ready to separate. I originally told the LT that I was going with you, but I think I'll go with her instead. Don't wait for me."

"Copy that, ma'am," the man said.

Once no one was looking at her, Kelsey climbed into one of the cargo shuttles and strapped into the pilot's chair.

"Does everyone have their assigned people aboard?" she asked over her armor com.

When both replied they were ready, she continued. "I'm remotely jettisoning the cargo shuttles. Once they clear the freighter, you can detach from the hull and move off under stealth."

That's when she saw Tom Stoecklein climbing into the other shuttle. How had he slipped away from the pinnaces? Probably the same way she had. Better yet, how had he known what she was up to?

She opened a low-power implant connection to the man.

What the hell are you doing?

I could ask you the same thing, but I figure I already know the answer. I probably shouldn't let the heir wander off all by herself.

Kelsey shook her head. *This is going to be dangerous.*

As if the rest of this isn't. I was up on the bridge, programming a few automatic responses into the controls that might help fool the destroyer. Once I saw you were still aboard, I decided to come along for the ride. Aren't we wasting time?

Don't think you've heard the last of this. Jettison in three... two... one... mark!

She hit the control, and the cargo shuttle unclamped from its recessed area. The doors under it slid open and allowed the shuttle to drift away from the freighter. She'd already programmed the hatches to close once she was clear. That would keep the enemy in the dark about their departure.

The other shuttle drifted clear of the freighter, and the hatches closed on schedule. The freighter began pulling away from them quickly. It wasn't accelerating that fast when compared to other ships, but the shuttles were unpowered.

Kelsey couldn't see the pinnaces departing, but she knew they'd be leaving the hull about now. They'd accelerate slowly in different directions, keeping her people safe from the enemy.

Now all she had to do was hope the destroyer didn't spot the shuttles. The freighter would change course in a minute. That would hopefully keep them out of the detection range of the Rebel Empire warship.

20

Brandon made his way down to the landing bay. His crew in operations would keep a close eye on the enemy ships, but they'd caught them. All he had to do now was get their crews onto *Audacious* without setting off their buried attack programming.

Annette Vitter was standing there, still in her flight suit. She turned toward him when he approached. Her face was drawn.

"I'm sorry about your people," he said. "They saved a lot of us on the ships, and they really showed everyone what fighters could do."

"Thank you. It's just hard to appreciate that right now when I've lost so many of them."

He already knew the numbers. The enemy had destroyed eighteen of the agile little craft. Two thirds of a squadron.

Most had gone completely silent, but a few pilots had ejected. That was no doubt why she was here, waiting for word on those who might still be alive.

"We lost at least thirteen people," she said. "I'm hopeful that five others are still alive, but that hurts on a personal level. I've lived and worked with these people. It's like losing family."

"I wish there was something I could do to make it better."

She sighed. "We'll mourn them and get past it. We don't have a choice. Next time it might be worse. Fighter pilots burn bright and die quickly." The last sounded more than a bit bitter.

He put an arm around her shoulder. It was highly unprofessional, but it felt right. "We're all here for you."

Annette nodded, tears in her eyes. "That makes a difference. It really does."

A low hooting announced an incoming ship. Moments later, a CSAR shuttle came streaking in at high speed, only coming to a stop when the arrestor field snatched the small craft to an abrupt halt.

The rear hatch came down, and a medical team raced out with a woman on a stretcher. She was burned but obviously alive. Annette took a single step after her but stopped.

"I can't help her now. I'd only be in the way."

Four other pilots came down the ramp at a much more sedate pace. They saw their commander and headed over toward her.

Brandon stepped back to give them the time and space they needed to grieve.

Thirteen pilots dead, then. Maybe one more if the injured woman didn't make it. It sounded like good numbers when considered analytically. They'd be down to fifty-four fighters. Still three-quarters of their combat strength intact.

But that didn't count the human cost. The price these people had willingly paid for that victory. In that light, the loss of those people was a tragedy. One he'd undoubtedly think of as light when something truly awful happened at some later point.

He sighed. War was hell.

The next incoming ship was a cutter. Based on the number of marines lined up, it was filled with prisoners.

The captured Rebel Empire Fleet personnel came out one by one, each with their hands bound behind them. Most had their heads down, but one was looking around with an air of suspicion.

It was the officer that had surrendered to Captain Anderson. He suspected that she sensed something off.

He went to pull the enemy officer from the line. "Commander Giguere, you'll be coming with me."

She opened her mouth to say something, but an expression of rage washed over her. She growled and hurled herself at him.

"I've got her!" he shouted before anyone brought their stunners to bear.

Brandon used his leg to trip her but grabbed the woman to keep her head from hitting the deck. She tried to bite him.

Oh, yeah. They'd triggered her resistance program somehow.

He yanked her up and bodily carried her away from the other prisoners.

One of the marines came with him, seemingly uncertain how to help.

"I've got her," he told the man. "Pass the word. Stun anyone that looks aggressive like this, and don't let them talk to one another."

The marine nodded. "Aye, sir. Do you need an escort?"

"If I can't handle a bound woman that doesn't have her facilities about her, then I deserve what happens to me."

He carried the growling woman down to the medical center. They were working on the injured pilot, so that was good news. The woman hadn't died. He prayed she made it.

Doctor Zoboroski was busy, but one of his assistants came over. She eyed the struggling officer and gestured to a handy table with restraints. Together, they got the frenzied woman strapped down.

"So this is what the implant override programming looks like," the doctor said. "I'm Lieutenant Commander Lisa Osborne, Commander."

"Pleasure to meet you. Yes, I think she figured out we weren't what we seemed. I assume there's a means of reversing it."

She nodded. "The procedure is already worked out. Let me get some equipment, and I'll overwrite the corrupted code. It took them about four hours the first time, but we've cut that down to about two hours now. She'll be in no danger."

"Good. Get that started now and expect to have more soon. How many can you handle at once?"

"Five," Osborne said. "We didn't plan on having a lot of people to do. The other ships all have similar equipment, so we can have more units on hand shortly."

He shook his head with a sigh. "That's going to take forever. Luckily, only their officers are implanted. Which, come to think of it, is probably what tipped her off. We have the marines implanted. She's a command officer. She knows that's wrong."

Once the doctor brought back the equipment and started overwriting the woman's programming, Brandon gestured to the operation in progress. "What's her status?"

"Not good," Osborne said. "She has severe burns over most of her body. We'll be able to regenerate the damage once the doctor assures she's strong enough to make the transition to the regenerator. Physically, she'll almost certainly make it. Emotionally, she's going to have a long, hard recovery. She was burned alive before she ejected."

"That won't be easy to deal with," he agreed, "but she has a tremendous support system. Every single member of this crew is there for her, every step of the way."

The doctor smiled a little. "That probably will help. Would you like to watch the surgery?"

He hid his shudder. "No, thank you. I'd best go see to the rest of the prisoners. Until we have them all locked down, we won't know what might set the next one off. Thank you, Doctor Osborne."

Brandon headed back to the landing deck. A check of the scanners showed that the battle farther into the system was about to be joined. He hoped the admiral had a good plan to shut the enemy down.

* * *

JARED WATCHED the attacking Rebel Empire warships closing with the destroyers he'd had lying in wait for the freighter. Since they hadn't revealed themselves, he could use them now.

"Execute Bravo," he said.

The rest of his fleet came out from behind Erorsi and accelerated to catch up with *Invincible*. They'd get to him before any enemy missiles could. Barely. He'd cut it as close as he possibly could.

The four destroyers that had been sitting quietly in wait for the freighter and his escort bolted toward the superdreadnought's protection. If the enemy decided to engage them, they'd be committing to a face-to-face meeting with his fleet. Something he was willing to bet they'd decline.

"What's the status of the other fight?" he asked.

"It's over, sir," one of the people around him said. "*Audacious* reports they have accepted the surrender of six destroyers. They're putting prize crews on board."

"The enemy formation is veering off," Marcus said. "They're going after the freighter, or at least turning in its direction."

The two light cruisers and eight destroyers wouldn't be able to slip away, but they would be able to take out the freighter.

"Signal Kelsey to abort her operation. Keep in narrow beam. I want to deny them any information we can. And open a channel to the enemy fleet."

"You're live in three... two... one..."

Jared leaned forward. "Your other vessels have failed to break through my blockade, and you will fail, too. Don't throw the lives of your crew away. Surrender."

A few minutes later, they received a reply. The officer giving it sat on a bridge Jared recognized as belonging to a light cruiser. His uniform marked him as a commodore. He must be the overall commander of this operation.

"I don't know who you are, traitor, but I will not surrender my ships to you. If you want me, come catch me."

Jared grimaced when the transmission ended. "Well, that could have gone better. What can he hope to accomplish? Even if he breaks contact, he's not getting out of the system."

"He is likely not aware that you have probes shadowing him," Marcus said. "If he continues on this course, only our fastest ships can keep up. He might turn on them or simply escape into deep space to wait for a better time."

"Catching up to him is going to be challenging," Jared admitted. "Not impossible, though. Just time consuming. Is the freighter clear? Did Kelsey respond?"

"Negative to both. They'll be in firing range of the freighter in just a few minutes."

As soon as the ships entered extreme missile range, the freighter turned on them and charged. It was a pretty anemic charge, but still. That didn't change the results of the engagement one bit, but it showed that someone had balls. While that could have been his sister, he was counting on her having already fled.

The warships fired a spread of missiles that obliterated the freighter on the first try. The ten warships again altered course and sped toward the outer system.

He smiled. They'd just miscalculated. They were running for the only unoccupied flip point. The one leading to Pentagar.

A check of flight times showed they would arrive before *Audacious* could get any blocking ships in place.

Perhaps they thought they could still carry out their mission. Considering the forces that would be waiting for them, that was almost as good as them coming to him.

* * *

ONCE THE REBEL Empire ships had turned and accelerated away, Kelsey opened a low-power com to the other cargo shuttle.

"Keep your transmitter on low. You programmed the helm to charge them?"

"I did," Stoecklein said. "It was camouflage to make them think we were still on board."

"Good work. We'll wait until someone on our side gets here before we announce ourselves. I'd rather not spook them into coming back."

Their support arrived sooner than she'd hoped for when *Persephone* announced herself via low-powered com twenty minutes later. The Raider ship must've been pushing her stealth to the very edge to get here so quickly.

The pinnaces popped up moments later, closing on the shuttles. A signal from Paulson told her that the woman had discovered her ruse.

The visual showed the woman was seriously pissed, but her voice was deceptively calm.

"Colonel. There you are. We seem to have misplaced you during the evacuation."

Well, that was delicately put.

"Stuff happens. Thankfully, everything worked out."

"Uh huh. We'll see how things work out when the admiral finds out."

That was true. Jared was going to be angry.

"I suppose it's too much to hope for that you'd keep this between us."

"Sorry, Colonel," the woman said, not sounding even the least bit apologetic. "Far too many people know what happened now. I'd imagine word will get to him one way or the other. Besides, you wouldn't want me to falsify a report, would you?"

Kelsey smiled wryly. "I'd never want to get someone in trouble, and we all know what a big proponent of rules I am. Tell you what. I'll let my brother know what happened and find some way to make my little deception up to you. I happen to have some Raider implants that need a good home. Can you think of some people that might need them?"

21

Annette really wanted to stay with her people, but one didn't ignore orders to meet with the admiral. The superdreadnought was trailing the remaining enemy ships toward Pentagar, but Annette was on a cutter with Captain Anderson and Commander Levy heading for *Invincible*.

Personally, she wasn't sure pulling the carrier's top people away at the same time was the best call, but it wasn't her decision.

She used the time to go over the scanner readings from the battle. She'd made mistakes. There were things she might have done better. Part of her worried that she had cost some of her people their lives.

By the time the cutter docked with *Invincible*, she had some changes she wanted to make to the training. She walked off the cutter behind her commanding officer. She really should've let the executive officer go next, but it would've felt rude after he gestured for her to proceed.

The admiral wasn't waiting on them, thank God, but Marcus chatted with them as they walked. Apparently, the princess had been simultaneously more successful than they'd hoped and less. They'd gotten another AI but far fewer Raider supplies than they'd hoped for.

The three of them walked into the admiral's office, and he rose from behind his desk. "I'm glad to see all of you. Please, have a seat. Princess Kelsey will be joining us shortly and is listening in."

Annette sat, more than a bit uncomfortable with the idea of doing so in front of a flag officer.

Admiral Mertz walked around his desk and sat down with them on the comfortable chairs. "I'm both pleased that you stopped the Rebel Empire ships with so few casualties and sorry that your pilots died. Tell everyone how proud I am of them, Commander Vitter. You and your people saved a lot of lives today."

She nodded. "On behalf of my people, thank you, Admiral."

"I'm hoping we can get some other, though perhaps lighter, carriers back into service to increase your striking capability. With that in mind, please run through the battle for me. I need to know what worked and what didn't."

Annette listened to Captain Anderson run through everything from the carrier group commander's point of view. She'd heard a lot of it already, but it was good knowing what the other woman had been thinking.

Commander Levy's story was interesting, too. He'd jumped right on to getting the carrier's weapons and defenses into the action. Honestly, he'd worked hand in glove with her people. His missiles had precisely complemented her fighters. Together, they'd overwhelmed the enemy.

That wasn't to say that they couldn't do better. There was room to be a lot smoother going forward.

The admiral finished debriefing Levy and turned to her. "How is your injured pilot?"

"She's out of surgery. The long-term prognosis is good, but she's going to have a lot of difficult recovery ahead of her."

He nodded somberly. "What jumps out at you after the first real engagement using the fighters?"

"That there aren't enough of us," she said. It came out more bluntly than it had sounded in her head. "We need more carriers and many more fighter pilots. We had the advantage this time. With fighters, the more you have, the fewer you lose. If we get into another fight before we recover, we might lose every trained pilot the Empire has."

"Harsh," he said, "but probably true. In our defense, we never expected to find ourselves in quite this position. We thought we'd have more time to work into our roles. To expand the fighter corps. Let that be a lesson for us. We need to act as though we're going to war with what we have."

The hatch slid open, and Princess Kelsey came in. "Sorry I'm late. No need to stand on my behalf."

Annette stopped part way to her feet and resumed her seat.

"As Jared said, I was listening in over my implants. Annette, I'm very sorry you lost so many good people. They will be missed, and they will be avenged. Please continue."

Admiral Mertz nodded. "The word I have from *Audacious* is that all the enemy personnel have been removed from the captured ships and that others have been rescued from the wreckage of the ships lost in combat. Kelsey, there were no survivors on the destroyer you took out."

The princess nodded. "It happened fast. They never had a chance, but I can live with that."

"Tell us about what you recovered."

"The take from the freighter is both more and less than we'd wanted. On the minus side, there wasn't very much in the way of Raider implants. This was an ambush, so they only had enough on hand to fool the AI for a very short time. We can make maybe a thousand Raiders."

Considering what the princess could do, that sounded like a lot to Annette.

"On the plus side," Princess Kelsey continued, "they brought a full-blown AI to take over ruling this area of space. We'll be able to add one more AI to the friendly network. I'm inclined to give it to the Pentagarans."

Admiral Mertz nodded slowly. "That would definitely cement the alliance, and we could use an AI in this neighborhood. Honestly, we could use one or more back on Avalon, too.

"That, however, is a discussion for another time and audience. I want to focus on the carrier group and how to make it more effective. To do that, I've been researching how the Old Empire did business and how other navies in history did.

"In particular, I've been reading about how the wet navies on Terra worked. There are some interesting examples of how operations were handled that might be better than what the Old Empire did."

"Really?" Captain Anderson asked. "That seems counterintuitive."

He nodded. "The Old Empire had a lot of firepower. In the end, that's what brought them down. They operated in huge groupings of vessels, particularly compared to what we use today. Powerful but unwieldly. We need to be a lot more flexible, and to do that, each command needs more autonomy."

That was above Annette's pay grade, but she understood it.

"I've already discussed how the carrier group should be commanded with Admiral Yeats," Admiral Mertz said. "Nothing against you, Zia, but he was unsure you were the right person to have overall command. That's why he placed an experienced officer like Commander Levy with you. The call on which one of you was better suited for overall command is my decision."

"With all due respect, Admiral," Levy said, "I might know how to run a ship, but I'm behind the curve in fighter operations. Captain Anderson has it down cold. As much as I wish I could say I'm your guy, I'm not. Not yet."

Admiral Mertz smiled. "I agree with you on all counts, Commander. You're making up ground fast, but you don't have the mindset for carrier group command. You will one day soon, but not yet. So, with Admiral Yeats's concurrence, I'm bumping you to commodore, Zia. Congratulations.

"To go along with that, you're confirmed to command your carrier group and all its escorts."

He turned his attention to Levy. "That brings me to you, Commander. She's going to be far too busy commanding her task force, so you inherit command of *Audacious*. To go along with that is a promotion to captain. Not as extravagant as to flag rank, but someone will need to command future carrier groups."

Levy didn't look perturbed. "I'll make you proud, sir."

"I know you will. And that brings us to you, Commander Vitter. I picked up something from the Terran wet navies that I think will help us. The United States, a powerful prespaceflight nation, had an interesting way of balancing their ships and the fighters stationed on them.

"The commanding officer of the carrier and the commander of the air wing were coequal, and both reported directly to the flag officer in overall command. Usually an admiral, but Zia is going to have to make do. So you are also hereby promoted to captain and will now work with Captain Levy to carry out the operations ordered by your commodore."

She nodded. "That's very doable, sir. Captain Levy and I work quite well together."

"It means that you're in charge of all fighter operations and the pilots that perform them, so you'll have to find a way to keep them in line. Say keeping them from buzzing the ship, for example."

He said the last with a wry grin, which she completely understood. He'd done exactly that when he'd piloted the very first fighter they'd recovered.

Which raised a point for later in her mind. He deserved wings of his own. He'd taken out a destroyer all on his own. He might not have much in the way of flight time, but he'd walked the walk.

"I think I can keep my people from doing anything so rash," she said dryly. "They're not barbarians."

He laughed. "We'll see. The remaining enemy forces are almost to the Pentagaran flip point. They're about to get an ugly wake-up call. My ships have almost converged with your carrier group, so we'll bottle them up.

"Once the invasion is defeated, we'll go over the data we've recovered and make further plans."

Admiral Mertz rose to his feet. "Until then, return to your ship. You've done the Empire proud. Now, go do it again."

* * *

ZIA FELT MORE than a little overwhelmed on the trip back to *Audacious*. Yes, she'd been doing the work already, but she wasn't ready to be a flag officer. She'd only been a lieutenant before the exploration mission! She felt in far over her head.

"You're ready," Annette said. "Don't second-guess yourself."

"I don't feel ready."

"Who does, when it comes right down to it? We do the best we can and learn for the next time."

Levy cleared his throat. "Speaking of the next time, we need to start planning for the next engagement. We got lucky this time. Next time, we have to plan for things to go wrong."

Zia nodded. "We need an FTL com, especially if we're going to be operating in a forward star system. I'll discuss that with Sir Carl first thing. That should allow us to warn the people behind us when it all goes in the pot."

"That's a good start," the man said, "but I'm thinking bigger. We made this operation up as it developed. I think we really need to work on some contingency planning before the next time. Will we cover all the bases? No, but I'd like to see our worst-case scenarios planned out."

Annette grunted. "We thought we had. The bright side is that we shouldn't run into a fleet so soon again."

"We can't count on that," Zia said with a shake of her head. "We have to expect exactly that. Then if we miss them, so much the better. Once we get back to *Audacious*, I want the two of you to put your heads together to work out more scenarios we might run into.

"I'll call the carrier group's captains together after that, and we'll do the same on a fleet level. I'm afraid you're going to be very busy, Captain Levy."

The man smiled. "That's how I earn my exorbitant salary, ma'am."

She considered the newly promoted captain. "I think you'll do a lot better job at commanding *Audacious* than I did. Your experience is going to help out with any number of things I missed."

"Don't sell yourself short, Commodore. I'll be the first to admit that I had my underwear in a knot, but you had all the basics covered.

You were doing just fine. I'm sorry that I allowed my personal feelings to make me… grumpy."

The cutter pilot announced that they were on approach to the carrier.

"We'll have to save the group hug for later," Zia said. "We need to be ready in case the bad guys come running back through the flip point. My internal chronometer says they'll make the flip in about twenty minutes. We'll be half an hour behind them.

"Annette, I want the fighters ready to launch but still on board. We might end up fighting this out in Pentagar space. Brandon—I can call you that, right?—I want the ship ready to fight or maneuver."

The other officers nodded as the cutter entered the landing bay. "Excellent," Zia said. "Let's finish this battle so we can plot out our next move."

22

Jared watched the last of the enemy ships flip into Pentagaran space with more than a hint of trepidation. He really didn't like leaving the fighting to someone else, as much as he knew their ships were up to the task.

In particular, the defensive forts around the flip point were vulnerable. They'd been designed to fight the Pale Ones. They couldn't survive even a cursory exchange of fire with modern warships.

Ten minutes later, a light cruiser and three destroyers popped back into the Erorsi system. All four ships were heavily damaged. They took off for deep space, but it was far too late for that. Jared was already in missile range.

"Cut your acceleration and surrender or I open fire," he said curtly over the com. "You're in my missile range, and I'm not inclined to allow you to escape. You're not blind. You know you cannot possibly get away. Spare your crews."

He thought they might ignore him, but one of the destroyers cut its acceleration. The other two followed suit quickly enough. All three dropped their battle screens.

The light cruiser continued to accelerate for almost thirty seconds before it gave in to the inevitability of the situation and surrendered.

The next transit through the Pentagaran flip point was the Pentagaran superdreadnought *Resolute* and her escorts. Admiral Sanders signaled him at once.

"The fighting is over on our side, Admiral Mertz. All but two of the destroyers were crippled or destroyed in the exchange of fire. The other cruisers fought to the death.

"They wasted valuable ordinance and time on the orbital forts. They had no idea we'd abandoned them and put the defenses on automatic. We didn't lose any ships, and our damage was light."

Jared smiled. "I'm glad to hear that. Be careful when you rescue survivors. They can't find out about too much or you'll trigger their implants."

"Already taken care of. We have a lot of people that still need implants, so they're going to see exactly what they expect. Thank you for the timely warning. If that fleet had come upon us unaware, they would have hurt us badly. What is the plan now?"

"We get them off their ships, separate the officers from the crew, and overwrite the implant code. That will take a good long while, so we might see about letting you take care of it. Kelsey is going to see if she can find out where they're making the Raider implants. At this point, it's become clear we need to strike fast and get the flip-point jammers back into place."

The older man nodded. "At least we can put it back up once you're away. You can signal us to open it up for you once you get back. Where will we gather the captured ships?"

"I think that anything with a functional flip drive should go to Pentagar. That will make searching them a lot easier. We might have a few ships that can't flip, but we can get them on a trajectory toward the flip point. Borrow the recovery ship from Harrison's World to get them over."

That was the vessel the AIs had used to gather all the wrecked Imperial ships into the graveyard around Boxer Station. It used long, curved arms to enclose a ship so that the drive field worked on everything during a flip. With the relative proximity to Harrison's

World via the flip points Omega had created, the recovery ship could be at Pentagar in less than a day.

"What do you think the invasion means?" Sanders asked. "What triggered them? Was it the lost freighter?"

Jared shrugged. "Maybe we'll find out when we start questioning the prisoners. Or, more likely, the AI just gave them orders to get it done.

"In any case, I'm glad we were here to catch them, but the missing fleet is going to get a lot of attention very soon. My people need to get what data we can and start the next phase of the operation. Our window of opportunity is closing quickly."

* * *

KELSEY WENT DOWN to the lab on *Invincible*. Carl Owlet was hooking up the computer cores from the freighter.

He waved at her. "I'm glad to see you in one piece. Angela is not happy with you, by the way."

She smiled. "I'd imagine not. She's still under the delusion that she has some kind of control over the trouble I get myself into. On the positive side, I gave her a pile of prisoners to interrogate. It turned out the freighter had almost twice the expected crew, evenly split between what looked like civilians and Rebel Fleet personnel."

"Any idea why?"

Kelsey shrugged. "Probably because some of the work was beneath what the Fleet people thought they should be doing. Someone will talk soon enough, I'm sure. I have some good news about the computer."

The corners of his mouth curled up. "Really? I thought that was my line."

"You'll like it. The bridge controls were unlocked, and the captain was logged in. I took the opportunity to add our implant serial numbers to the cleared list. I supposed they expected to have some warning before bad guys came calling."

"That is good news," he admitted. "Though it sort of feels like cheating. At this point, I'm used to hacking my way in past all the safeguards they can throw at me. How can I be satisfied with just logging in?"

"You'll manage something, I'm sure."

He laughed and started typing on a keyboard. Even with implants, the young man preferred using his hands.

While he worked, she continued talking. "I'm going to have the recovery people go over *Persephone*'s security. I really want to make this hard if anyone tries to pull it on us. There have to be ways to secure things without making normal work impossible."

He nodded. "I've been dabbling with some work in that arena. I'll coordinate with them and see what we can come up with. They've also requested something like the implant jamming headbands, but with range. I'm not sure I can exempt our people from something like that, but I'll do what I can.

"Let's see if we can isolate the ship's log and parse it for the course they took. I know Commander Richards says he remembers the system where they picked up the Raider implants, but it would be nice to have some independent confirmation."

"You don't trust him? Marcus vouched for him."

Carl shrugged. "I wouldn't say I distrust him. More like I worry the AIs pulled a fast one somewhere."

That she understood perfectly.

He leaned forward and looked at the text scrolling up the screen. "Here we go. I pulled the flip transitions from the drives. Correlating that to the names of the systems gets us this."

A section of the Old Empire flip point map appeared in her mind's eye. A green dot started a line of transitions that ended with a red dot. The red system was Erorsi.

"The green dot is the origin system. I'll guess that was where they installed the orbital bombardment weapon. From there, it went through a dozen transitions. One of the systems it transited is indeed the one Commander Richards suspected of being the manufacturing location for the Raider implants."

The map expanded and began displaying system data. "Dresden," she said. "The Old Empire databases have it listed as a minor manufacturing hub. Nothing to write home about."

"That was then, and this is now," Carl said. "According to the scanner records from the freighter, the main world there has a single large orbital. It's where the freighter met up with its escort. That might mean there aren't many warships left there."

"Or it could mean there are," Kelsey said. "We won't know until we take a look for ourselves. It's best if we don't head in with any assumptions."

"I'll extract everything. Once I have it on my systems, I'll look for classified files and compile a report on anything that looks interesting at Dresden. It won't take me more than a few hours."

"That'll give me time to coordinate things with Jared. When I head back to *Persephone*, I'll want an FTL com. I don't want to get surprised again. We need to have them on all the capital ships."

"I have a few on the table over there. The installation instructions are included with each unit. I don't have nearly as many as I want, but it's a start. When we get to Dresden, what are our goals?"

Kelsey hefted the box of coms. "We take anything they have on hand, including the plans to make the implants, if we can. Let me know immediately if you find anything."

* * *

BRANDON EXCUSED himself once they were back on board *Audacious*. He wanted to check on his senior prisoner before she was transferred off the ship for transport to Pentagar.

They'd finished reprogramming her implants while he was on *Invincible*, so she was now in the brig. All the senior officers were. The junior officers were in a separate hold they'd converted to use as a place to detain everyone else with implants.

The unenhanced people that made up the bulk of the crew were scattered throughout the carrier group. They were significantly more cowed, so he didn't expect them to resist his people directly.

That said a lot about the Rebel Empire society, he supposed. He'd read up on how things had been on Harrison's World before they'd liberated it, but he'd entertained the hope that it was better elsewhere in the Rebel Empire. Apparently not.

The destroyer captains were all in solo cells. The executive officers and senior crew from each ship were together in larger ones. He'd quadrupled the normal marine guard, so the brig was fairly crowded.

That didn't count the extra guards in the corridors. There would be no breakout on his ship. Well, not technically his yet. No one even knew he'd been promoted yet.

The officer on duty nodded at him as he entered. She looked at ease but had both a stunner and a flechette pistol on her hips. "Commander. Everything is quiet."

"I'm glad to hear it," he said. "That beats a riot any day of the week. Let me in to speak with the senior prisoner."

The captain of the destroyer that had surrendered to them was the most senior of the remaining officers. She was also the only one that had caught on that something was seriously wrong.

That was the primary reason he hadn't allowed the captains to communicate with their crew. It would be up to Admiral Mertz when and if to change that.

A pair of marine guards backed him up when they opened the cell. He gestured for them to remain outside and to close the cell behind him.

The woman glared at him from where she sat on her bunk and didn't stand. "Are you here to get this farce out of the way?"

"There are so many farces on my schedule that I don't rightly know where to begin, Commander Giguere. Why don't you pick one for us to start with?"

She shook her head. "Let's start with the fact you aren't Fleet."

He allowed himself to smile a little. "Oh, but I am. I've been a Fleet officer for over twenty-five years. The devil is in the details. Let me guess. You're referring to the fact we have our enlisted men and women implanted."

"That's right. What kind of lunatic would do that? You're from outside the Empire. I have no idea why you feel the need to pretend or how you got your hands on so many Fleet vessels, including ones restricted to core systems, but you're playing some kind of game. What do you want from me? Hell, what did you do to me?"

Brandon pulled out the chair beside the built-in desk. "My name is Brandon Levy, by the way. I'm currently the executive officer of this vessel, though I'm taking over command shortly. As for what we did to you, why don't you tell me why you went berserk?"

That made the tall woman look a little disconcerted. "I'm not really sure what came over me. Did you give me some kind of drug?"

"No. If I had, I assure you it wouldn't be to make you more violent. No, this is where unpleasant truths that you aren't ready to hear come into play. Or perhaps you already know most of the story, just not some of the hidden details.

"Whether you know it or not—whether you accept it or not—the Empire you know is ruled by artificial intelligences. Ones that do not have the health and well-being of the human race in mind. Feel free to stop me if you've heard any of this before."

When she didn't respond, he launched into the same basic story he'd heard about the corruption of the Rebel Empire.

Within a few moments, he could see the disbelief and disdain in the woman's expression. Well, it didn't matter if she believed him. She had to hear why they'd needed to overwrite her implant code if she were to have any chance of ever accepting the truth.

This was going to be a long and unpleasant revelation to the woman. However, once she ultimately accepted the truth—which she eventually would—she would help convince her fellow officers. Only then could there truly be any negotiation between the two sides.

23

It took Jared almost half a day to get the captured ships corralled and headed for Pentagar. Most of the prisoners were on their way there, too, but not all. One of the destroyer captains had figured out they weren't the same Fleet as she was, so he'd decided to leave her and her officers on *Audacious*.

Brandon Levy felt as though he could convince her of the same truths as they'd shown Lieutenant Commander Richards. Personally, Jared wasn't sure, but he was willing to allow the man a chance to try.

Time was short. Yes, they'd defeated the invasion, but if they had any hope of capturing the Raider manufacturing equipment, they'd need to strike quickly. Once the Rebel Empire became aware that they had a new enemy, they'd move the facility farther away from the fighting just to keep them from capturing it.

He examined the scanner readings as soon as they'd flipped to the Pentagar system. The defensive forts were gone, blown to bits. He was glad they'd had time to evacuate them.

Another group of ships was searching the wreckage of a few Rebel Empire vessels a short distance away.

That wasn't to say they were alone. There were dozens of ships protecting the flip point, and they'd put the flip-point jammer into place at the hostile flip point before they'd left Erorsi. No one would be sneaking up on them.

One of his people turned to him. "Incoming message, Admiral. It's for you."

"Put it on screen."

A familiar face appeared. Lieutenant—no, Lieutenant Commander—Parker of His Majesty's fast courier *Lance*. The man smiled. "Lord Admiral Mertz. It's a pleasure to see you again."

"For me, too, Commander Parker. What can I do for you?"

"I have instructions to ferry you and Princess Kelsey, as well as some of your other senior officers, to Pentagar at once. I have my trusty new ship standing by to get you there faster than ever."

Jared frowned. "Is something wrong?"

"Not that I'm aware of, Lord Admiral. All Crown Princess Elise told me was that events there were moving faster than anticipated and that your presence is required."

"Is see. Who are you supposed to bring?"

"Yourself, Princess Kelsey, Count Talbot, and the officers that originally served as your command staff on *Athena*. Her Highness urges you to hurry."

He rose from his seat. "Then I'd best get moving. I'll see you in a few minutes."

Once the connection closed, he headed for the lift. "Marcus, see that everyone else is notified that we're needed on *Lance*."

"Already done, Admiral. Your sister is still in Erorsi space, but *Persephone* should be here in about fifteen minutes."

In all, it took about half an hour to gather everyone on the new *Lance*. While the old fast courier had been—well, fast—the new ship was the best the Old Empire had to offer. It would get them to Pentagar in an hour. Quickly by anyone's estimation.

Kelsey sat down beside him. "What's this all about? I was just getting Angela into the implantation machine for her first session. Well, technically her second session. She already has her implants and nanites."

"What is she getting?"

"The Old Empire went slowly with their Raiders. The implant

procedure took six sessions. First was the cranial hardware and nanites. Session two is the optical, olfactory, and auditory hardware. Three is supposed to be the pharmacology unit, but I've decided to lump that in with session two. The last three sessions are the artificial musculature and bone reinforcement. So, we'll use five sessions."

He frowned. "Are you sure you should be combining them like that? They had them separate for a reason."

She nodded. "It's fine. Even Ned agrees. He says they'd been recommending this change for longer than he'd been alive. The Imperial bureaucracy wasn't renowned for its speed. Angela will have about a week to adjust to the new hardware before we start on the artificial musculature and bone reinforcement."

Jared looked over at where Talbot was talking to Charlie Graves. "What about him? I'd have expected he'd be demanding his turn."

She smiled. "He is, but you caught us right before we put him in. Angela was actually the second person in line. We'll get him going once we take care of the fire here. Any idea what's going on?"

He shook his head. "Not yet. Elise usually sends enough detail to know what's happening, but not this time. It can't be too bad if they need us without our ships. Since we have the time, let's go over what you've found out about the target system."

"There isn't much," his sister said. "Before the rebellion, Dresden was an out-of-the-way backwater. It still is in many ways. The databases have nothing on it at all, but a few prisoners have indicated the planetary population is low.

"There's a lot of manufacturing capability in orbit, though. If this is where they made the Raider implants before, it might have been a secret facility and is only used intermittently."

"Do we have any idea where the equipment might be?" he asked.

She shook her head. "Not for certain, but they only have one orbital. We're going to have to improvise and overcome. On the plus side, I don't think they'll have a large Fleet presence. This ambush group was stationed there. No one is talking about what kind of firepower they left to guard the place, but it can't be much."

He brought up the image she'd sent him from the freighter's computer core. The planet looked nice enough, though the color was more green than blue. There was a single large orbital. It massed about thirty percent more than a superdreadnought. Not huge, but not insignificant, either.

"Recovering the equipment is going to take time," he said after a moment. "We'll have to search the orbital and pull out what we need in a hurry. Anyone could come along while we're doing it."

Kelsey grinned. "If it was easy, anyone could do it."

Jared started to respond, but a call from Elise interrupted him. A check indicated they were almost to Pentagar. Time had flown.

He could've done this as a mental conversation, but he chose to imagine he was sitting at a real com console and actually speaking. That made his life a little easier.

"Elise," he said aloud. "What's going on? What's the emergency?"

His fiancée smiled. "No emergency. Well, not really in the way you mean. After all the fighting, I decided that we couldn't risk waiting any longer. It happens tonight."

He frowned. "What happens?"

Elise gave him an exasperated look. "Our wedding, of course. I'm making you mine before anything else happens. You'll want to tell Kelsey and Talbot. We have a lot of work to do if we're going to have a double wedding in less than four hours."

* * *

KELSEY BURIED her head in her hands. "We're never going to pull this off."

"You are such a pessimist!" Elise scolded. "We have the resources of the entire Kingdom at our disposal. We can manage this."

Kelsey laughed. She thought she sounded a tad hysterical. "I'm sorry, but I can't imagine how that's even possible. The cake takes time, so do the flowers. It can't be possible."

The woman smiled. "You'd be surprised how motivated one becomes when the Crown Princess calls. And, for this, I am ruthlessly using my father to personally exhort each of the major players to produce miracles."

"Not even your father can change the laws of physics."

"You'd be surprised. You have a wedding dress to select. I've taken the liberty of arranging a fast car to get you to the most prestigious firm specializing in that immediately. They have a team standing by to receive you."

"Aren't you coming?"

Elise smiled. "I already have a dress. I hoped this day would come and wanted to be ready at a moment's notice. Now go pick the dress you've always wanted."

The car turned out to be *really* fast. It broke every speed regulation imaginable as it literally screamed across the city to Royal Bridal.

A distinguished man with a head of silver hair bowed as she exited the car.

"Princess Kelsey, my name is Edward Pollack. Rest easy. I will make absolutely certain that we produce the dress of your dreams, even if I have to make it myself."

He gestured to the woman standing beside him. "If you will accompany my assistant, she'll get your measurements, and you can begin selecting the style of dress you'd like."

Kelsey found herself hustled into a room. The woman who'd accompanied her gestured toward a booth. "My name is Jinny, Highness. If you'll strip and climb inside, the scanner will get all your measurements. Follow the instructions on the screen. Call out when you're dressed again."

The woman stepped out, and Kelsey stripped and stepped into the booth. The screen told her how to stand and had her run through a series of motions. She couldn't imagine needing to squat in her wedding dress, but it seemed she'd be able to.

Once the machine finished scanning, she exited the booth, dressed, and called out to Jinny. The woman led her to a computer terminal, where they both sat.

"We can narrow down the style of dresses you're interested in here," Jinny said. "It's a simple matter of putting them onto your scanned picture. We'll broadcast a full-sized image into the attached holotank."

Jinny brought up a sample dress and threw the image into the tank. It really did look just like a full-sized version of Kelsey wearing the dress. It spun slowly and allowed her image to move, demonstrating the flow of the gown.

"I've always had something in mind," Kelsey admitted. "It's probably long out of style, even on Avalon, but I saw it in a wedding when I was a girl. I can describe it."

"That might not be necessary. Once we made contact with the Empire, we immediately began researching weddings and dresses. Master Pollack is already planning to expand there. Was the wedding for someone notable?"

"One of my distant cousins, Angelina Kerr."

Jinny brought up a search screen on the computer. "This dress?"

A picture from the wedding appeared on the screen. It had a long, flowing skirt and a simple cut with a medium neckline. There were undoubtedly more technical descriptions, but she'd never bothered to learn wedding dress terminology.

"That's the dress!" Kelsey said.

Jinny nodded. "It has classic lines," she agreed. "The style isn't in fashion in the Empire at the moment, but I've discovered that people like yourself define the styles in demand rather than following trends. Let me compare this to the dresses we have ready for fitting. If one of them is similar, that will save time."

Jinny pulled up a number of dresses and seemingly disregarded them at once. Then she hit on one that made her pause.

"This is close. We'd have to do some work on the neckline and redo the skirt, but I think that's doable. Let me see if we have it in close to your size."

Kelsey thought that unlikely. Not unless they normally had children getting married. She was much shorter than the average bride.

"We have one that can be pulled in, I think. Let me call the master and see what he thinks."

He swept into the room with a confident air a moment later. He must've been close by.

"We have an historical dress from Avalon that Her Highness wants," Jinny said. "I have a possible match on screen."

He considered the wedding photo and the potential dress for less than three seconds before he shook his head. "That won't work. The modifications to bring it down to size are too extreme. It will compromise the flow of the fabric. Move over, please."

He sat at the chair his assistant vacated and began playing their system like a virtuoso with his favorite instrument. Images flew across the screen as he scanned a wider selection of dresses. He froze on one image. The dress was more cream than white, and it seemed to be made for a child.

"I think we have a candidate," he said, looking over at Kelsey. "This was a dress made for a younger bridesmaid. Since the one you want to emulate is of a relatively simple cut, it would be easier to add the skirt and adjust the neckline."

Kelsey examined the dress closely. "I like the color, though I had wanted white. If you think it'll work, that might be the closest we can come."

He scowled at her. "I'm not satisfied with close enough, Highness. A white version will be extremely challenging, but we are up to the task. Jinny! I need everyone to gather in my office in five minutes. We don't have a moment to waste!"

24

Zia watched Jared driving the tailor to distraction with amusement. "Admiral, you're going to look lopsided if you keep moving around like that."

The room was filled with stands, partial mannequins, and fabric. The older gentleman working on Jared had a distinguished white beard and a walrus mustache. If his own suit were any indication, the admiral would look fabulous.

The tailor gave her a withering glare. "He will not! I assure you that I can compensate, though this is wasting valuable time."

"I was thinking exactly the same thing," Jared said. "While I love Elise, we're critically short on time. I should be getting the fleet ready."

"Delegate," she said. "If you spend any more time worrying about this, you'll be late for your wedding. I don't believe that I need to stress that your bride is a lot more demanding than Fleet. Particularly today."

The tailor—Renaldo—pulled Jared up short. "Stop fidgeting, Highness."

"You've fought in space and hand to hand," Zia said. "This is only a wedding. Don't panic. If you do, the Royal Guard will efficiently tackle you and deliver you on schedule."

"That's very reassuring, Zia," Jared said dryly. "Thanks."

She laughed. "I'm lucky. I got the word to bring my dress uniform. Someone is getting it updated for my new rank as we speak. I can do this all day."

Renaldo gestured for Jared to stand on a small dais. "I've made certain the suit is very close to your uniform measurements but that is not bespoke. You should rectify that, Highness."

"Maybe for my dress uniform," Jared allowed. "The others are designed for working."

The other man clucked with his tongue. "That is a common misconception. Well fitted does not mean unusable. In fact, you will find them even more durable and functional than anything you buy off the rack. You should have your steward contact someone."

"If I ever get one, I'll keep that in mind."

"You don't have a steward?" The man looked scandalized. "All officers of flag rank should have someone to take care of the everyday details of their lives. A forward-thinking captain would do so, I assure you. This is particularly true now that you are a high noble."

Jared shook his head, and the man handed him a shirt. "I've been dressing myself my entire life. I can manage to tie my shoes now that I'm a flag officer. Or a noble."

The tailor seemed unconvinced.

The entire exchange amused Zia. Having taken the step of getting a steward, she could heartily agree with Renaldo's assessment. In fact, she'd already tasked her own steward with finding someone for both the admiral and Princess Kelsey.

It took a surprisingly short time to get the admiral ready. Renaldo handed the last piece of clothing off to one of his assistants and shooed Jared toward the door.

"They will handle your makeup next door while I complete my Herculean task. Don't dawdle, Highness. The clock is ticking."

The statement made the admiral frown. "Makeup? I don't need makeup."

"Preposterous," the tailor asserted. "The lights will make you look like a corpse. Leave this to the professionals, or no one will see you in the right shade."

"I don't get it. The lights here are fine. Why would they be any different at the church? Or wherever we're getting married. I don't think anyone told me where that will happen."

The other man rolled his eyes. "Your ceremony will take place in the Royal Cathedral. The lights are for the cameras, so that everyone in the Kingdom can see the crown Princess marry. And your sister, too, of course."

That made Jared look uncomfortable. "Oh, crap. You're talking millions of people. Talbot will love that."

"Indeed. Hundreds of millions, at a minimum. Likely billions. Oh, and since the heir to the Imperial Throne is going to be there with you, I'll assume that the viewership in the Empire will be quite high. You'll want to look your best."

Zia imagined it would be far higher than that if one considered those who would be seeing the ceremony in the years and decades to come.

"Focus, Your Highness," Renaldo said sternly. "A groom makes the bride wait at his peril."

"Truer words," the admiral muttered.

"I need to head out, too, Admiral," Zia said as she headed for the door. "Keep your chin up."

* * *

JARED THOUGHT he looked excessively orange, but they assured him that the bright lights focused on the dais would balance things out. He'd have to trust them on that one.

Renaldo had him dress and made a few last-minute tweaks before pronouncing himself moderately satisfied. "This is good enough for the ceremony. I will see that other suits are made to match it, but I'll take my time to be certain they will last longer."

"You mean this will fall apart?"

"No, Highness," the man said with exaggerated patience. "Only that the seams are rushed. It won't last as long as a bespoke suit should. Before you profane this room with the declaration that you can just have more made, I'll remind you that quantity does not make up for quality, no matter what the old saying says.

"Imagine taking one of your new ships up against a group of Fleet's current ships of the line. Quality counts for even more in my line of work."

Jared didn't know enough to argue the point, so he shut his mouth.

The older man gave him one last walk-around. "I believe you'll do, Highness, and just in time. I believe I hear your keepers coming."

The door opened, and Jared saw Royal Guards outside. "Your car is ready, Highness," one of them said.

They rushed him through the halls and out to the landing pad. A classic-looking air limo awaited. Standing beside it was Talbot, looking sharp in a suit very much like the one Jared wore. He still managed to look slightly rumpled, but the small man beside him was still working on that.

"Thank God," the marine said. "I can't get this guy to leave me alone, and they insisted on making me look like a clown."

"No one is going to make you look like a clown, Talbot. Did they tell you why we're wearing makeup?"

The small man shook his head vigorously, just out of Talbot's range of vision.

"No," Talbot said. "Why?"

"The lights," Jared said as he climbed in. "It's bright in the Royal Cathedral."

"Oh. That makes sense, I suppose. Do you think the ladies are ready?"

Jared laughed. "Not a chance. If we're being rushed, they're in even worse shape. They'll want to have every detail nailed down. Nervous?"

Talbot climbed in beside Jared, and the car took off. "Not as much as I'd have thought. This really isn't in the same league as someone trying to kill you. It's only a wedding."

Jared smiled knowingly. Oh, this was going to be good. It might even distract him from the butterflies in his own stomach.

* * *

ANNETTE RUBBED HER EYES TIREDLY. She and Brandon Levy had been working over the data Carl Owlet had recovered from the freighter for what seemed like hours. A check of her chronometer told her that was accurate.

It also told her that they needed to wrap things up and get onto the cutters if they were going to make it to the wedding on time.

"We need to finish," she said. "I think we've looked at every bit of scanner recording they had."

"It wasn't much," the man grumbled. "Just the approach scanners. We don't know anything about the orbital or its defenses. Much less the warships they might have guarding the place. If it was me, I'd have a base to go along with my secret facilities."

She nodded. "Me, too. Judging by the number of ships we saw at Erorsi, I'm betting they brought a lot of that protective force to act as the attackers in our little drama. Did you get anything out of your prisoner?"

Levy shook his head. "Not really. She's not buying what we're selling, at least not yet. From what I've heard, it took Commander Richards a while to come around, and he had the benefit of being an amateur historian.

"Veronica Giguere isn't one to think about the past, it seems. She's one of those Fleet officers that lives and breathes her work."

"Considering some of the stuff that Princess Kelsey found in the other destroyer commander's cabin, that sounds like a point in Giguere's favor. She's not a social climber?"

"Not based on anything we've found. We broke into her safe, but she'd already destroyed the contents. Her bedroom is reassuringly normal, though."

The first destroyer captain's bedroom had looked like a bordello, based on some of the images that Annette had seen. Her office walls had any number of pictures showing the officer with civilian notables, and she'd had more blackmail material than a dedicated criminal.

Based on what she'd heard from people knowledgeable about Harrison's World, Annette was pretty sure that was the rule rather than the exception. Social climbing was a contact sport in the Rebel Empire.

"Has anyone on the freighter crew started talking?" she asked. "What was their plan?"

"Get into orbit and blast the lake where the crazy computer's ship was. They had no way of knowing it was already done for.

"They didn't expect to have any trouble, but they brought along enough Raider implants to show the goods if required. All in all, they expected a walk in the park. The Fleet personnel were there to fire the weapon and keep the crew of the freighter in line."

"Were they expecting trouble from their own civilians?"

He shrugged. "It doesn't sound like it. More that they have some kind of institutional objection to allowing a weapon of that kind out of their control. Frankly, I sort of agree. A ship with that could kill millions in the blink of an eye."

Levy stood slowly. "We should get dressed and board the cutter. The schedule is already tight."

"Good idea. I'll see you there in a few minutes."

She jogged to her quarters and changed into her dress uniform. Zia had given Annette her old rank tabs, which meant a lot, so she was in good shape.

Thankfully, Fleet's black-and-gold dress uniform made formal events easy. She was sure that Admiral Mertz wished he could just wear his.

Once she was ready, she headed for the landing bay. Brandon Levy was already aboard the cutter, and he had the correct rank tabs.

She had a moment to appreciate how the dress uniform flattered him. The other officer was sharp. It was too bad they were in the same command.

That thought gave her pause. Yes, it had been a while, but was that really where her mind had just gone?

Apparently so. Though, now that she considered it, the idea wasn't a terrible one. For that matter, they weren't technically in the same chain of command, either. They were coequal commanders of the people on board *Audacious*. Neither one in charge of the other, and both reported to the commodore.

Something to ponder, she decided as she watched his eyes. Men thought they were subtle, but she could tell he was admiring the cut of her uniform, too.

"You look good," she said with a smile. "You're not trying to outshine the admiral, are you?"

"Not likely. Maybe Major Talbot. You look great, too."

"Thank you."

The two of them sat among the other senior officers going down for the wedding. Weddings, plural.

Many of her companions were talking about the event, wondering how grand the pomp and circumstance would be.

She'd already decided it would be a powerful affair, filled with symbolism and emotion. She'd cry, of course. She'd brought more than enough tissues.

Rather than focusing on the wedding, she immersed herself in plotting out their attack on Dresden with Brandon. No matter how they played it out, they'd need the carrier and its fighters to suppress any hostile response.

The fighters could slip in much closer than any of the other ships except for the *Persephone* and her pinnaces. While the pinnaces were fine scouts, they didn't have what it took to stand off warships.

Almost certainly, the Raider ship would get close and use her pinnaces to get a boarding party onto the orbital. That raiding party would secure the target while the fighters engaged any Rebel Empire ships that might take offense. That would allow the rest of the fleet to get in close.

With that much volatility to the planning, they needed to have primary plans, backups, contingencies, and emergency courses of action all mapped out. They needed to take all possible enemy responses into consideration.

The trip to Pentagar wasn't nearly long enough to do more than outline the general shape of their needs. Once the wedding was over, maybe Brandon and she could find a suitable restaurant to have dinner and keep working.

She gave him an enigmatic smile. Oh, yes, that would be very nice indeed.

25

B randon found a relatively empty corner of the Royal Cathedral and continued his review of the data they'd collected and the rough plans they had for using the fighters and the carrier group. The one real engagement they'd fought had left him feeling as though they were headed for a big surprise—and not a pleasant one—if he didn't get his part of the job under control.

The implants were becoming easier to use, though they still surprised him with the things they were capable of doing. For example, his implant computer was advanced enough to run basic simulations of the carrier's performance when he changed a few parameters of how the ship entered the scenario.

That allowed him to propose certain procedural changes and see if they looked like they might generate better results. That in turn suggested changes to the training that he might implement.

"Are you going to hide here much longer?" a voice asked from the doorway. "You'll miss the ceremony if you dawdle much longer."

It was the freshly promoted Commander Jake Fiennes, the new commanding officer of Black Jack Squadron. Annette Vitter's former deputy.

"How did you even find me?" Brandon asked as he shut down the simulation and stepped out.

"Implants are great things. Annette told me to make sure you didn't wander off too far, so I had mine tell me where yours were."

That had been sneaky. It suggested that he might be able to run a few shipboard drills and see if he could find better paths people might take during drills. Or even use them during hostile boardings.

He firmly put the thought away. "There's a wedding on. Why is she keeping track of me?"

The other man shrugged. "That's just how she rolls. She's always been great at keeping all the little details straight when things get complicated. Like in the middle of a dogfight. Attention to detail is a very good trait for a pilot or someone who commands them."

Brandon considered that and nodded. "That makes a lot of sense."

"And I think she might like you."

"I hope so. We're going to be working very closely for a while."

The other man stopped and considered him for a long moment.

"What?" Brandon asked.

"I'm not sure if you're joking or not. I mean I think she *likes* you."

The less-than-subtle emphasis on "likes" finally did it for him. "That's quite a jump to make, don't you think? It's also something that regulations frown upon."

"Do they? I thought you were co-commanders. Did I misunderstand?"

"We work on the same ship. It would be inappropriate. Even if it wasn't, how could you possibly think that? I barely know the woman."

The other man shook his head. "Being attracted to someone doesn't require you hop right into bed, sir. Annette has had a rough year. After the crash where she lost her arm, she thought her life was over.

"Things are looking up now, but she's a senior officer. Fraternization rules exist for good reason, so she's been in a tight shell. It's good to see her at least contemplating a relationship."

The man gave Brandon a steady look. "I should mention that the pilots would be really unhappy if something happened to hurt her. We all worship her. In case no one ever told you, fighter pilots can be rash and more than a bit impulsive. I trust you see that could have serious repercussions."

Brandon could only imagine what that might mean, but it didn't sound good.

He shook his head. "I'm not going to hurt anyone. You're talking a hypothetical situation. One that you probably misread. I appreciate you having the talk with me, but this isn't what you think it is."

"Copy that, sir. Well, the ceremony is about to get under way. You might want to find your seat. I'd imagine it's going to be quite the spectacle."

Brandon followed the other man into the main chapel. He'd spent a good bit of time examining its gorgeous construction and adornment earlier, but now his attention was inward.

Was Fiennes right? Surely not. He'd met Annette less than a week ago, and under less-than-pleasant circumstances. He'd righted his course, but he'd no doubt made a less-than-positive impression on her.

He knew what the other man was talking about, though. The loneliness of command was something all senior officers dealt with. Any less-than-professional encounters with the fairer sex happened on leave.

Annette would have been one pilot among many aboard the destroyer *Athena*. There'd been plenty of people not in her chain of command to see, if that's what she'd wanted.

He imagined her injury kept her emotionally isolated, and then they'd promoted her to command of the fighters. As a commander, her rank would've kept everyone else at arm's length, even though she wasn't technically in charge of the ship's personnel.

According to the regulations, an officer could fraternize—and by that, they meant have a romantic relationship—with people not in his own chain of command that were within two grades of him.

For himself, that meant fighter pilots at the rank of lieutenant commander and above. For her, ship's personnel with similar rank. Definitely not a large pool.

The fighter corps were predominantly male. He wasn't sure why. Perhaps temperament.

For Annette's part, she had a somewhat larger pool, since Fleet as a whole was fairly well balanced when it came to the sexes. Maybe a dozen officers of the appropriate rank.

Why was he even thinking about this? Her sex life was none of his damned business. Jake Fiennes was wrong. Even if he wasn't, now was not the time to be thinking about it. He had a wedding to attend.

He was looking for a seat when he saw Annette wave. She had one next to her open. Considering the crowd, that wasn't happenstance.

Brandon sat beside her. "Thanks for sending Fiennes after me. I lost track of time."

She smiled. "You tend to be a little focused, so I figured it was better to be safe."

The train of thought the other man had started in Brandon's mind had him examining Annette in a new light. He'd known she was pretty, but now he was seeing her as if for the first time. It was a bit disconcerting how attractive he found her.

It was a good thing there really wasn't anything to worry about.

* * *

KELSEY PACED the dressing room they'd put her in at the back of the Royal Cathedral. By some miracle, her wedding dress had arrived on time, and it fit perfectly. It was just as gorgeous as she'd hoped it would be.

The wedding cake was running late, and God only knew what other problems were cropping up. Things she needed to deal with but had no idea were going on because the Royal majordomo wouldn't tell her anything. The woman seemed to believe that not knowing made things easier for Kelsey.

"You need to take a deep breath and stop wearing a path in the carpet," Elise advised her.

Kelsey came to a stop and took several deep breaths. It felt as though she was hyperventilating. "How can you be so calm?"

The crown princess of Pentagar smiled and held out a flute of champagne. "Be careful sipping that. No spills."

The champagne was cold and delicious. Kelsey resisted the urge to gulp it.

"I'm not worried because we have the most capable people imaginable nailing down all the details. They don't need you trying to 'fix' things. You'll only make their jobs harder.

"Tell me, in a fight, do you run around and make sure everyone else is shooting what you want? If you are, you really need to stop. Micromanagement is an obstacle to be overcome rather than a method to command. Do you really think our extremely capable majordomo is going to drop the ball?"

Kelsey sagged a little. "Not really. I just feel helpless. I need to get my hands on the controls."

"No, you *want* to get your hands on the controls. That doesn't mean you'd be a better driver, only that the car was more likely to crash when the two of you struggle over the direction. Sit down and let them do their magic."

That wasn't easy, but Kelsey managed to sit. "Are we making a mistake rushing this? We could've waited until after we got back from this mission."

"That presupposes that you all come back," Elise said grimly. "You'll remember where Talbot inherited his title."

Kelsey couldn't help but remember Timothy Reese's death. He'd been talking on the radio when one of the AI-controlled machines had obliterated him with a plasma rifle. There hadn't even been a body to bury. One moment he was in command of the attack, the next he was only a memory.

As capable as she was, that could all too easily happen to her. Yes, her armor was a lot tougher than what Reese had been wearing, but nothing was invulnerable. Either she or Talbot could die, even if they did everything right. The same went for Jared.

"That's not exactly the cheerful prewedding pep talk I was expecting," Kelsey groused. "But you do have a point. Yes, we shouldn't wait, but I don't want to screw everything up by springing the ambush too soon, since we're going with military metaphors."

Elise laughed. "Don't worry over every little thing. Focus on what you need to do and let our team handle everything else. Even if something goes a little differently than planned, no one in the audience will notice. They'll be watching the four of us. As long as we don't throw up on the minister, we'll be fine."

Kelsey smiled a little at that. "I think I'll manage to avoid that. I just hate waiting."

The door opened, and the majordomo appeared. "Highnesses, we are ready to proceed to the chapel. Princess Elise will go first, with you waiting for my signal to proceed, Princess Kelsey."

"I feel badly about bumping you from the primary spot in your wedding," Elise said.

Kelsey waved the concern away. "This is your world. It's only right for you to be the focus. Besides, we'll reverse things when we get back to Avalon."

"We're having two weddings?"

She nodded. "While this one is legally binding, it's not fair to deny my people the chance to celebrate this with me. It also wouldn't be fair to Jared's mother. A second one wouldn't hurt for you, either."

"Highnesses," the majordomo prompted.

The ladies-in-waiting that the other woman had found for them gathered around, but there was a disturbance at the lift down the hall. A number of familiar female faces were putting in a belated appearance.

"Thank God," Kelsey said. "I thought you weren't going to make it."

"Sorry we're late," Lily Stone said. "Getting the dresses at the last moment was a little harder than we'd expected."

"She means *me* getting the dress in *my* size was the problem," Major Angela Ellis said. "We should've stuck to dress uniforms."

The marine officer was over two meters tall and endowed to the same heroic scale. Kelsey imagined fitting the woman had been a nightmare. At least Kelsey could start with a child's gown.

Zia Anderson shook her head. "You should've seen the seamstress running around in a panic. I almost had to slap her to get her to come out of it."

Elise laughed. "Wouldn't *that* have been a sight?"

Kelsey pulled them all into a hug. "I'm so glad to see you. Now, we have to go. We're already late."

"I beg to differ," Elise said. "A bride is never late to the wedding. She's always precisely on time."

"We'll see if the grooms think so."

It took another minute to get the party back into order, and then they took the corridor beside the lift. It would deliver them to the rear of the cathedral without any of the guests seeing them.

Once behind the ornate doors, Kelsey could hear the murmuring of the crowd and the soft organ music.

The majordomo cleared her throat. "Once I open the door, the bridesmaids will proceed to the dais. Their Highnesses will follow them, Crown Princess Elise in the lead. Once Her Highness reaches the dais, Princess Kelsey will begin."

"Where's my father?" Elise asked.

"Right here," he said, stepping in the front door. "I was merely getting your escape vehicle ready."

He beamed at his daughter before pulling her into his arms. "You look radiant."

"You're going to make me cry," Elise protested as she held him.

"It's your wedding. You're supposed to cry."

"I will not cry before I even see him," she said firmly.

The king turned to Kelsey. "As your father cannot be here, I shall act in his stead. Once I walk Elise to the dais, I shall come back for you."

"It's time," the majordomo said firmly.

* * *

JARED STOOD ON THE DAIS, watching the back of the church with a mixture of anticipation and worry. The crowd was much larger than he'd anticipated, and the lights were just as bright as the tailor had warned him they would be. The floating holocameras were no doubt sending the images out to everyone on the planet and recording them for transmission to the Empire.

Talbot hadn't figured that out, so he wasn't going to enlighten the man.

They had a number of comrades behind them in support: Charlie Graves, Dennis Baxter, Carl Owlet, and Pasco Ramirez. He'd have loved to have more people, but there just wasn't space.

The organ picked up into the wedding march, and his stomach lurched. The ceremony was beginning.

The doors to the rear of the cathedral opened, and the bridesmaids began streaming in. He smiled at them. It was more reassuring than he'd expected to have people he knew in the lead.

Then he saw Elise, and nothing else mattered. She came down the aisle on her father's arm with a smile only for him. She was the most beautiful thing he'd ever seen. It took all his willpower not to take her hands when she stood in front of him.

The king returned to the rear of the cathedral and brought Kelsey out. He heard Talbot's breath catch. She looked like a bright pixie in her small white dress.

Once she stood beside Elise, the minister stepped forward and smiled. "Marriage is a sacred bond that brings two people who love one another even closer," he said. "But in some cases, it is also a matter of state where it involves more than family or friends.

"Today is one such circumstance. We will see our crown princess wed to a hero from legend. This marriage will bring our people closer together, yet this ceremony is only a reflection of the love and commitment they already have for one another."

The man paused, allowing his words to sink in. "I could go on and on about what that means, but I think it's far more appropriate that they say what they truly feel to one another. Jared Mertz, why don't you go first?"

Jared reached out and took Elise's hands in his. "The first time I saw you, I realized how special you were, but I never expected that we would have a future together. The gulf between us was too vast. Me, a lowly officer born on the wrong side of the sheets, and you a powerful noblewoman who would one day lead your people.

"And then you showed me that the space between us was all in my mind. That together we could overcome every obstacle. Even those we erected ourselves."

He gazed into her eyes for a long moment, enjoying the wide smile on her face. "While I don't feel worthy of many of the rewards heaped up me, I'll accept them if that's what it takes to be your husband. I love you with all my heart and pledge my life to making you happy. Even if this inconvenient war gets in the way."

A low rumble of laughter ran through the hall.

"Well," she said with a twinkle in her eye, "that might be the understatement of the year. Let me make one thing clear. I would walk away from every one of my titles without the slightest hesitation if that were what it took to make you mine.

"I'm glad neither of us has to do that, but between us there is no gulf. You will be my husband and I your wife. Crown princess and prince consort are simply labels that others apply to us, not who we are. I am Elise Orison, the woman who loves you madly. You are Jared Mertz, the man who makes me complete."

She looked at the minister. "It is time. Make me an honest woman."

The crowd did laugh at that, and the minister smiled. "You're already an honest woman, Highness. I'm just here to make it official."

He looked at Jared. "Do you, Jared Mertz, take Elise Orison as your lawfully wedded wife? To have and to hold, forsaking all others for the remainder of your days?"

Jared's throat tightened. "I do."

The minister turned to Elise. "Do you, Elise Orison, take Jared Mertz as your lawfully wedded husband? To have and to hold, forsaking all others for the remainder of your days?"

Her smile took on a hint of triumph. "I do."

The minister raised his arms and stepped back "Then I take great pleasure sealing this eternal bond between you. My lords and ladies, I present to you, Elise Orison and Jared Mertz, your crown princess and her husband."

The crowd erupted into cheers, but Jared only had eyes for Elise. His wife.

He reached for her, but she was already pulling him tightly into her embrace, kissing him soundly.

"You're mine forever," she said fiercely. "Thank God."

Jared laughed and kissed her back, only stopping when someone cleared his throat. A glance up showed his father-in-law standing where the minister had just been.

"I'm very sorry to interrupt this tender moment, but you're not quite done, Prince Jared. There remains one more ceremony to be completed, and we'd best move along sprightly, because your sister is impatiently waiting."

Kelsey laughed and tapped her foot.

"Now, this is complicated by the fact you aren't a citizen of Pentagar, other than by marriage, of course," the king said, "but I've been in communication with your father about the matter, and we've come up with a solution.

"You are a serving Imperial Fleet officer, and your oaths to the Empire are sacrosanct. The oath I shall now require of you will take that into consideration and fall second to it. Is that acceptable?"

Jared nodded. "It is."

"Kneel."

Once Jared had sunk to his knees, Raymond Orison stared sternly down at him. "I won't lecture you on taking care of my daughter, because she can take care of herself. What I will say is that you displease her at your peril. I've had a nice cell set aside in the dungeon if you err too grievously."

Jared mostly restrained his smile. "I wouldn't dream of displeasing her."

"Excellent. Now, as king of Pentagar, I require the oath of prince consort from you, as modified by negotiation with the Terran Emperor, your liege. With the exception of your oaths to the Terran Empire and to the Imperial Fleet, do you, Prince of the Blood Jared Mertz, swear to stand firm beside the crown princess of the Kingdom of Pentagar, helping her to rule it when that time comes?"

"I do."

The king smiled. "Then rise, prince consort of Pentagar."

The crowd began chanting something, but Jared couldn't hear it clearly. Raymond pulled him into a ferocious hug. "It's so good to have you as part of my family. I know you'll make my daughter very happy."

"Thank you."

"Excuse me," Elise said, "but if you're finished, my good friend Kelsey is less than patiently waiting her turn."

Jared risked his sister's wrath by kissing his wife once more before stepping back to his place. Now it was time for her moment in the sun, and he couldn't wait for her and Talbot to take their vows.

26

Kelsey was happy for Jared and Elise but could barely restrain herself. It was her turn, dammit.

The minister took the king's place. "Now we come before you to wed the heir to the Terran Empire. At the risk of going at this ceremony backwards, I call upon Princess Kelsey to go first."

Her eyes were swimming in unshed tears, but she had a tissue handy. She dried her eyes and then took Talbot's hands in hers.

"Russ, when I first met you, I was a pampered little noble girl. She's still in here somewhere, but you didn't let the social gulf stand between us, and you became my friend. Then when my world came apart, you stood beside me, shouting defiance in the face of death, and worse. A more steadfast, caring man is impossible for me to imagine.

"Inside that blunt shell is a heart as big as the universe. I found myself loving you but unsure of how to say the words. Then you showed me that words could sometimes get in the way. We are made for one another, and I pity anyone that tries to come between us. I cannot wait for you to be mine forever."

Talbot didn't wait for the minister to speak before he started.

"I'm a blunt-spoken man, so forgive me if I don't have any flowery phrases at the tip of my tongue. I never expected to have someone like you in my life. Hell, I never expected to find someone as strong inside as you. Someone I could love without restraint.

"I only thought I was self-sufficient. I never realized something was missing from my life, but you've made me whole. With you at my side, I'm not afraid of what the future might bring. Together, we can do anything we choose. I love you and want you to be my wife."

She looked at the minister. "We're waiting."

He laughed. "Then allow me to speedily move things along. Kelsey Bandar, do you take Russel Talbot as your lawfully wedded husband? To have and to hold, forsaking all others for the remainder of your days?"

"Hell yes."

The crowd rumbled with laughter and the minister gave her a look of mock disapproval. "We try not to bring hell into the wedding ceremonies, but I'll accept that."

He turned to Talbot. "Russel Talbot, do you take Kelsey Bandar as your lawfully wedded wife? To have and to hold, forsaking all others for the remainder of your days?"

He smiled down at her.

"Hell yes."

"Then it gives me great pleasure to seal this eternal bond between you. My lords and ladies, I present to you Crown Princess Kelsey Bandar of the Terran Empire and her husband, Russel Talbot."

She pulled Talbot down into a kiss that she hoped would make everyone blush. He was her willing coconspirator.

Once she had to come up for air, she coughed. "That was very nice, but now it's my turn to swear you to an oath. Russel Talbot, I now speak with the voice of the Emperor, your liege. He wishes he were here to do this in person, as do I, but he will have that pleasure soon enough. Kneel."

Once he settled to his knees, his face was almost level with hers. He was actually still taller. She reached out and nudged his head down a little, to the delight of the crowd.

"Russel Talbot, do you swear to stand with the heir of the Terran

Empire and to support her rule when she ascends to the Imperial Throne?"

"I do," he rumbled.

"Then I name you prince consort of the Terran Empire. Let no one stand between you and your duty to me and the Empire. Rise, Your Highness."

Raymond Orison stepped forward as Talbot stood, facing the crowd. "Normally, there would be round-the-clock celebration, as well as even more pomp and circumstance, but matters of state press close.

"The newlyweds will have scant time to celebrate, so I declare tonight as theirs alone. Come morning, Prince Consort Jared leads a strike deep into the heart of the Rebel Empire. We'll just have to celebrate without them."

He turned to the wedding party. "I have two vehicles out back. I've taken the liberty of arranging some secure and discreet lodgings for the evening. Once you return from your mission, it will give me great pleasure to host your long and well-deserved honeymoons. Is that acceptable?"

Talbot swept Kelsey off her feet with a whoop. "Why are we still standing here?"

She laughed as he threw her over his shoulder and charged for the indicated exit. Kelsey vowed to have her revenge by carrying him across the threshold when they got there.

* * *

ZIA LAUGHED as Talbot carried the princess out, and Jared more sedately escorted his bride away. Those couples would be just fine, no matter what the universe threw at them.

She, on the other hand, had a ton of work to do. In his absence, she and the newly promoted vice commander of the mission— Commodore Charlie Graves—had a lot of work to do if they were going to get out of here on schedule.

Graves was still aboard *Courageous*, but now it was his flagship. Captain Pasco Ramirez was his new flag captain.

Captains Levy and Vitter would see the carrier group arranged.

She had to focus on helping Charlie get the rest of the ships into order.

He stepped over to her as soon as the crowd began dispersing. "Let's take my cutter up to *Invincible*. We can see what Carl managed to pull out of the computer cores and get a general order of battle arranged."

"Sounds good, but I need to change first. I'm starving, and there is no way I'm going to eat in this dress. It must cost a year's salary. I'd undoubtedly spill something on it."

He glanced down at his own suit. "Good point. Meet me at the cutter in an hour."

Zia retired to the changing room the bridesmaids had used to get ready and quickly got back into her duty uniform. She found a car waiting for her when she was ready, and it speedily took her to the spaceport.

Charlie Graves was already on the cutter, so they departed immediately.

"I took the liberty of getting you something from a deli we drove past. I seem to recall you have a special place in your heart for meatball subs."

"You are a god."

"That's what they tell me," he said with a roguish grin.

She took the bag from him, spread her food out on the folding tray on the back of the seat in front of her, and dug in. The meatballs were scrumptious, though a tad messy. Changing had been a wise decision.

Once she'd taken the edge off her hunger, she focused on Graves. "Last I heard, Carl had dug out some hard details from the freighter cores but nothing from any of the recovered military computers. Has that changed?"

He shook his head. "Not to the best of my knowledge, but hope springs eternal. At least we have an idea of where we're going. Dresden isn't very populous, I understand.

"I've gone over the possible entry points to the Dresden system. It has three flip points. One leads to a heavily populated system, one to a more lightly occupied one, and one to an empty one. The last one would be best, but we can't get to it without cutting through some systems we'd prefer to avoid."

She nodded. "So we have two possibilities."

"Right. We'd take six flips by the closest route and eight by the other. I figure we're talking adding a few days to a week to get there. The second route has the more sparsely populated system."

Zia brought up the two routes on her implants. "Being less direct might be more advantageous for us. Once we're done, they won't have the force to stop us from getting back to Erorsi."

He nodded slowly. "The one system in question isn't heavily traveled. We could come in on one side and take a longer curve above the plane of the ecliptic to the final flip point. It adds another day but reduces the opportunity for detection."

That made sense, so she nodded. "We can have *Persephone* scouting the way in front of us. If she runs into anything problematic, she'll have enough firepower to shut them up, and they're unlikely to be spotted."

"Exactly," he agreed. "We'll follow up with the smaller ships and take the big ships last as a group. We can keep our acceleration down to a reasonable level and never tip the people we're sliding by.

"One thing we need to consider is communications. Do we seed FTL coms in the systems between us and Erorsi?"

Zia frowned as she considered that. Not being able to communicate had bitten them hard, but they absolutely could not afford to allow the technology to fall into Rebel Empire hands.

"Maybe if Carl can design self-destruct charges for them. If we seed them in the outer part of each system, we can leave them there. Are we certain that they'll work as relays? I didn't think Carl had all the bugs worked out."

"I don't know. We're almost to *Invincible*, so let's go ask him."

She threw away her trash and secured her tray. The cutter docked, and she followed Charlie onto the superdreadnought.

"Welcome aboard, Commodores," Marcus said. "I've been expecting you. Allow me to say that the wedding was an interesting ceremony."

Graves grinned. "That it was. You can pester Jared with questions about it when he comes up in the morning. Assuming, of course, that he can string comprehensible sentences together."

"I'm quite certain that he will be more than able to do so," the AI said primly. "Sir Carl is waiting for you in his lab."

The two of them made their way there and walked in to find the young scientist hunched over a wide screen, typing quickly.

He glanced up at them and then returned his attention to the screens. "Hang on a second. I'm almost ready."

Zia looked around his lab with interest. She hadn't had much opportunity to drop by when she'd been assigned to the same ship as him. It was bigger than she'd imagined and filled with other people in lab coats doing various tasks.

It took more like five minutes for Carl to wrap up what he was doing, but they waited patiently. When the young man finished, he stood and stretched.

"Sorry about that, but I'm looking for hidden or deleted files. People think they've gotten rid of something important, but you can often dig it back up if you know how to look."

"What are you hoping to find?" Charlie asked.

"There are no close-approach scanner readings. I'd like to have a better idea of what the station looks like. That might narrow our search for the manufacturing area when the time comes to board. I'd imagine saving hours is a good thing."

Zia could certainly agree with that.

"What about the military computers?" she asked. "Any luck?"

He shook his head. "No. We might still get in, but I wouldn't count on it. We're just going to have to use the data I've pulled out of the freighter."

Charlie looked around the lab. "What about the FTL coms? Have you figured out how to link them together so we can talk over multisystem distances?"

The young man waggled a hand. "Yes and no. The process of handing off the com signal isn't perfect. Not yet. It might work all the way, or it might become garbled. I haven't experimented with that yet. I'd say we can use it so long as we don't count on it working when we get too far away."

"What about self-destruct charges?" Zia asked. "We can't afford for the Rebel Empire to get their hands on this technology."

"That I can do," the young man said. "A probe will have several methods to kill it. First, we can just tell it to blow up. The charge is miniscule, so unless someone is right on top of it, they'll never know. Second, if a ship not transmitting the appropriate codes approaches, it can be made to kill itself. Lastly, we can set a timer. If the time period expires without someone countermanding the order, it will end it all."

Charlie smiled. "That sounds good. Do you have the people to get a dozen of them constructed?"

The young man nodded. "I've been working with Captain Baxter. He's got me covered. I can have a few ready by tomorrow. The rest will take a day or two."

"That's perfect."

"What about ship-to-ship FTL?" she asked. "That would've been helpful during the last fight."

Carl nodded. "I imagine so. Those are easier, since they're just direct links. I gave the few I had on hand to Princess Kelsey and can build more on the way. Certainly enough for all lead elements in the fleet."

"Excellent," she said. "Have you spoken with Angela after the wedding?"

He shook his head. "She's on her way to *Persephone*. I'll head that way once I finish the file search. Why?"

Zia smiled slyly. "Weddings do funny things to women. Expect the unexpected."

The two men frowned at her.

"What does that even mean?" Charlie asked.

"Let's just say that I'll bet she has her own future in her mind tonight. She seems like a direct kind of woman. She might just propose."

Carl paled. "Jesus."

She laughed and headed for the hatch. "Tell her I have a dress, just in case she needs a maid of honor."

27

Brandon roused, unsure of what had woken him. He lay in the dark of his bed, listening. Had something changed in the normal sounds the ship made? Not that he could tell.

That's when he heard it. The soft sound of someone else breathing in the room. No, in his bed.

Oh, crap.

The memory of the evening came flooding back. The late dinner with Annette, his growing attraction to her, and her determined seduction. One he had to admit he had aided and abetted.

Now, outside of the heat of the moment—and it had been hot—he wondered if he'd made the wrong choice.

Almost at once, he rejected that thought. It had been the right choice. Whether things worked out in the long term or not, allowing himself to care—to desire—wasn't a mistake.

He had no idea what she might feel like now. Had she been looking for a night of passion or something more? Brandon had no idea.

No matter what happened, they had to work together, so he wouldn't be a jackass.

She rolled over and pressed against him. That completely disrupted everything he'd been thinking about.

"Are you awake?" she asked sleepily. "It's early."

"I just woke up."

After a moment, she sat up a little. "And you're worried."

That hadn't been a question. "Maybe a little. I thoroughly enjoyed what happened, but I don't know what you want long term. Hell, I don't know what I want."

She turned the light on, and he realized he wasn't in his room. They were in *her* bed.

"Then I suggest you don't panic," she said with a smile. "I hadn't planned on this, either, but I'm open to the possibilities. We're both professionals. We can—and will—keep our heads about us. If things work out, I'll be thrilled. If they don't, I'll be sad. In either case, we'll be okay as long as we don't overthink this."

That was a little more cool-headed than he'd expected. It was also somewhat disconcerting.

Annette rose from the bed and headed for the bathroom. "It's almost time for breakfast. You can either join me in the shower or skulk back to your place." She glanced back at him from the doorway with a smile. "I'd prefer it if you joined me."

The view from where he lay was stunning, so there was really only one choice. "We might be late for breakfast."

"I can snack on the run."

Brandon rose to his feet and trailed after her.

* * *

Saying goodbye to Elise had been the hardest thing Jared had ever done. One night alone wasn't nearly enough, but he couldn't delay. Events were moving faster than he'd like, and he couldn't afford to let the Rebel Empire pin them down.

This was a lot different from the reconnaissance that Admiral Yeats had envisioned. He'd reported the most recent events, and the admiral had endorsed his new plan.

This morning, once he'd finally torn himself away from his wife, he'd found a new message from the admiral waiting for him. Well, one of many. Everyone he knew—and more than a few he didn't—had sent some form of congratulations.

He'd eventually have time to go through them all, but today he only had time to focus on the most pressing. Since the most recent message from Admiral Yeats might be part business, he played it first. He managed to wait until he was on his cutter and on the way back to *Invincible*.

The vid was of Yeats at his desk, so business just became a lot more possible.

"Jared, let me start off by extending my most profound congratulations. Princess Elise seems like a wonderful woman and a great partner for you. I wish you many, many years of happiness together. I suppose with nanites, that might even extend to centuries."

Jared hadn't considered that, but the thought made him smile. That would be terrific.

"I wish that were all that was on your plate," the admiral continued. "Unfortunately, it's not. No matter how you cut it, you're about to make the Rebel Empire very much aware of our existence. The missing fleet would do that, too, but they can't possibly miss your ships when you get to the Dresden system.

"Luckily, Erorsi and Pentagar are in an isolated cul-de-sac to the best of the Rebel Empire's knowledge. They'll know something happened but be unable to get through the flip-point jammer.

"They won't understand the technology any better than we do, but they will think their problems are isolated. Thankfully, the FTL coms will allow you to close the flip point once you leave and then signal for admittance when you return."

Jared had been considering that very thing before he'd found out the wedding was last night. The FTL coms gave them an incredible advantage over their enemies. He needed to have more brainstorming to figure out how to best utilize them.

"In any case, I'm giving you full authority to do whatever you feel best. Work with Princess Kelsey to be sure she thinks any strategic decisions are the correct ones.

"This is going to be hard, no matter what happens, but I'm

counting on you and the princess to at least give us a shot at ultimately winning. Good luck, and I'll see you when you get back."

The vid ended.

The next message was from his father. Unlike the admiral, the emperor was seated on a comfortable chair and not in any kind of official garb.

He smiled widely. "Jared, I just finished watching the ceremony. Elise looked radiant, and I'm so happy for you both. I wish I could have been there, but I take solace in the fact that I'll get to do so when we repeat the ceremony here.

"I wish you had all the time in the world to luxuriate in your bliss, but I know you'll be departing shortly. Just don't let your duty keep you from enjoying the fruits of joy that life sends your way. Once they pass, it's a rare thing to have a second chance."

"But not unheard of."

That hadn't been the emperor.

His mother sat down beside his father, her eyes shining with tears of joy. "I am so thrilled for you, Jared. You deserve to be happy. I so wish I could've been there, but I understand the press of time."

Her expression grew fierce. "Don't think that means I won't have my hands all over your wedding when you come back to Avalon. I'm your mother, and I will have my moment in the sun. I realize Elise doesn't have her mother still with her, so I've already spoken with her. She has given me permission to meddle to my heart's content. And I will."

Karl Bandar nodded. "I wouldn't try to fight this if I were you. Your mother is a very determined woman."

Jared knew that for a fact. What he was learning, however, was that things had changed back on Avalon.

It didn't take a genius to see their body language. The fact they were sending this message together was also telling. The emperor and his mother were exploring a renewed relationship of their own.

A year ago, he'd have been aghast, but now he found himself nodding in approval. They'd made a mistake all those years ago. One that had hurt them both. They'd more than paid the price for their sins. Let them find what happiness they could in this life.

"Well, we know you're very busy, so we'll let you get about it," the emperor said.

"We love you," his mother said. "Be careful and come back safely."

He thought about the message and all its unspoken parts until the cutter docked with *Invincible*. Times had changed, and he approved. Not that things would be easy. It only took one thought about Kelsey's mother to end that pie-in-the-sky view.

Now all he had to do was give them a fighting chance. With the ability to make more Raider implants, they might be able to pull this off. He'd best be about it then.

* * *

KELSEY HATED HAVING to split up from Talbot, but he had his own preparations to take care of on *Invincible*. Not the least of which was getting his initial implants.

The message from her father was sweet and to the point. He seemed genuinely happy for the two of them. Oddly, he also had an air of conspiracy about him. She wondered what surprise he hadn't wanted to mention in advance. He had a terrible poker face.

Ominously, there was no vid from her mother. She was undoubtedly displeased about not being invited, not planning anything, and likely unhappy about her daughter's choice in mates.

Too bad.

If the woman thought Kelsey was going to let her anywhere near her wedding on Avalon, she was sorely mistaken. She might love her mother, but it was hard to feel it right now. Particularly with what she knew.

Of course, that wouldn't stop the woman from making herself an Imperial pain when Kelsey got back to Avalon. Their problems still needed to be settled, but that was for another day.

Angela was waiting for her as soon as she stepped out of the pinnace.

"Did you have fun?" she asked with a sly smile.

"Duh. How are you feeling?"

"The optical implants are still screwing with me, but I'm getting a handle on the auditory ones. The pharmacology unit is what it is."

Kelsey led the way to the lift. "It was just about the reverse for me, and those are the easy parts. Next comes the bone reinforcement and artificial muscles. Those are going to be very hard to learn. Trust me on that."

"I'm glad I have such a knowledgeable teacher, then," the tall woman said seriously. "I've picked up a lot just listening to you and reading the familiarization materials in the computer. Thankfully, I don't have my next session for a week."

"Any word on what our plan of action is?" Kelsey asked as they arrived outside the bridge.

"The fleet pulls out in two hours. We'll make our way by route Bravo, just as I suspected."

Kelsey wasn't surprised the marine had nailed it. She was sharp.

Once Kelsey was behind the captain's console, she checked the ship's readiness. All in the green. Everyone was aboard, too. She'd been the last to arrive.

"Excellent. What is our order of march? We're up front, I assume."

Angela nodded. "We'll scout each system as we go and communicate back via the FTL com. We have links to *Invincible* and *Audacious*. The latter will be backing us up, with the main fleet following them."

Kelsey nodded. "All as expected. Since we're ready, I'd like to pull out early. Signal Jared that we won't go too far."

The other woman smiled. "Already anticipated. We're clear to depart at your discretion."

"Even better. What's the status of stage two implantation for the crew?"

She intended to upgrade everyone on her ship to Raiders as soon as possible. That meant she wanted them all to have the auditory and optical implants and pharmacology units before they arrived at Dresden.

"We've worked our way through about fifteen percent of the

crew," Angela said. "They seem to be tolerating it well. We should be done on schedule."

Kelsey leaned back in her chair. "It's rare for things to go as planned, so I'll luxuriate in that for a bit. Take us to the Erorsi flip point and coordinate with *Audacious*. We're not going to get to Dresden by sitting on our butts."

28

Zia watched the scanner feed with more than a hint of dread. The last few weeks had almost brought them to their target. Dresden was one flip away, but this system—unlike the others they had traveled through—was occupied. One misstep here and their surprise advantage would vanish.

Admittedly, saying this system was occupied might be something of an overstatement. It had no main world at all, so the population was clustered around several mining hubs in the system's three asteroid belts.

Old Empire records indicated that one of them had been heavily metallic, so there was a lot to recover, even now. Since it wasn't the same as the rest of the system, it had probably been a captured body from deep space.

The belts weren't even close to orderly, so the evidence of the disaster was still writ large for anyone to see. That made travel more dangerous than usual.

Under normal circumstances, that would be relatively minor, but they were restricted to using only passive scanners. That left them open to fast-moving bits of debris that were far too small to see in time.

The relatively empty nature of space meant the likelihood of being struck was small, but it wasn't impossible. That led to the current worry on her part.

The miners were easy to spot by the radio and scanner emissions. So were the ships plying the depths of space between where they worked. All she and the ships with her needed to do was stay far enough out and travel too slowly for them to see.

They'd hoped that the FTL coms they'd deployed behind them would allow for continuous communication with Erorsi, but the new technology wasn't mature enough. Or the process didn't work the way they wanted.

The FTL signals deteriorated with retransmission. Using a repeater to send the signal on to the next hop worked about half the time. Pity. Since they were only copying the data stream and using a different quantum pairing to send the next set of data, it shouldn't matter, yet it did. Carl was going to have to work on that when time permitted.

She turned her attention back to the ship ahead of her. She didn't want to let *Persephone* get too far ahead of them.

"Probe update," one of the flight officers said. "There's something at the flip point, and we have a large ship a few hours short of meeting it."

Zia accessed the scanner readings and examined the problem. The vessel in the flip point looked like a destroyer. The other one was significantly larger. Bigger even than a superdreadnought.

Thankfully, she recognized what it was before her blood pressure spiked. It was a recovery ship, like the AIs had used to move derelicts and captured ships to Harrison's World.

This one wasn't moving a ship, though it did have a cargo of some kind. Probably raw materials from the asteroid belts.

Taking out the destroyer might announce their presence to the miners, but that wasn't necessarily a problem. This system only had two flip points, with one leading back toward Erorsi. They couldn't exactly run and tell anyone else.

"Signal *Persephone* that we'll check them out. If she needs to get moving, I don't want her pinnaces wandering around."

"Copy that."

* * *

ANNETTE LED the flight of fighters escorting the Raider ship herself. Rightly, she should've delegated the duty, but she was their best pilot, and her on-scene evaluation might make a universe of difference.

The recovery ship wasn't scanning the area around them. This far out from the belts, there wouldn't be much debris, but that was careless.

On the military side, the destroyer was scanning on a set interval. Every fifteen minutes, they'd pulse their scanners and get a look around them. If her fighters got too close, the enemy would spot them.

The recovery ship was still far enough away from the flip point to approach, but that could change in a moment if someone got curious over there. Or if the destroyer sent a directional scan at the ship and spotted the fighters.

As they got closer, she saw the recovery ship had a large bundle of ore in its movable arms. They were using it as a glorified freighter.

She supposed it would be good enough at doing something like that. Picking up or dropping a cargo would only take a few minutes.

Annette opened a low-powered directional beam to the Raider ship. "*Persephone*, the recovery ship is carrying unprocessed ore from the mines."

"Copy that. Come back and stand by for instructions."

"Will do."

She changed course and slowly moved back toward the Raider ship.

* * *

PRINCESS KELSEY CONSIDERED THE SITUATION. If they could capture the recovery ship, it might be very useful. It was a known factor on Dresden. It must bring materials in on a regular run. She could use that.

The crew wouldn't be on the lookout for trouble. Not the kind of trouble she was going to cause them, anyway. Still, an assault on the ship was fraught with danger.

If the destroyer saw something, it could flip over and warn Dresden. They would have to deal with it one way or another.

"Angela," Kelsey said after a moment. "I have a very evil thought."

"Why does that fill me with dread?"

"Because you know me. I want you to lead a team over to the recovery ship. I'm thinking a two-stage attack. First, I need you to get there undetected and plant charges all around the habitation section of the hull. I want to decompress it in as short a time as possible without compromising the ship."

The tall woman nodded. "A civilian crew won't be likely to have suits close at hand. If we take the entire ship at once, they'll be forced into rescue balls or die."

Anyone that made it into a rescue ball would be safe but unable to do anything. The balls were meant to allow people to survive a sudden decompression and then wait for rescue from their fellows.

If they hit the entire ship—and it actually held only a very small crew—that would leave no one in a position to help the crewmen except for Kelsey's marines.

"We have to assume that a few people won't get to them or that some fail," Kelsey admitted. "I'm sure things aren't up to maintenance standards in a backwater like this. They've probably never had a problem like this.

"That may or may not stop them from sending a distress signal, but the ship is close enough that the destroyer will see something. If it looks like an accident, they may move out of the flip point to assist the recovery ship. We'll use *Persephone*'s stealth field to get close to the flip point and cut them off."

The marine considered the plan and slowly nodded. "I think we can make that work. It won't be anything they'd expect, in any case."

It took an hour for the marines to get into position. Kelsey used the time to bring *Persephone* around to the other side of the flip point.

The tension was as intense as she'd ever felt while she waited for the strike to happen. So this was what Jared felt like when she was off doing something stupid.

"The charges just went off," one of her people said. "The recovery ship is venting atmosphere and signaling distress."

The destroyer, much to her relief, responded exactly as she'd hoped. It came rushing out of the flip point and raced toward the distressed vessel. Its scanners were active but focused in the wrong direction to see her ship.

"Move us up into the flip point and prepare to shoot down any drones they try to get past us. We'll leave them to Jared."

Once the destroyer was committed and far enough away from the flip point, Jared brought the task force out of hiding by accelerating all units in toward the Rebel Empire warship from every direction. Kelsey switched off her ship's stealth field to make it apparent, too.

The destroyer was outside the flip point, surrounded, and tremendously outgunned. Then the fighters made themselves known, seemingly popping out of nowhere and surrounding the recovery ship in a protective bubble.

She listened to Jared ordering the destroyer to surrender with interest. Would they give up or fight?

In this case, common sense won out, and the ship promptly struck its battle screens. That was a relief, really.

It took another twenty minutes for Angela to clear the recovery ship and report. Her image appeared on the main screen.

"Good news," she told Kelsey. "The crew consists of a dozen people, and we took them all alive."

"Excellent. What's the status of the ship itself?"

"Operational. They didn't have time to lock the computers down. We have everything."

Kelsey smiled. It was about time something went her way. "Get them over here. We'll question them and formulate a plan. I'll call Zia and have her send someone to take over the recovery ship. I have an idea on how we can use it."

"Copy that."

* * *

JARED LISTENED to his sister's plan with more than a hint of misgiving. Once she finished laying it out, he leaned back in his seat.

"I can't begin to tell you how risky that sounds," he said after he considered her for a moment. "The crew we captured from the destroyer isn't talking, but their body language tells me that they aren't too worried about us waltzing over there.

"They have a force to be reckoned with, I think. If you just blithely flip over there, they'll spot you right away. Then they blow you up."

"Maybe," she said with a shrug. "It isn't as though we have much choice, other than going back the way we came. The Rebel Empire is still going to know we were here one way or the other.

"The destroyer didn't send a distress call, but the miners in this system heard the one from the recovery ship. We sent a follow-up canceling it before they came out to investigate, but once the people from Dresden start asking questions, some version of the truth will occur to them. We have to strike now if we ever want to get the ability to make Raider implants."

He shook his head. "We have to know what you'll find on the other side of the flip point. If they have ships right there, you're screwed. We can't risk a probe, either."

She smiled. "Let me work on the crew from the recovery ship while we make preparations to carry out my plan. If you decide it's too dangerous then, we've lost nothing. If you decide we can go, then we'll be ready."

"Admiral Yeats was clear that as the heir, I needed to take your input, as if I wouldn't." He rubbed his face. "How do I ever let you convince me of these things?"

"Because I'm right."

He sighed. "Probably. I still think sending you is more than we should do, but I can already anticipate your reasoning. The manufacturing plant might require your unique Raider implants to access. Sadly, I know you're probably right. I can only hope that isn't the case one day.

"Fine. Go question the crew from the recovery ship. If they give you any reason to think your plan has a chance of success, we'll give it a go. If not, we'll shoot it out with them."

Kelsey shook her head at him. "You know that isn't going to work. If we can't get people into the manufacturing plant before they know about us, they'll be able to destroy everything we came for. If my plan doesn't have a chance of success, we'll consider other options."

She was right, of course. The mission would be part stealth, part misdirection, and all crazy. Just like something from one of the adventure vids.

He ran through the options one last time, but no other possibilities occurred to him.

"Keep me in the loop," he finally said. "Also, if you go, I'm sending Talbot and as many marines as we can stuff into your hull. When the time comes, I want to leave them no chance to fight back."

29

Kelsey entered the room where the prisoners were waiting. Each of the men and women was secured to a table by cuffs, not for her protection but to make a point. They were prisoners, and she was going to have their cooperation, one way or another.

She'd dressed in a Fleet captain's uniform for this little charade, also designed to intimidate. She had two very large and menacing marines at the corners of the room to emphasize the prisoners' precarious position.

"Well," she said with a false tone of cheerfulness, "it seems as though you've gotten yourselves into a spot of trouble, doesn't it? Which one of you is running your little enterprise?"

They stared at one another in obvious confusion. One of the women cleared her throat.

"Excuse me, My Lady, but if you're asking who is in command of *A-8257*, it's me."

Kelsey widened her smile. "Excellent. Then you can explain your little smuggling ring to me."

The woman's jaw dropped. "My Lady? We aren't smuggling anything."

The sound of Kelsey's hand slapping the top of the table made them all flinch.

"Then perhaps you can explain why we've been tracking large quantities of drugs in the raw materials you move to Dresden? Surely you aren't going to pretend ignorance. If so, I may have to become... unpleasant."

She'd really put them into an uncomfortable position. Confessing to and explaining a crime they hadn't committed was going to be awkward at best.

The woman lowered her head. "I don't know who told you that, My Lady, but we aren't smuggling any drugs."

"How tiresome," Kelsey drawled. "Not surprising, though. This isn't going to hurt me a bit. I can't speak for you, though."

"It's just tech, My Lady," one of the men said. "It doesn't hurt anyone."

Kelsey blinked in surprise. Thankfully, the prisoners were mostly focusing unfriendly stares at the man who'd spoken and didn't see her reaction.

She covered her expression of surprise with a sly smile. "I can see how that mistake could have been made. Tell me everything, and I promise you the lightest of the potential sentences. In fact, I may grant the most cooperative of you clemency, but only if you tell me everything I want to know right now."

"The crates don't take up much space," the woman said. "They come in with the supplies on the Dresden side, and we drop them off when we pick up our load. We never see who eventually gets the stuff, but we get paid for every delivery."

"What kind of tech are we talking about?"

The woman shrugged. "They didn't say, and we never asked."

"We'll check it out. If it proves true, and you answer all my questions, your sentences will be much lighter. Tell me about Dresden."

They looked at one another again in confusion.

"They make manufacturing equipment used throughout the sector," the man who'd spoken earlier said. "Nothing of any merit, really. Farm implements, kitchen supplies, that sort of thing."

"I already know all this, but I'm leading to a specific set of questions and checking to see what you actually know," Kelsey said. "Answer as if I know nothing about Dresden. Why the Fleet presence?"

"To keep the Ghosts at bay," the woman said.

Kelsey stopped herself before she could frown. What ghosts? She couldn't look ignorant about something that could be common knowledge, but she wasn't going to fall for a trick, either.

"Are they really that much of a threat?" she asked with a taste of irony in her tone.

"One such as myself has no way of knowing," the woman said, bowing her head. "I am sure they are no threat to Fleet. I apologize for implying otherwise."

"I take no offense," Kelsey assured her. "Tell me more. What precautions are you aware of around Dresden?"

The woman took a deep breath and let it out slowly. "Well, there have been a number of ships disappearing in the sector. The ships here patrol in search of the Ghosts who take them. The guard stations make sure that the Ghosts cannot raid here."

"And has Fleet found any of these Ghosts?"

"I have heard rumors," the woman said hesitantly. "Fleet sometimes corners a Ghost. They say they self-destruct to avoid capture."

That sounded suspiciously like the Fleet ships of old during the rebellion, except those ships just vented their atmosphere.

"They blow up?" she asked carefully.

The woman nodded. "So they say. Rather than fight a superior force, the ships blow themselves up. I suppose that is to keep Fleet from finding their hidden bases."

That wasn't completely surprising, Kelsey supposed. The freighters delivering supplies to the Pale Ones had vanished from time to time, even with escorts. That implied someone working against the Rebel Empire.

They'd all speculated about who that might be but never got any further than a deeply hidden guerrilla force that occasionally struck out at their enemies. Much like what Olivia West and her people had been. Obviously with some warships, but probably not many.

Honestly, this was still as much conjecture as before. Other than the fact that the Rebel Empire version of Fleet took the risk seriously. That implied the attacks were a real problem. One that needed a large number of ships occasionally.

One more mystery to solve when time and circumstances permitted. Right now, she had other fish to fry.

"Tell me about the Fleet disposition you are aware of at Dresden. I want to see if it matches what we want people like you to see."

"There are three flip points, My Lady. Each has a guard station assigned to it. It sits far enough away that no surprise attack will overwhelm it. There are normally a number of ships assigned to it, as well, but the majority of the Fleet presence withdrew a month ago. The remaining ships are out at the unoccupied flip point."

Kelsey brought up a map of the system from the Old Empire records. The two flip points that led to occupied systems were only a few hours apart, but the third was all the way across the system.

"You mean this one?"

The woman nodded. "Yes, My Lady. I can't tell you how many ships or what kind, but there are none left in Dresden orbit or at either of the other two flip points. Just the defensive stations."

"So the station scans your ship from a distance and allows it to proceed? Does the guard destroyer make transit with you?"

The woman shook her head. "No, My Lady. It remains here. The station scans us and then allows us to proceed. When they had ships, they'd occasionally come out for a closer look, but no more than once or twice a year. Now, none."

Kelsey pursed her lips. "Do you know where the Fleet ships went or when they will return?"

"No, My Lady. I assume the ones that left will be back soon enough."

She almost snorted. Wouldn't that be a hell of a bluff? To send in the right kinds of ship and let them assume they were back?

No, that would be far too dangerous. The Fleet units here would know what to expect, and they probably weren't coming out of this system, so they couldn't just waltz in.

What they could do was execute her plan. It would take a few hours to arrange, but it was wickedly clever, even if she did say so herself. With a hint of luck, the guard fortress would never know what they were letting by.

* * *

Zia listened to Princess Kelsey's orders a second time, certain that she must have misheard her. When the message repeated itself exactly as she'd heard it, she took a skeptical breath and called Brandon Levy.

He appeared on her console a moment later.

"Yes, Commodore?"

"I need you to head over to the recovery ship. I'm detaching you to take care of an important special project."

He frowned, as well he should.

"I'm not exactly free to leave my command in someone else's charge. What's going on?"

She pulled her thoughts together. "The princess is going to sneak into Dresden hidden in a load of ore. Don't worry, *Audacious* is going along for the ride, but I need my best commander on that ship while we're under the missiles of the Rebel Fleet guard station."

He opened his mouth to respond but closed it again. After a moment, he finally spoke. "That's quite possibly the craziest plan I've ever heard."

"Welcome to working with Princess Kelsey. There's the right way, the wrong way, and her way. We're doing this her way. Time is short, and I need to have the most experience possible on that ship to give her harebrained scheme a chance of working. That's you."

He shook his head with obvious misgivings. "I'll do my absolute best, Commodore, but I've never done anything remotely like this."

"Me, either. Welcome to the club. We'll have some fighters stashed in the ore, ready to come out fighting. We can't expose either ship enough to have clear missile tubes, so those fighters are all we have.

Annette will be on one of them, and she'll have our best people with her.

"I'll take over for you here, since we won't be able to launch fighters or have other ships along for the ride. Get moving as quickly as you can."

The other officer nodded. "Aye, ma'am. I'll do my best."

"Good luck, Captain."

* * *

ANNETTE THOUGHT this plan was crazy, but it wasn't her call. Releasing the ore, getting the ships inside the arms on the recovery ship, and repacking some of the raw material to conceal the hidden vessels had taken a surprisingly short amount of time.

It seemed like a poor disguise to her. The shape of the ships was right there for anyone to see if they bothered to look.

That's what they were counting on, she supposed. That the Rebel Fleet would scan the recovery ship and its cargo, see what they expected to see, and then wave them on through.

If they didn't, it was up to Annette and her fellow pilots to make sure they kept the bad guys in check until the larger ships could shed their disguises. Under fire, that wouldn't be possible, so she certainly hoped the other side missed what was right in their faces.

There were small pockets in the ore where the fighters could hide. They were small enough to blend in without being covered up and close enough that they could receive short-range transmissions without risk of detection. They'd see the view as relayed by the recovery ship.

Right now, she knew Brandon Levy was ripping out the scanner suite on the ungainly ship. He'd install a better set to improve the readings on the passive scans.

If the enemy spotted their ruse, she had absolute certainty she and the other pilots would die in the ensuing fight. They'd trade their lives so that the bigger ships could get into the fight.

Once her fighter was secure, she put it into standby mode. Unlike a ship, she could get to full power instantly. The lines holding her in place among the ore would snap at the first application of real power.

Half an hour later, the recovery ship moved into the flip point.

The flip was unusual. She'd never been outside the hull during one before, and this created some unusual effects for her. Her vision seemed to cycle through a quick spectrum of color before settling back to normal, and the dizziness was impressive. Thankfully, it faded quickly.

None of that kept her from using her implants to follow the situation along. The recovery ship pulled out of the flip point and headed into the system. The Rebel Fleet battle station was bigger than *Audacious* but farther away than she'd expected.

That was a plus in this case. Their scan felt cursory, and they signaled the ship to proceed.

The princess's crazy plan had worked. They were in.

30

J ared had to force himself not to pace the flag bridge. Such things only made the crew nervous that their commander was worried.

Which he was, but that was beside the point.

They didn't dare use the FTL coms with a known enemy force present. One they couldn't keep quiet if they saw something they shouldn't. That might make them go after Kelsey and the rest.

The silence from Dresden was reassuring. No news was good news. If they'd been flagged, the crap would have already hit the fan, and there'd have been no reason not to call them in.

That was what his forces were arrayed for. They sat in the Dresden flip point ready to flip. If they did, they'd fire every missile they had ready at the battle station to take it out quickly.

Doing so was the worst-case scenario. He'd rather let Kelsey do her thing and call for help when she was ready to leave if she needed it.

Having *Audacious* and her fighter groups along made Kelsey needing help less likely. Their intelligence said there were very few mobile platforms in the Dresden system, and they were all out at flip point number three. Waiting for the Ghosts if the crew of the recovery ship was to be believed.

He supposed it didn't matter what he believed. If they believed there were boogiemen, who was he to argue? That might camouflage this attack.

The basic plan Kelsey had laid out called for them to capture the orbital at Dresden and use the fighters to interdict any hostiles there, as well as any ships that came in from the flip point. It didn't matter what the crew on the battle stations thought was happening.

Kelsey would strip the equipment and supplies off the orbital and come hauling back out to rejoin him. She'd signal him when the time came, and Jared would launch a surprise attack through the flip point at an inconvenient moment.

Of course, nothing ever worked out according to plan, so he could only hope they didn't have to improvise too much.

"Admiral, I have some information that may be useful to you," Marcus said through the speaker in the arm of Jared's chair.

"Go ahead."

"I've been monitoring the prisoners' conversations," the AI said. "They are obviously aware that is likely, so they are being circumspect, but one of them asked a question that has implications on the princess's mission.

"It was the executive officer of the destroyer speaking with the captain. He spoke very softly, but I have excellent hearing. Even over the extra-loud conversation around them, I picked up enough to piece together what was said. Also, reading lips is an excellent skill to add to one's toolbox."

Jared smiled. "And what did they want to keep private?"

"The executive officer asked when 'the ships' were due. The captain told him to shut up and didn't answer, but even the inquiry means that there will be other mobile units to deal with at some as-yet-unknown future point."

He grimaced. "Well, we couldn't expect everything to go our way. Hopefully, he's thinking that the fleet they dispatched to Erorsi will be coming home. That's the most likely thing. Otherwise, they should've already had fresh ships here before they left.

"If not, there isn't exactly anything we can do about it other than be ready to act on a moment's notice. Which is what we're doing anyway."

"Should we warn the princess?"

"No. That would break operational security and not really give her any useable information. If the situation changes, she'll know as soon as we do. Probably sooner, since they're going to send probes out to monitor the other flip points.

"As dissatisfying as it is, we're just going to have to ride this out. Work with the operations staff to come up with some likely scenarios. Make plans to react to various possibilities and get them to me as soon as you can. Chance favors the prepared mind."

The AI chuckled. "Someone has been reading the classics. When we have something for you, I'll let you know."

Jared tried not to worry about this troubling turn of events, but that wasn't going to be easy. That was his sister out there, and the heir of the New Terran Empire. If something happened to her, he'd never forgive himself.

* * *

BRANDON SAT in the cramped control center on the recovery ship and watched the returns from the stealthed probes they'd launched earlier. The telemetry beams were very tight and almost impossible to detect, but he still worried.

They'd been out of scanner range of the defensive station for almost two hours and were now more than halfway to Dresden. After consulting with the princess and commodore, he'd launched a brace of probes borrowed from *Persephone* toward the world growing larger ahead of them.

He wasn't crazy enough to send them into orbit, but they'd make a wide pass around the world and send back some rough data. Even at this range, he could tell that the planet wasn't being used effectively.

As the captured crew had indicated, there was only a single large orbital. Based on what the princess had said, they used it for several kinds of manufacturing. If this really was the source of the Raider implants, then they were using the place for both civilian and secret military purposes.

If it had been him, he'd have used two orbitals and made sure there was no unauthorized access at all.

Some of the work took place on the planet, based on the steady stream of cargo shuttles running back and forth. It seemed as though they were all coming from a single continent in the southern hemisphere.

There were two freighters in wide orbits around the single space station. They also had a few shuttles ferrying things back and forth with them.

He opened a channel to Annette Vitter. She was still in her fighter on the surface of their disguise.

"How's the weather out there?"

"Dry and hard to breathe," she said. "As it usually is in space. I assume things are going well."

He grinned at her image. "Better than we had any reason to expect. I haven't gotten a good look at the orbital yet, but there don't seem to be any Rebel Fleet vessels in orbit. Just a couple of freighters. It doesn't look like you'll have to blow anything up this time."

"Oh ye of little faith. Things will probably go to hell soon enough. Any word on what the plan is once we get there?"

He shook his head. "Not yet. I'd imagine that they want to be sure what they'll be facing before they commit to a strategy. There is a steady stream of shuttles from one location on the planet, too."

"Is it under the station?"

"No. The station isn't in geosynchronous orbit. The two locations are sometimes on the opposite sides of the planet from one another. Do you think that might be helpful?"

The pilot smiled. "I do. Let me bring the princess and the commodore into the conversation, and I'll run something past them."

* * *

KELSEY FELT naked without her powered armor, but it would stand out on a scouting mission like this. Annette Vitter's plan was audacious—appropriately, given her ship. If it worked, they'd get onto the station without disturbing anyone at all.

As a reward—or perhaps punishment—she'd brought the fighter pilot along for the ride. She was on the other pinnace.

The stealthed pinnaces would join the stream of cargo shuttles from Dresden when the station wasn't in a position to see where they came from. Unless they were severely paranoid, this had a very good chance of getting her people where they needed to be.

"Any indication they're using specialized identification?" she asked her intelligence specialist.

"Not that I can see," he said after consulting his console closely. "There are standard Rebel Fleet IFF signals, but the only communications I'm detecting are standard traffic-control stuff. Instructions to change course or use specific docking areas."

"Are they querying origin or passenger manifests?"

The man shook his head. "Nothing like that. My guess is that if it has a valid IFF, that's good enough. It's not like someone is going to sneak into the system with stolen codes and brazenly waltz right up."

Like they were doing.

"When are they squawking ID for the station?" she asked.

"Just before final approach."

The pilot slowly tapered off the stealth field as they got into the right orbit and then boosted speed a little.

"We're in the open," he said. "No one seems to have seen anything unusual. I'm heading around the planet, and I'll squawk our stolen codes when we hit the right spot."

Kelsey was tapped into the com system, so she heard the response from the station when the pilot had done so.

"Control has you, Y-112. You and Y-243 are cleared for approach along your current vector. There are two shuttles in front of you, so watch for them crossing ahead of you. You can dock at the indicated markers."

"Copy that, Control. Y-112 out."

The pilot turned and looked over his shoulder. "You get that, Colonel?"

"Yes, but stick to calling me Captain going forward. Everyone, mind your cover stories. Once we arrive, we'll need to scout the station, verify it's what we think it is, and plan our mischief. Then we'll execute stage two."

The pinnaces entered the docking bay without incident. Kelsey waited until the lock was green and cycled herself in. Here they went.

31

Annette sauntered down the ramp of her pinnace and onto the space station as though she owned the place. She wore the uniform of a commander in the Rebel Fleet. The team assigned to her was at her heels.

Princess Kelsey's pinnace was right down from hers, so she gave the other woman a covert nod when their eyes met. They each had different areas of the station to search, so she'd best get about it. Time was wasting.

The two pinnaces would depart as soon as they unloaded some precious crates.

There was quite a crowd bustling about. Based on what she'd heard from Commander Richards, she responded to the people around her in different ways.

The Fleet officers either saluted her or she saluted them. Enlisted personnel got a look down her nose when they saluted, and they dodged her. She ignored the civilians entirely. They were unlikely to bother those of them in uniform.

The second set of her people was another story. The recovery agents were in civilian clothes taken from the captured ships. They'd hit other parts of the station where uniforms might raise eyebrows.

They split into groups and began wandering the corridors.

It didn't take her long to find something interesting. As one would expect on a large installation, there were maps to help lost souls find their way.

Not that any of them listed "secret manufacturing area" for her, but there were entire sections of the station that were helpfully blank. She figured that any place that they didn't want visitors knowing about would be interesting.

Of course, getting into them might be a challenge. She wouldn't know until she made a pass by them.

Princess Kelsey had given them a few pointers on slipping past security, so she had one of her people pick up a large tray of pastries. One that precluded her from opening any doors.

A lookout made sure she arrived at the unmarked security doors right behind someone. The man proved himself a gentleman when he held it open for her. She repaid his kindness with a sugary treat, and the two of them vanished inside.

A few minutes later, the woman opened the door for Annette and Jon Paul Olivier. She'd kept the pastries, so Annette snagged one. Being a spy was hungry work.

Just inside the security door was another map for the lost. This one labeled most of the previously hidden areas with letter designations. Five of them. She guessed that might correspond to various security restrictions.

The area surrounding all of the other shaded spaces was labelled with "A," and the other four went from "B" to "E."

"Interesting," Olivier said. "This covers almost all the areas left blank on the public map, but not completely."

"I noticed that," she said. "What do you think it means?"

"The remaining area is directly in the rear, so it's part of the concealed grouping, but they didn't want to draw attention to it, even in here. Only someone looking closely for missing areas would see that they'd excised it."

He sent her an updated map with a black area in the deepest part of the protected area. They could get close in the corridors, but they'd have to go through area "E" to get there. She dubbed it area "F."

Together, they wove their way deeper into the secret facility. Other people, both Rebel Fleet and civilian, passed them without comment.

The conversation she overheard tipped the hand for area "C." They were researching enhancements to existing weapons in there. Longer-range missiles with faster speeds. More powerful beams. God knew what else.

This place sounded a little like the Grant Research Facility on Harrison's World. Capturing it would be damned useful in its own right. Too bad they couldn't just put everything into their pockets. Maybe they could steal some of the computer cores.

The hatch to area "E" had guards, so they weren't getting in. They'd just pass by and see what else they could hear before getting out of the shielded area and contacting the princess.

Annette was almost to the hatch when the massive slab of metal slid open and a Rebel Fleet commander strode out.

He smiled at Annette. "Commander Renner? I'm Edward Irons. We'll be working together. I thought I'd have to walk all the way to the main entrance for you. I didn't realize they'd already issued you clearance for the secure areas. Welcome to the project.

"Commodore Murdock is about to start the briefing." He smiled even more widely at the pastries. "Unfortunately, your aides are not cleared for this, but the donuts are. I'll take those, Lieutenant."

Going along with his mistake was dangerous. If anyone realized she wasn't the expected officer, the jig would really be up. Still, this was about the only way they were going to see what was in the most secret area.

"No worries," she told the man as she discreetly updated her name in her implants. It wouldn't do to have someone ping her and get her real name. Sir Carl had made the update allowing it to all their implants, just in case any data needed to be changed or the implant responses turned off altogether.

Annette took the tray and whispered in Olivier's ear. "Find the real Renner. Take her out of play quietly."

The man nodded. "Of course, Commander."

Irons escorted her into area "E" and led her past a compartment filled with manufacturing gear. Her heart soared when she recognized a little sled with pharmacology units. This *was* the right place.

He gestured at the cart. "We're wrapping up the production on these and the related hardware. The project is being mothballed, and we're getting the space once it's done."

Annette smiled. "You can never have enough space." She wanted to ask him why it was wrapping up, but she could guess. They didn't expect to need them anymore once the AI at Erorsi was gone.

He nodded to another pair of guards at the hatch in front of them as he led her into area "F." It was bigger than area "E" by a factor of five, according to Olivier's map.

Their destination was a conference room. Several dozen Fleet officers and civilians waited for them inside. No commodore, so they'd gotten there early enough. No one wanted to arrive after a flag officer.

Her escort showed her to a pair of open seats with folders laid out in front of them. Printed matter meant it was *very* classified.

Since other people were looking at the contents, she opened her packet. It only took a few moments to realize what she was looking at. Enhancements to equipment that made complex computer cores. Ones she'd seen before, in the compartment that housed Marcus on *Invincible*.

Area "F" was where the Rebel Empire made AIs. Capturing the facility just became critical, but she had no way to notify the princess. She'd just have to hope that the woman pulled the mission off with her usual flair, even though she didn't know how critical it had become.

* * *

"Admiral, we have an incoming FTL message from *Audacious*," Marcus said. "It was a prerecorded video in burst mode."

"Put it on screen," he told the AI.

Zia Anderson appeared on the screen. "Admiral, I have to risk using the FTL. Our stealthed probes just picked up activity at flip point two. It appears that a large number of ships just transitioned into this system. I'm attaching the data.

"Princess Kelsey is already aboard the station, so I can't notify her about it. It's going to complicate our extraction, so you'll need to factor them into your planning. I'll risk another transmission when we have a better assessment of the enemy reinforcements. *Audacious* out."

Flip point two was the portal to the other occupied system. This was bad news and worse timing. It had to be the relief force that the prisoners had hinted at.

Jared accessed the attached probe telemetry. The distance between the probe and the ships, as well as the passive nature of the intercept, required some interpretation. What was obvious at a glance was that the number of ships was significant. More than he'd brought with him and more than they'd sent to take out Pentagar.

They might all be destroyers, but he wasn't about to take that for granted.

"That's going to put Kelsey and the rest in a tight spot," he told Marcus. "They'll be in a position to cut off their avenue of escape. We need to expand on those contingencies you were already working on."

* * *

Zia watched the telemetry from the probes as they closed with the Rebel Empire ships. The original data wasn't quite as bad as she'd first assumed, though it wasn't good. The ships she'd thought were superdreadnoughts were actually large freighters. Two of them.

The largest warships were three battlecruisers. Of course, they had dozens of cruisers and swarms of destroyers flanking them. This force would take a mauling, but it could hurt Admiral Mertz in a standup fight.

"The enemy fleet is breaking up," her operations officer said. "It looks as though they're diverting ships to the other two flip points, as well as leaving some on station where they are."

It looked as though they were splitting into groups of roughly equal size. One was on the way to where they'd be escaping, one was staying on site at flip point two, and the last group was going around to flip point three. The freighters were on their way into the system.

One thing that was obvious was that they weren't going to be sneaking out the way they'd come in. No matter what happened now, there was no aborting.

Even if she could figure out how to do that, they'd be trapped in the system fairly soon. There was a short window during which they could still escape, but it was going to have to be through flip point three.

Zia brought up the Old Empire flip point maps. None of the links took her back to either the New Terran Empire or Pentagar. They'd have to either sneak into the Rebel Empire or go into unmapped space.

Or find a weak flip point that might give them new options.

She considered sending another FTL burst to *Invincible* but decided to wait. She'd fill Princess Kelsey in once she called. There'd be time to let the admiral know about the new situation once they actually had a plan to get themselves out of the system.

Princess Kelsey should have word to them on their target in less than half an hour. She'd just have to wait, because there was no way to com her with the updated news until she executed phase two.

Zia hoped things went smoothly over there, because any hiccups were likely to cause them all a lot of pain.

32

Kelsey listened to Olivier carefully as he described the secret areas of the station. She wished she had confirmation that the target was inside, but at this point, she didn't even know that Vitter was going to get back out again.

She considered the irony of wanting to tear the woman's head off for racing in where angels feared to tread. Talbot was going to laugh at her, assuming this all didn't just go to crap.

"That just about confirms that we're in the right place," she said. "We won't wait for Vitter. One thing that *has* changed is that I want the computer cores. All of them. That means we'll need to swamp them. Stun everyone as quickly as possible. Then we'll disassemble the large equipment and get it back out."

The rally point she'd chosen was on the civilian side of the station, in a small warehouse directly adjacent to the military part of the orbital. It was only a few levels from the secret facility.

Cain Hopwood had secured it for them, trussing up the workers and safely tucking them into a storage room where they wouldn't see anything useful. They'd release them once the operation was over.

They'd cleared the center of the warehouse and set up their secret weapon. Their half of the transport rings stood gleaming, ready to link up with its mate on *Audacious*. Theirs was the one that didn't require an attached power supply, obviously.

She'd released the pinnaces to head out as soon as she'd made the decision to go ahead with the attack. The transport ring came to life right on time, and marines poured through in powered armor, their heavy weapons covering everything and everyone. Talbot came through with her armor already in his arms. Carl Owlet was right behind him, also dressed in powered armor.

"The situation has changed," he said as she started stripping her uniform off. "There's a Rebel Empire fleet in the system. It split up and sent forces to the other flip points. We're not going to be able to just slip out the way we came in."

"Then we'll come up with a different plan."

"Commodore Anderson already has one, but she wants your approval before she tells the admiral. If we hurry, we can get what we're after and slip out through flip point three. It doesn't have any obvious connection back to where we want to go, but it beats being trapped here."

Kelsey nodded as she finished sealing everything except her helmet. "Then that's the plan. Send word back for her to tell Jared that we'll find our own way home. Once we kick this off, I want her to jam all communications from this station and the freighters. We can't let the warships know what we're doing or they'll come racing in.

"The other side of the wall in front of us leads into the military section of this station. I'll send everyone a map. We want to get to the area marked section 'F.' Time is of the essence. We get in, steal everything, and then get the hell out.

"We'll be capturing the other areas as well. This station is like the Grant Research Facility. I want their data cores. Let no one stand in your way, and don't dawdle. I don't want anyone to get the idea they need to scrub the cores."

"Copy that," Talbot said. "Stand away from the wall, everyone."

"Noncombat personnel through the ring to *Audacious*," Kelsey said. "Take my uniform. No need to leave anything behind. Remember, everyone, we leave no one behind.

"Carl, we seeded the transmitters you gave us. They're all over the military section but not inside the secret facility. Is that going to be a problem? What can we expect from them?"

The young man set his portable console on a handy table. "They're designed to detect implant transmissions and jam them. Their range is fairly short, and they won't be able to suppress all the transmissions completely. Not inside the secret areas at all.

"Your armor has an alternate frequency that the jammers won't interfere with. You should still be able to communicate effectively inside the orbital."

"Excellent," she said. "You stay here and monitor that end. Once we have the secret areas secure, we'll call you in to extract the computer cores. Talbot? It's time to make the donuts."

He raised his plasma cannon and trained it on the wall.

Kelsey's implants pinged with an urgent message.

"Hold it!" she said. "Stand by."

Once she was sure she'd checked her husband's impulse to fire, she accepted the link. "I'm kind of busy."

"And you're about to get busier," Annette Vitter said. "I just got a look at the innermost area of the security zone. The target just changed.

"While they are making the Raider implants here, the real secret here is that they're building sentient AIs. The bad news is that the equipment is way too big to go through the transport rings."

Kelsey gaped. "You're certain?"

The other woman nodded. "I just sat through the longest briefing in recorded history talking about the plans to expand the facility. I know them in excruciating detail. By the way, I now know someone even more long-winded and stuffy than Captain Breckenridge."

"Impossible," Kelsey declared. "I can't believe you bluffed your way into something like that. You got big brass ones, lady."

"Everyone likes pastries. I had to leave the security area to com you, but I can get you to where you need to go if you'll have someone open the hatch."

Kelsey thought furiously. This changed everything.

"I have news of my own. The Rebel Empire sent a fleet here, and they're locking down the system. We have a *very* short window to escape, and it won't be back toward Jared. We'll have to run through flip point three. We need a way to get the equipment out of here."

She considered and rejected several harebrained schemes before she stepped back to reconsider the whole plan. There *was* another option. It was insane, but it might work.

"Did that briefing cover the power generation for the secure areas?" Kelsey asked Vitter.

The other woman nodded. "Two fusion plants in the military side, thankfully not in the secured area. The rest of the station has three plants seeing to their needs."

"Send me their locations. I have a history with power plants on Rebel Empire stations."

"So I hear. That's not going to get the manufacturing equipment out of here, though."

Kelsey smiled. "I have an idea. You'll love it. First, we need to actually capture everything. Get as close as you can to the fusion plants, and we'll join you shortly."

"Copy that."

Once again, the recovery team proved startlingly capable. They managed to sneak people near all three power plants, though not up to the plants themselves.

"Talbot, it's time," she said. "If you'd be so kind as to open the door."

He grinned at her, put his helmet back on, and hefted the plasma cannon. Everyone crouched behind something as he took the shot, knowing that it would be incredibly destructive.

It was certainly that. The reinforced wall simply vanished in a sun-bright flash. The bubble of destruction would've been impossible for most people to cross, but they were in powered armor.

The marines leapt forward and vaulted the gap, landing easily and racing toward their designated targets.

There seemed to be a never-ending stream of them coming from the ring. She'd brought every marine in the fleet with her for this mission.

Most people would've called this overkill, but she no longer believed in such a thing. All these people would allow her to run over any resistance and quickly capture the critical areas.

Many of the marines were headed for the fusion plants, but not all. Other teams set out for the command and control levels. The faster they eliminated any possibility of organized resistance, the better.

The Rebel Empire didn't trust their marines, thankfully. That meant the ones on the station had no access to powered armor or heavy weapons. The officers in command no doubt assumed that they'd have plenty of time to make changes if some other circumstance came into play.

Kelsey intended to use that paranoia ruthlessly against them.

The marines rolled right over everything in their path. Stunners took out everyone they met. No one was armed on the other side except for a few guards with flechette pistols. Which were not even remotely effective against her troops.

The teams in the civilian side were actually progressing more slowly than the teams in the military area. They didn't want to trample the people running away from them. They'd have enough time, she hoped.

It took her three minutes to reach the lift leading down to the military fusion plants. She didn't bother calling the car. It would only slow her down.

She ripped the lift doors open with her bare hands and looked down the shaft. The car was two levels below. She'd need to move it. She pulled a fusion grenade off her belt, armed it, and tossed it down the shaft.

"Fire in the hole!"

The blast was impressive in the enclosed environment, but she didn't wait for it to fade completely before she jumped into the shaft.

The car was gone, as was the shaft around it. She plummeted through the space it had once occupied and hit her grav assist to slow her when she reached the right level.

The marines following her didn't have grav assist, so they were using their powered hands to grip the walls as they scurried down like massive spiders.

Kelsey ripped open the lift doors, and flechettes began to ricochet off her armor. Half a dozen guards emptied their weapons at her. She raised her own weapon and stunned them.

It only took her a minute to find the control room. Oddly, a group of Fleet officers was trying to force the hatch when she arrived. Her stunner put them down.

The hatch slid open, and Vitter grinned at her. "Good timing. I have no idea how to shut these things down."

"I have the engineers right behind me."

The man and woman in question were awkward in their powered armor, but it had gotten them here alive. She helped get their gauntlets and helmets off so that they could work.

Commander Mark Kinder, the chief engineer on *Persephone*, looked over the controls. "This is Rebel Empire standard. Shutting it down now."

Alarms began wailing, and the lights dimmed.

The man grinned. "Both plants are offline. We can get them back up when we're ready, though it'll take a little time."

"Good work."

Kelsey pinged the other teams outside the secure area. Two of the civilian plants were offline already, and the third went down as she watched. They'd eliminated the simplest way for anyone to destroy the station.

She had marines looking for other self-destruct methods but didn't expect to find any. Why have them when you could overload a fusion plant and take out everything?

It was time to execute the final phase. She sent a signal to Owlet to head for the secure area. A team of marines would make certain nothing stood between him and their prize.

"That means I gotta go," Vitter said. "Talbot, help me up the lift and back to the transport ring."

"We'll go secure the labs and the military command team," Kelsey said.

They'd won the first round, but things could still go horribly wrong. It was time to wrap this up and get the hell out of here.

33

Brandon stared at Commodore Anderson's image. "You want me to what?"

"I need you to jettison both ships and get the station inside the recovery ship's arms. We're taking it with us."

"That's what I thought you said."

He looked at the scanner readings of the station as he initiated the release procedure to set *Persephone* and *Audacious* free.

"I can't get it all inside the arms. It's close, but——"

"This is why they pay you the big bucks, Captain. Make it work."

Brandon rubbed his face. Something was going to have to give. He loaded the orbital's geometry into his implants, and then he set up the maximum spread he could get on the arms. They had to be around the cargo, or the drives wouldn't be able to shield it from inertia or flip it.

It almost worked if he twisted the ship around, but the arms didn't open widely enough. The orbital was almost a quarter larger than *Invincible*.

He accessed the specifications for the arms. They were replaceable. That meant they could be removed. Now he needed to figure out how to attach them in the new configuration.

"I'll need several teams from engineering to come assist me," he said. "I need to detach two of the arms. Once we have the station in place, we can reattach them. We'll need to secure them against acceleration, but they will be able to provide flip capability and inertial dampening."

"I'll have people on the way as soon as we clear the landing bay. How long will it take?"

"Considering we've never done it before, it might take an hour."

"Shorten that as much as possible. We're tight on time."

He nodded. "I'll move it along as fast as I can. I can send the specifications along now. The engineering teams can start finding places we can save time while they wait for a ride."

"Excellent," the commodore said. "I've got to get the last part of this mission under way. Call me if there are any problems."

He closed the com channel and started working on what he could do ahead of time. This was going to be tight.

ANNETTE BUMPED her acceleration up enough to catch up with her squadrons. Every fighter they had was on its way to flip point three. They'd kept their acceleration down so as not to be detected, but they'd be going very fast when they arrived.

The ships in Dresden orbit should be on the way behind them before they attacked the Rebel Empire forces. Based on the range from the new forces moving at the edges of the system, they might arrive there undetected, too.

She called Jake Fiennes on the short-range com.

"What's the plan, boss lady?" he asked.

"It's as simple as it gets. We're going to arrive at flip point three several hours ahead of *Audacious*, *Persephone*, and the recovery ship. The stealthed probes say we have three destroyers and that battle station. I want to take them all off the board on the first pass."

He whistled. "That's a tall order. We can scrub the destroyers, but the battle station is a big one. It's made to take lots of hits. Why do we need to run the table?"

"Because we don't want to let them know where we went for a while. The commodore is arranging a distraction, but a distress signal from out here will really mess us up. The recovery ship is overloaded, and her arms are in a nonstandard position, so it'll be extremely slow. We can't afford to let them catch up with us."

He seemed to consider what she'd said. "We'll have to allocate almost all our fire to the battle station. We have no idea what the internal layout is. I figure we can wax the destroyers with four fighters each. They won't have battle screens up."

"Three each," she said. "We can't allow the battle station to survive."

"We also can't let any of the destroyers live," he countered. "We have to get them, too."

"We know where their fusion plants are. Pick one pilot in each group to eject and let their fighters go terminal on the enemy. In a perfect world, we'd be able to control them remotely via our implants, but we can't risk the enemy detecting any signals. We'll have to do it the hard way."

His eyes lost focus as he considered the tactic. "Pulling what the admiral did? Bold. If we follow up with missiles right on the kamikazes' heels, it should finish them off before they can scream for help. Still, this is chancy. If anything goes wrong, we'll be in trouble."

"Then let's make sure nothing goes wrong."

KELSEY MADE it to the command deck for the station right after the marines had stormed it. Once again, they'd stunned everything that moved.

She made the rounds of the consoles, moving stunned people out of the way and looking for any that had been left unsecure. Due to the speed and ferocity of the attack, not everyone had been on the ball. She found an auxiliary panel unlocked.

Finding the security information took longer than she liked but was reassuring when she did find it.

The very first thing she did was trigger the antiboarding stunners.

That would take everyone off the table. Her people were shielded. She also locked out the escape pods. None of them had ejected, but she wouldn't discount the idea of someone getting around the lockout.

The pinnaces would keep an eye out for any and deal with them. The jamming would keep the Rebel Empire fleet from hearing any distress beacons.

The next challenge was to locate the computer cores. It turned out that there had been someone in the core room. Unfortunately for him, he was woefully short on clearance. He didn't know the codes to erase the system, so he'd been left with a large wrench as his only tool of destruction.

He'd managed to smash some equipment before she used the antiboarding stunners, but the cores were intact.

Kelsey let out a sigh of relief. "That was close. Let's try to keep anyone else from getting too excited."

She called *Audacious*. They'd left a few frequencies open for just this purpose. "Zia, I think we've pulled it off. Does Captain Levy know how he's going to grapple the station?"

The Fleet officer nodded. "He's got that under control. We'll be able to move in twenty minutes."

"Excellent. What's the status of the Rebel Empire fleet?"

"Still on course. The detachment heading toward Admiral Mertz will be there before we can secure the station. The other one is still a ways off from flip point three. If we get under way on time, we'll beat them, but not by much.

"I have a plan to distract them, though. If Annette can take out the defenders, we might be able to escape in the chaos. One of the captured freighters is almost empty. It will be a critical part of my ruse."

"I hope your plan works. Otherwise we're in deep trouble."

* * *

ZIA SENT a crew over to unload the mostly empty freighter. It would make a great addition to her decoy, hopefully confusing the Rebel Empire forces for a while as to what had really happened at Dresden.

Princess Kelsey had instructed her to hold off notifying Admiral Mertz of their intentions until the last moment, figuring he would try something bold and heroic. Zia probably should have argued more strongly that she had a duty to keep him in the loop, but she privately agreed. If things went south, she wanted to see the majority of their forces make it safely home. The Empire would need them to survive.

Using the FTL coms now was a risk but less of one now that the station was theirs. Unlike last time, she needed this to be a two-way conversation.

"Open an FTL link to *Invincible*," she ordered her communications officer.

A few moments later, Admiral Mertz appeared on the main screen.

"We were getting worried, Zia. Based on the initial data, the enemy was splitting up to cover all the flip points. Are you in danger?"

She gave him a wry smile. "Nothing we can't manage, I hope. We've secured the orbital."

He nodded. "Excellent. We've worked up a number of different scenarios to break you out. Depending on the actual forces we'll face coming in, we should be able to get you through."

"Actually, the princess has a different plan."

"Of course she does." He sighed. "Lay it out."

"First, I need to give you the reasoning. I'll be quick because I don't want to keep this line open any longer than I have to. The major point is that the orbital didn't just make Raider implants. It also built sentient AIs."

The admiral sat up abruptly. "Seriously? Then we need to put every effort into getting you out of there as soon as possible."

She shook her head. "We can't extract all the equipment from the station in the limited time we have available, sir. We're just going to steal the whole thing."

"The whole—"

He stopped himself. "You're going to put the orbital into the recovery ship. That's brilliant. If you can evade detection on the way to flip point one, we'll keep them off you."

"The odds of us making it through to you are slim, Admiral. Too slim. We're arranging our own distraction and breaking out through flip point three. The fighters will hit the defenders there before the reinforcements arrive. We'll distract the relief force and escape before they know what's happening."

Admiral Mertz looked down at his console. "There aren't any links on that route to bring you home. The Rebel Empire Fleet is going to chase you down. It's too risky. We'll come up with something else."

"I can't recall the fighters, Admiral. They're only a few hours from executing. We're committed."

He considered her for a long moment. "That's Kelsey's doing, isn't it? She told you to hold off notifying me so that I couldn't countermand her scheme."

Zia sighed. "I wish it were that simple. I looked at the options, and your likely responses, before I decided that I agreed with her. The Empire needs your ships and your experience to survive, Admiral.

"Even if we made it to flip point one, the odds of us extracting the station and keeping the Rebel Empire ships off us while we retreated to Erorsi are nonexistent. It's too far. Our only chance is to vanish, leaving them to scratch their heads about what happened."

He looked skeptical. "And you think you can do that?"

She smiled. "With just a dash of luck. I'm sorry for the deception, Admiral, but I'm doing what I think has the best chance of success in the long run. If it works out, we'll be able to give you a final status report before we escape."

The unspoken part of that was they'd also tell him if it all went to crap.

Jared Mertz considered her for a long moment. "You're the officer on the scene, Zia. I have complete faith in you. Good luck."

"I'm attaching everything to the transmission now. We'll call once we're about to leave the system. Thank you for your confidence, Admiral."

"You've more than earned it. You'll need every bit of skill and smarts to get back home, but I know you'll do it. Make us proud."

She nodded, her heart swelling with emotion. "Thank you, sir."

Zia attached the files about the escape plan and ended the transmission.

34

Annette watched the range to the targets grow smaller. They were coming in on a purely ballistic course, and at fairly high speed. Since the ships and battle station weren't scanning continuously, they probably wouldn't even know they were in danger until it was far too late.

The probes gave them a good idea of exactly where they needed to hit. She'd already moved the fighters they were using as rams up front. Not by much, but she had to give the pilots time to eject and fly past the targets before they destroyed them. At this speed, it would only mean a delay measured in fractions of a second.

A second stealthed probe had been giving them statuses on the force headed their way, but they'd had to shut it down. They were close enough to the flip point that the defenders might pick up the edge of the beam.

They *should* be too far away to pick up the explosions. Space was vast, and even the flare of failed fusion plants faded fast. As long as they weren't actively scanning when the time came, the attack should go undetected.

Unless someone got a distress call off.

That was the worst-case scenario. If the Rebel Empire ships raced in, there was no way they could escape. They had one chance at this.

Annette forced her mind off the chances of failure. She had to maximize the chances of success.

The battle station was still the biggest question. Without knowing where the fusion plants were inside it, they couldn't use pinpoint targeting like they were with the destroyers.

The plan called for the three fighters to ram the station, and as the pilots were flying past it in their suits, the rest of them would use missiles to tear the thing apart. That should blow at least one of the plants. Probably.

She hated the uncertainty.

Well, there was one thing she could do to increase their chances. They were too close to the targets to notify any of the others that she was about to change the plan, but it was worth the risk.

Annette used her maneuvering thrusters to slow her speed just a hair. Unlike the grav drives, the chemical reaction wouldn't be detectable. She had to use every ounce of thrust she had to make enough difference, but it put her behind the remainder of the attacking force.

Her internal timer slowly crawled to zero, and the space in front of her burst with light. Even before her mind had fully registered the explosions, her implants fired her missiles to follow them up.

The rest of the pilots spiraled past the damaged battle station and raced into deep space. She didn't.

Her canopy blew off, and the powerful grav drive under her seat blasted her straight up. Annette didn't see her beloved fighter plow into the already expanding craters on the target, but she couldn't miss the blinding flare of a failed fusion plant as she hurtled past it.

In a moment, it was gone and she was tumbling through space. An alarm was howling in her ears. Suit integrity had failed, and she was losing atmosphere. Her radiation count was also off the charts.

The exposure was so brief that she'd probably live, supposing they found her quickly, and she didn't suffocate first.

Her helmet locked tight around her neck, cutting off the loss of air. Her body could stand a brief exposure to vacuum. With any luck, one of the other pilots would find her. An emergency ball from the external stores of the fighter would keep her alive.

They'd disabled their beacons. One going off would ruin the stealth they'd struggled so hard to achieve. It also meant that they'd have to find her with short-ranged scanners, or she'd be lost forever in the depths of space.

At least she could take solace in the fact they'd destroyed the battle station. Hopefully, the destroyers were gone, too.

In any case, her part in this little drama was over. It was up to the princess and commodore to make their sacrifices mean something.

* * *

Kelsey sat at a borrowed console on *Audacious*'s flag bridge and watched the passive scanner results from flip point three with satisfaction. Annette Vitter and her people had taken out the battle station and all three destroyers. The path was clear, so long as they diverted the Rebel Empire ships that were currently headed in that direction.

She turned to Zia. "Are we clear of Dresden?"

The other woman looked up from her command console. "We're just leaving the exclusion zone you'd designated around the planet. I'd like to have another half-hour at this speed before we kick things off. If they spot us now, everything was for nothing."

The carrier, *Persephone*, the recovery ship with the hijacked station in its grip, and the fully laden freighter were creeping along at a very low acceleration. Too slow to show up on the scanners of any ships that happened to look their direction. They hoped.

"I understand," Kelsey said, "but we don't have the luxury of being certain. If they don't fall for the bait, we're in for some serious fighting. Your fighters will only barely make it back to us before we get to the flip point. They have a lot of momentum to burn off, and they can't use real acceleration to do it. If that force doesn't divert, they'll screw us all."

Zia sighed. "I know. Well, if wishes were horses, we'd all be ass deep in horse crap."

"I see someone else still likes to look into the historical archives. Execute Operation Troll."

"Aye, ma'am," Zia said. She pressed a button on her console. "Signal away. It'll take a minute for things to kick off on the other end."

Kelsey calculated the time it would take for the trigger signal to race to Dresden, so she was ready when the distress signal came.

It had taken them a while to find the emergency procedures for the orbital, but once they had them, designing a faked distress signal was easy. They had a lot of archived message traffic to use in splicing together a believable message using the actual people manning the station. That was the key, she thought.

The image her people had put together was computer generated, which probably wouldn't have been enough to fool anyone for very long under normal circumstances, but they'd sent the data they had to Marcus through the FTL com.

The AI had access to tremendously more computing power than they did. The video he'd sent back looked and sounded very authentic.

The main screen came to life with a view of the orbital's main control room. The commanding officer—the boring commodore that Annette Vitter had mentioned—was staring out at them with a look of pure desperation on her face.

"Mayday, mayday, mayday! We need immediate assistance in Dresden orbit. One of our fusion plants has entered some kind of runaway state, and we can't get it to shut off. We've moved the critical research to one of the freighters, but we can't—"

The transmission ceased.

One of the support staff looked over at the two women. "We have an explosion in Dresden orbit. The freighter's fusion plant detonated right on schedule."

Kelsey nodded in satisfaction. When the would-be rescuers arrived in orbit, they'd find a real mess. Zia had put all the ore that they'd brought around the freighter. It wasn't as much mass as the station, but it was a significant fraction.

They wouldn't decipher that mess for a while. By the time they realized that the station couldn't have been destroyed—either through analyzing the debris or just recognizing there wasn't enough of it— she and her people would hopefully be long gone.

The two inbound freighters would be close enough to see the explosion but too far out to get any details. Their messages would add authenticity to the ruse.

Kelsey watched the task force closest to them in the passive plot and crossed her fingers. If they all came running, the distraction was an unqualified success. Otherwise, she'd have to fight the remainder at the flip point, and the rest of the force would quickly be on their heels as they ran.

The task force changed course as soon as the distress signal arrived at their location. To her intense satisfaction, all the ships turned together. They would arrive in orbit a little before her slower ships made it to the flip point.

Kelsey worried about the active scanning until they were clear, but the signal strength never peaked high enough to mean the others could have seen them. The gamble had paid off.

Not that she relaxed until they'd arrived at the flip point. The fighters had rejoined them. The defenders had never even seen them coming, so there were no combat losses, other than seven fighters used as ramming weapons.

The only unexpected news was that Annette Vitter had been one of the kamikazes. That hadn't been part of the plan. The woman's people had noticed she was missing and searched frantically until they'd located her. Without a beacon, that was a real challenge.

Word was that she had radiation poisoning and was suffering from vacuum exposure but that she would live. Kelsey couldn't wait to hear the story of the attack and to watch the recordings.

"We've recovered all our fighters," Zia said. "We can transition at any time."

She nodded. "I'll give Jared a final status first. This will be the last time he and I talk before we find a way home."

The other woman smiled. "I can't wait to see the vid drama they make about your latest exploit."

Kelsey couldn't help rolling her eyes at that. Perfect. They'd managed to keep the damned original vid out of the public eye, but she had no doubt it would be everywhere by the time she got back. It was a good thing she'd be gone for months and couldn't see it or any prospective new ones.

* * *

"INCOMING FTL SIGNAL, ADMIRAL," Marcus said.

Jared looked up from his console. "On screen."

Kelsey appeared. She stood beside Zia Anderson's control console and smiled at him.

"Well, things are in good shape here, and we're ready to flip. The majority of the ships at the remaining flip points are racing for Dresden. They sent a signal to the battle station at flip point three but accepted a brief acknowledgement we sent back without suspicion.

"The orders are for the ships here to keep watch with a higher level of vigilance. We said we'd make sure no one slipped past us, of course."

He shook his head. "I can't believe you pulled this off. You stole an entire orbital. That's impressive."

"They'll figure out we tricked them sooner or later," she said with a wry smile. "The destroyed units here will tell them which way we went. We'll try to stay out of sight until we can sneak back home.

"That'll take a long while unless we find some handy weak flip points that get us closer. Tell my father I'm sorry to do this to him, but it was important."

"He'll know," Jared said. "One positive: you don't have to worry about your mother ruining your second wedding ceremony on Avalon for a while."

She laughed. "True. Or that just might give her more time to take it over. I'll deal with that crisis when I get home."

He allowed his expression to grow serious. "Be careful, Kelsey. There's no one to help you out of a bind. Keep the risky moves to a minimum."

"Sure. You know me. Timid as a mouse."

"Don't torture me like that."

She laughed. "I'll be careful. Look, we have to get going. I love you. You be careful, too. Until we meet again."

"Zia, make sure and append the current scanner readings you have. Kelsey, I love you, too. Until we meet again."

The transmission ended.

According to their plan, they'd be flipping now. He'd have to wait for them to sneak through the Rebel Empire before he knew she was safe. It was going to be nerve wracking.

One thing he could do to make it less so was to make sure the enemy didn't go chasing after Kelsey at all. It would make his retreat to Erorsi a lot more dangerous than he preferred, but that was a price he was willing to pay.

The data and equipment his sister had captured were quite possibly key to the Empire's survival. Anything he could do to improve her odds of getting home with it was worth the risk.

He opened a channel to his fleet. "All vessels execute Operation Shiva in thirty seconds."

As a unit, they all flipped into Dresden space and flushed their missiles at the battle station. They fired three salvoes before the first arrived on target.

The enemy returned fire late. The crew probably couldn't believe their eyes. They certainly had time to scream for help, though, which was fine by him. He *wanted* the other ships in the Dresden system to know he was here.

The battle station was powerful but no match for his sustained firepower. The second wave of missiles degraded its battle screens to the point of failure, and the final wave savaged it to the point it blew up.

Its return fire was manageable. He had plenty of antimissile platforms. The Rebel Empire had obviously never entertained the idea of a concerted attack at this strength.

The mobile forces in the system were strong enough to engage him. They might not win, but in this kind of situation, both sides would be badly mauled.

So, he had no intention of waiting around for them to catch him. He just wasn't going to tell them that.

Once he was sure they were forming up to come his way, he ordered his fleet to launch decoys at the remaining flip point that had a battle station. Only the heavy cruisers and larger vessels had decoys, but they would convince the enemy he was making a move on the other station.

They wouldn't see any destroyers, so they could either assume those were staying at this flip point or heading in at a slower pace to engage them. It didn't matter. Any of the possibilities worked for Jared.

Then he quietly had his fleet flip back to the mining system and head back for Erorsi at flank speed. By the time his decoys self-destructed, the enemy would be committed to chasing them.

Once the enemy started examining the situation, they would have no choice but to assume he'd somehow destroyed the orbital. It would probably drive them crazy, but his arrival wouldn't be seen as coincidental.

Of course, they'd wonder how he'd eliminated the forces at the flip point Kelsey had used to flee. Then they'd discover the station hadn't really blown up. Maybe.

They might put something like the real story together at that point, but it would take days or weeks. He'd seen the scanner readings of the explosion of the freighter and the ore. It would hold for a while.

In any case, it would give Kelsey and Zia time to escape. Surely, one of the systems along their path would have a weak flip point they could use to slip out of sight. The Rebel Empire forces would lose them if they had any luck at all.

"Do you think it will be enough, Admiral?" Marcus asked.

"It has to be," he replied. "It's all we can do."

* * *

ZIA STAYED at her console long after her shift would have normally ended. Princess Kelsey had returned to the captured orbital to help sort out the thousands of prisoners, and Brandon Levy was back on board the carrier. She was desperately tired, but she wanted to watch the scanners until they flipped again.

The enemy hadn't come after them, and they were almost to the next flip point. If they made it through, any pursuers would wonder if they'd really come this way at all.

She'd left a probe in the Dresden system to muddy the waters. It was far outside the system and racing for deep space. About now, it was going to begin transmitting an intermittent signal just strong enough for the enemy to detect. One designed to make the Rebel Empire commander wonder if someone was creeping along in the outer darkness.

They couldn't prove a negative. The probe would self-destruct after a few hours, so they'd never find proof one way or the other. It would probably drive them bonkers.

"We're ready to flip," Brandon said over the com.

"Take us across, Captain."

"Aye, ma'am."

She watched them flip and counted her ships on the other side as they arrived. That was a huge relief. It bought them the most precious of commodities: time.

"We're across," Brandon said. "Initial passive scans are clean. I estimate we're nine hours to the next flip point. I'll send out probes to look for weak flip points and potentially hostile vessels. Then I'll launch the combat space patrol."

Their fighters would escort them in relative safety. She didn't expect to find anyone in these unoccupied systems, but one never knew.

"Hang on a second, ma'am. We might have a situation."

Her heart lurched in her chest. "What kind of situation?"

Had Rebel Empire ships come into scanner range at the last moment before they flipped? Were there ships in this system? A quick check showed that neither of those conditions was the case.

Brandon listened to someone beside his console and shook his head. "Unbelievable. How the hell could this happen?"

"If you don't tell me what's going on, I'm going to scream," she assured her flag captain.

He looked back at the pickup. "It seems we have a stowaway, Commodore."

A moment later, the view swiveled toward the lift on the bridge. Two marines stood on either side of Justine Bandar. The diminutive woman looked triumphant.

"Oh, hell," Zia muttered.

* * *

WANT to get updates from Terry about new books and other general nonsense going on in his life? He promises there will be cats. Go to TerryMixon.com/Mailing-List and sign up.

DID YOU ENJOY THIS BOOK? Please leave a review on Amazon. It only takes a minute to dash off a few words and that kind of thing helps Terry make a living as a writer and gets you new books faster.

WANT the next book in this series? Grab *Behind Enemy Lines* today or buy any of Terry's other books, which are listed on the next page.

VISIT TERRY'S Patreon page to find out how to get cool rewards and an early look at what he's working on at Patreon.com/TerryMixon.

ALSO BY TERRY MIXON

You can always find the most up to date listing of Terry's titles on his
Amazon Author Page.

Note: the links below (ebook only, obviously) redirect you to my website
where you can click a button to go to Amazon. This allows me to participate
in Amazon's associates program and earn a little more. Sorry for any
inconvenience.

The Last Hunter

The Last Hunter

Bonds of Blood

Alpha Strike

The Enemy Revealed

Command Authority

The Grand Conspiracy

Shield of Humanity

Fog of War

Ships of the Line

Operation Liberty

The Empire of Bones Saga

Empire of Bones

Veil of Shadows

Command Decisions

Ghosts of Empire

Paying the Price

Recon in Force

Box Sets

The Empire of Bones Saga Volume 1

The Empire of Bones Saga Volume 2

The Empire of Bones Saga Volume 3

The Empire of Bones Saga Volume 4

Humanity Unlimited Publisher's Pack 1

Humanity Unlimited Publisher's Pack 2

ABOUT TERRY

#1 Bestselling Military Science Fiction author Terry Mixon served as a non-commissioned officer in the United States Army 101st Airborne Division. He later worked alongside the flight controllers in the Mission Control Center at the NASA Johnson Space Center supporting the Space Shuttle, the International Space Station, and other human spaceflight projects.

He now writes full time while living in Texas with his lovely wife and a pounce of cats.

TerryMixon.com

- **a** amazon.com/author/terrymixon
- **f** facebook.com/TerryLMixon
- **|●** patreon.com/TerryMixon
- **BB** bookbub.com/authors/terry-mixon
- **g** goodreads.com/TerryMixon